GHOST HAND

GHOST HAND

The PSS Chronicles: Book One

RIPLEY PATTON

First published in the United States in 2012 by Ripley Patton.

Cover design by Kura Carpenter Design
Typesetting by Centauri Typesetting

Library of Congress Control Number: 2012921384
ISBN 9780988491007

Publisher's website: www.ripleypatton.com

DEDICATION

For Pete, Soren, and Valerie, because you loved my stories first, and that made all the difference.

CONTENTS

1

THE NEW GUY

Five minutes into my Calc test, I glanced up and caught the new guy staring.

He sat across the aisle from me, his eyes locked on my glowy, see-through right hand and the pencil that hovered between my fingers, never quite touching them.

I slowly set my pencil on my desk.

His eyes tracked my movements, still staring.

I raised my fingers and wiggled them at him in a cheesy little wave. Normally, that was enough to make people turn away and try *not* to notice my ghost hand. But not this guy. Instead, he looked up, straight into my eyes with this way-too-intense gaze.

God, what was his problem? So I had PSS of the right hand. Psyche Sans Soma was a rare birth defect, but most people had at least heard of it. The internet had loads of stuff about PSS, and *Sixty Minutes* had done a whole segment on it for Christ's sake. Besides, hadn't anyone taught him that staring was rude?

I curled my hand into a fist and flipped him off, glaring at him through my own finger.

He raised his eyebrows and finally looked away, but I didn't miss the smirk that played across his lips as he did.

Why were the hot ones always such cocky, self-absorbed douche bags?

Unfortunately, there was no denying he was good-looking. He had black hair, brown eyes, dark skin; not a tan but the kind that comes with your DNA. And he definitely had a nice body.

He glanced up from his test, caught me checking him out, and smirked even wider than before.

I felt the blush rise to my face and picked up my pencil, pretending to focus on the test, but after reading the next question four times, I still didn't know what it said. What kind of a jerk comes into a new town and a new school, and spends the first day of his Calc class trying to make someone else feel like a freak? He was the noob; not me. He was the mid-semester transfer no one knew anything about except that he was from a school up near Chicago. And what was his name anyway? Seemed liked it began with a J. Or maybe an M.

At least he'd finally turned his attention away from me, his pencil scratching out answers the way mine should have been. He didn't even have to take the test. Since it was his first day, Mr. Giannopoulos had given him permission to opt out, but New Guy had said, "That's fine. I'll take it." Very studious of him. And annoying. Who takes a test when they don't have to?

"Twenty minutes remaining," Mr. G droned from his desk. Great. The test was twenty problems long, and I was only on number five.

The clock on the wall behind Mr. G ticked louder and louder as I scribbled down answers.

On question seven, my pencil tip snapped, the tiny mouse turd of lead rolling down the incline of my desk and dropping into my lap. I dug out another pencil from the coffin-shaped leather backpack at my feet, and that's when I noticed that my ghost hand felt warm, which was weird. PSS wasn't temperature sensitive. I'd held my hand over an open flame and stuck it in a bucket of ice, both times on a dare, and never felt a thing.

I rolled the new pencil between my warm ghost fingers. Weird or not, I had a test to finish.

"Ten minutes left," Mr. G said when I'd only just answered question eight.

Passion Wainwright, who sat in front of me, got up from her desk and turned in her test. She was done already? Then again, Passion was the best student in the entire senior class. She pretty much had to be because she was the local pastor's daughter. Her parents had named her after The Passion of Christ, this Easter play her church did every year in which Passion always played the Virgin Mary. The part actually fit her pretty well, because despite being blonde and skinny and beautiful, guys did not pursue Passion Wainwright. She wore turtlenecks, long-sleeved shirts, and long pants, even when it was warm, as if her wardrobe were some kind of "Do Not Enter" sign. She had a permanent parental waiver against changing for gym class because showing skin and wearing vintage nineties gym shorts was against her religion or something. Most days, I just felt sorry for her. Except when she turned in her Calc test with ten minutes to spare.

"Focus, Olivia," I told myself, but the heat in my fingers was bordering on uncomfortable. I could always write with my other hand; I was ambidextrous. But if I switched, New Guy would think he'd made me self-conscious with all his staring. No way was I giving him that satisfaction. I gripped the pencil tighter in my hot little hand and soldiered on.

Passion came back, sat down, and pulled out her Bible for a little light reading.

I flicked a glance at New Guy, but he wasn't there. He was up at Mr. G's desk turning in his test. I hadn't even heard him get up. I clutched my pencil and tried to answer question nine. I heard the rustle of New Guy sitting back down and caught a whiff of his cologne or deodorant—the smell of pine overlaid with a faint hint of smoke. It made me think of campfires, which made me think of how much my ghost hand felt like it was roasting over one.

I looked down at it and saw that my fingers were shimmering around the edges. I yanked my hand under the desk, sending my pencil clattering to the floor.

It landed in the aisle and rolled toward New Guy's desk. He put out a foot, trapping it, and kicked it back my direction, his glance following its progress as it came back to me, bumping up against the thick sole of my boot. His eyes rose up my multi-buckled calf to my thigh, then to my lap, stopping at the spot where I was doing my best to hide my hand under my desk.

I followed his gaze, looking down at the pool of blue PSS energy, shapeless and pulsing, writhing at the end of my wrist stump. I looked back up, locking eyes with him.

His expression was unreadable. He didn't look surprised, or afraid, or alarmed. He just looked, his eyes fixed on my wacked-out hand, as if curious to see what it would do next.

I gritted my teeth and tried to focus my PSS back into shape. I was not going to be this guy's personal freak show. I could fix this. It was just mind over matter.

But it didn't work. If anything, the more I tried, the worse it got, expanding and losing even more definition. The burning sensation grew so intense I squeezed my eyes shut against it. All around me, I could hear the scrape and shuffle of students getting up and handing in their tests. I bent over my desk, trying to block my hand from view. For a moment, I thought about getting up and running out of class, but someone would see my hand for sure if I did that. Maybe if I took a deep breath, and calmed down, it would go back to normal on its own.

As if in response to that thought, the pain suddenly eased off.

I opened my eyes.

New Guy was leaning over the edge of his desk, and there seemed to be something wrong with his neck. He kept jerking his head toward Passion. What did he want? An introduction to Virgin Mary the hotty? If so, his timing was utter crap.

"Leave me alone," I mouthed past clenched lips.

He shook his head and gave an exaggerated nod toward Passion again, rolling his eyes in her direction.

This time, I turned and looked.

Something was crawling up Passion's back.

Not just one something. Five somethings. Five elongated, wisp-thin tendrils, winding their way up Passion's chair, climbing her back, fluttering at the strands of hair that escaped from her ponytail, making a moving, barely-perceptible pattern of bluish light on the back of her white turtleneck so faint I could almost convince myself it was an optical illusion.

But it wasn't.

It was my hand, my five fingers stretching impossibly and rising from under the front of my desk, groping the back of Passion Wainwright.

I yanked my wrist in toward my body, but it made no difference. I couldn't feel my hand, couldn't control those fingers or call them back.

Passion, intent on her Bible reading, shivered as if she felt a draft and absently brushed an undulating tendril away from her neck.

The thickest finger, the one in the middle, rose up along her spine, stopping at a spot right between her shoulder blades. It held level for a moment, weaving back and forth like some ghostly snake dancing to the tune of an invisible flute. Then it dipped forward, slipping silently through the thin cotton fabric of Passion's shirt and straight into her back.

She didn't make a sound as she went limp, her torso gently slanting toward her desk; the tendril of PSS embedded in her back the only thing holding her up.

I didn't make a sound either, didn't move, didn't dare. What if moving made it worse? *Oh my God,* a voice yammered in my head, *you think this could get worse?*

I could feel New Guy's eyes boring into the side of my head. Obviously, he could see my PSS skewering Passion. Why didn't he jump up and scream and point? How could he just be sitting there so calmly?

I had to get away. From Passion. From everyone. But if I bolted, would my PSS come with me or stretch between my wrist and Passion like some horrible, incriminating rubber band? What would that do to my hand? What would it do to Passion?

I had no idea.

And before I could figure it out, the bell rang.

2

A BAG OF BLADES

All around me students slid from their desks and rushed the door. A short line formed in front of Mr. G's desk, kids waiting to hand in their tests on the way out. Thankfully, they made a nice wall, blocking his view of Passion slanting oddly over her desk in the fourth row. But, any minute, someone would notice her, or see the faint PSS energy protruding from her back. Any minute, I was going to be in serious trouble.

Suddenly, New Guy was crouching next to me. With his right hand he plucked my pencil from the floor while his left hand reached under my desk and grabbed my wrist stump. I tried to pull away, but his grip was firm. People didn't touch me there. I didn't even know this guy. What the hell was he doing? He squeezed my wrist between his fingers and it went abruptly and unexpectedly cold. And then he let go, standing up just as Passion did a face-plant into her Bible.

"Mr. Giannopoulos, sir, I think this girl fainted," New Guy said, putting his hand on her back, the picture of concern.

I stared at his hand—his normal hand—but there was nothing else there, no elongated tendrils of PSS or gaping hole to indicate where they had been.

I looked down in my lap. My ghost hand was back, normal as could be, glowing gently and nicely formed into a palm with four regular-sized fingers and one thumb. And there was something else in my lap— a clear plastic baggie full of a something grey and shiny. I had never seen it before, didn't know what it was or where it had come from. Maybe New Guy had put it there—slipped it under my desk when he'd grabbed my wrist.

"What the—?" Mr. G said in alarm, jumping up from his chair and rushing over. "Passion, can you hear me?" he asked loudly, gently taking her by the shoulders and restoring her to an upright position.

Passion's head lolled to one side.

Mr. G looked at New Guy and said, "Call 911."

"She's breathing," Mr. G said as New Guy dialed, and I realized I hadn't been. I'd been holding my breath, waiting for someone to discover I'd killed

Passion Wainwright in Calc class. But she wasn't dead. Mr. G said so. I took a deep, shaky breath.

When Mr. G pulled Passion's long white sleeve back, perhaps to check her pulse, he sucked in air between his teeth, like a reverse whistle. He quickly yanked her sleeve back in place, but not before I'd seen the long white scars and the fresh pink cuts crisscrossing the surface of her inner arm.

Mr. G and I looked at each other. He knew I had seen it, and I could read the conclusion written all over his face; Mr. G thought he'd just discovered the reason Passion had fainted.

I looked up to gauge New Guy's reaction, but he was on the other side of Passion, oblivious, phone to his ear, apparently still waiting for emergency services to pick up.

Passion gave a weak moan.

Mr. G seemed to come to a decision. "Hand me the phone," he said to New Guy. "Someone get Passion some water," he ordered toward the crowd of students gathering in the hall outside the door. There was no class in Mr. G's room last period, so at least students weren't streaming in.

New Guy handed his phone over to Mr. G just as the school nurse came pushing through the crowd. News of Passion's faint had obviously made it to the main office at the other end of the building. Some random freshman brought in a Dixie cup of water. Passion was sitting up a little and seemed to have revived enough for the nurse to dribble some of it into her mouth. Coach Edmunds was doing crowd control in the hall, shooing kids to their next class. "Nothing to see here, folks. Move along," his voice boomed down the long hallways. And Mr. G was on the phone with the 911 operator, talking them out of sending an ambulance.

I felt like I was watching all this from a distance, like there was some kind of screen between me and everything that was happening.

New Guy looked down at me, his eyes full of concern, as if I were the one who'd just been shish-kabobbed.

In a groggy, slurring voice, Passion asked the nurse, "What happened?"

Out in the hallway, the bell rang, signaling the start of the day's last class.

It was my chance to get away. I started to shift out of my desk, forgetting the baggie which began to slide off my lap. I caught it with my left hand and felt a sudden bite of pain. I looked down. One of the shiny grey things was poking through the plastic, its sharp-edged corner digging into my index finger. When I pulled my finger away, I could see the wound; a thin precise line of red where the blade had cut me. Cut me. And cut her. Cutter. Passion Wainwright was a cutter. That was why she wore long sleeves and didn't change for gym. It had nothing to do with her religion. She'd just been hiding her scars. Passion Wainwright, the pastor's daughter, was a cutter and my ghost hand had reached into her. I looked down at the baggie in my lap— a bag full of sharp, thin-edged razor blades. They hadn't come from the New Guy. He hadn't put them in my lap.

"You two," Mr. G said, looking at both of us. "Join me at the back for a minute." It wasn't a request.

As soon as they turned away, I slipped the bag of blades down into my pack and zipped it up. Then I made my way to the back of the classroom.

"Thank you both for your help," Mr. G said, arms crossed, his face serious. "You acted very maturely, especially you, Marcus. Quite a first day you've had."

"I just noticed she was slumped over, that's all," Marcus said.

New Guy's name was Marcus then. He didn't look like a Marcus. Marcuses went to private schools and had trust funds and traveled to Europe for their family vacations. He looked and smelled more down-to-earth than that.

"You stayed calm," Mr. G was saying, "and I'm sure you can both understand the need to keep this incident from becoming a major topic of conversation amongst the student body. I think Passion would appreciate your discretion," he finished, nodding toward the front of the class where the nurse was helping Passion gather her things.

"Of course," Marcus said.

Passion, finally lucid, was protesting weakly that she was fine; she didn't need to go to the nurse's office, but the nurse wasn't taking no for an answer. She guided Passion firmly out the door. Did Passion's parents know she was a cutter? They must. They were the ones who'd written her the note so she wouldn't have to change for gym. But how could they know and not get her help?

"Olivia?" Mr. G said.

I looked up to find Mr. G and Marcus both staring at me.

"Yeah, of course," I said. "I won't say anything."

"Good," Mr. G nodded, looking at us pointedly one last time. "You'll need passes to your next class," he said, heading down the aisle toward his desk.

"You're in shock," Marcus said, his voice low. "Just hold it together long enough for us to get out of here."

I barely heard him, barely noticed him move away from me. Mr. G had stopped at my desk and was looking down at something.

"Olivia, is this your test?" he asked, pointing.

"Uh, yep, it is," I said, moving numbly toward him, trying to act normal, be normal.

Mr. G scooped up my test paper and added to the pile on his desk. Then he began digging in a drawer for his pass slips.

Marcus was gathering up his things.

I walked to my desk, picked up my backpack, and put it over my shoulder. My arms were doing what arms do. My legs were moving my body around. My eyes were seeing things. But it didn't feel like it was me doing any of it.

Marcus was already at Mr. G's desk getting his pass. He took it and headed out the door, not even giving me a backward glance.

Maybe I'd imagined what he'd said. About me being in shock. About us getting out together. No, holding it together. That's what he'd said. He'd told me to hold it together.

I found myself at Mr. G's desk holding out my hand for a pass. Not my ghost hand. It was tucked behind my back, my body a solid barrier between it and him. At least, I hoped.

He finished scrawling his messy signature on the little yellow slip but, instead of handing it to me, he looked up. "Passion will be okay," he said. "We'll make sure she gets some help."

"Yeah, I know," I nodded, staring down at the pass, wondering why he wasn't giving it to me.

"Gossip could really hurt her though."

"Mr. G, I won't say anything."

"Good," he said, finally handing the pass to me.

I slipped it into my pocket and moved out into the hallway.

A shadow separated itself from behind the door and Marcus said, "Come on," taking my arm and steering me down the hall in the wrong direction, away from my Honors English class.

I stumbled along next to him, trying to keep my body between him and my ghost hand, trying to understand where we were going and why we were going there.

We rounded the corner to the Science Wing and he pulled me toward the south exit doors which opened onto a patch of asphalt and the school's collection of trash dumpsters. It was also the favored place for stoners to smoke during lunch hour.

Just shy of the doors I stopped in my tracks, planting my feet shoulder-width apart like I'd learned in self-defense class.

"Let's go," Marcus said, tugging my arm.

"I'm not leaving with you," I said. "I don't even know you."

"What do you mean? I just helped you back there," he said, letting go of me.

"Yeah, but that doesn't mean I know you."

"Fine. I'm Marcus," he held out his hand.

I didn't shake it.

"Listen," he said, obviously frustrated. "You're in shock and you're in danger, especially after what you just did. That's all you really need to know."

"In danger?" My mind was beginning to clear, but I still had no idea what he was talking about.

"Trust me," he said, glancing up and down the hall. "We need to get out of here now." He turned toward the doors again, apparently assuming I'd follow.

"Wait," I said. This time I was the one grabbing his arm. "My hand—I—just tell me what you did to fix it."

He stared down at me.

I became aware of the roundness of his bicep through his shirt, of its smooth solidity under my fingers. He was taller than I was, but not by much. My mouth was about even with his chin, and I could feel the warmth of his body radiating toward me, perfumed with his wood-smoked scent. The phrase "smoking hot" flitted through my mind like a moth, and I batted it away. It was very warm in the hallway. Or I was warm. Shit! My ghost hand was warm.

"It's happening again," I said, letting go of him and backing away. I couldn't help looking down at it. It was shimmering around the edges, just like before.

"I can help you," Marcus said, "if you come with me."

"Help me now!" I cried. Searing heat blazed up my arm as my fingers stretched away from me, twisting and straining towards him.

"We've got to get out of here first," he insisted. "If they see us together, I'll never get you out."

He wasn't making any sense.

One of my PSS fingers was almost touching him.

He extended his hand toward it, completely unafraid.

Was he crazy? Hadn't he seen what I'd done to Passion?

I tucked my ghost hand in toward my body, whirled away from him, and ran.

3

RESCUE FROM THE RESTROOM

I charged into the girl's restroom at the end of the hall, glancing under stall doors and checking for feet. Thankfully, they were all empty, so I chose one with a working latch and locked myself in. I sat down on the toilet seat, trying to catch my breath, and looked down at my hand. It still had tentacles instead of fingers. If anyone saw that, I was screwed.

I dug Mr. G's pass out of my pocket. As usual, he'd neglected to fill out the time on it, which gave me a few minutes to play with. But if I didn't show up for English soon, I'd get reported to the office, and my mother would find out. And I could not explain any of this to my mother.

I stuffed the pass back in my pocket and tried not to freak out. Part of me wanted to run. Run and keep running. But another part of me knew that was stupid. I couldn't run from my own hand. Maybe I should have gone with Marcus. He had made my hand go back to normal, but I was pretty sure of one thing; leaving school with some guy I didn't know without telling anyone was a very bad idea, no matter what he was promising.

Still, I wasn't done with Marcus. He had a lot of explaining to do.

First though, I had to make it through the school day without my hand going postal again. And for that I needed help. Help I could trust. I needed Emma.

Emma Campbell had been my best friend since third grade when we'd discovered we both had a crush on Eric Meyers. Emma's mom, Charlotte Campbell, was Greenfield High's drama teacher, so Emma always spent last period helping backstage with whatever school play was in the works.

I pulled my phone out of the back pocket of my jeans. The battery was low, but I tapped out a text to Emma and pressed send.

Four minutes later, my phone chimed a return message. Good. Emma was already on her way with a hall pass from her mom.

I looked down at my ghost hand. It was still all blurred around the edges, like someone had attacked it with a crimping iron. Why was it doing this to me?

An image flashed in my head from some bad horror film—a severed hand with a bloody stump dragging itself down a long hallway by its fingernails. Except this was worse. My evil hand was still attached to me.

The restroom door banged open, and I yanked my legs up, listening while Brittany Randolph and Leah Hodge used the toilets, washed their hands, and shared a quick cigarette and some mindless chatter. They were freshmen, so I didn't pay much attention to them until they mentioned Passion Wainwright.

"Maybe she's pregnant," Leah said, "That can make you faint and shit."

"You actually think the Virgin Mary screwed someone?" Brittany sneered. "Not likely. I don't think she's pregnant. I think she's schizo."

"Well yeah, but—"

"No, I don't mean just praise-Jesus crazy. I mean so messed up in the head she needs a shrink. My dad saw her coming out of Dr. Black's office the other day."

Dr. Black's office. The way she said it made my mother's workplace sound like a crack house. So, Passion had been seeing my mom and, as usual, I was the last to know. Dr. Sophie Black, psychologist extraordinaire, took her doctor/patient confidentiality very seriously. She never told me anything, which was pretty ridiculous in a town so small and nosey you couldn't take a crap without the neighbors overhearing and asking you how it had all come out. Still, that meant Passion's parents did know about her cutting and had gotten her some help.

After Brittany and Leah left, I lowered my aching legs, only to hear the door open again. I left my legs where they were and hoped for the best.

"Olivia?"

"Emma, I'm in here." I wagged my foot under the stall door. My backpack zipper was undone a little, so I slipped my phone into it. Then I opened the door and ushered Emma in. "What took you so long?" I asked. There wasn't much room. It was a challenge just getting the door closed again.

"I got here as fast as I could," she said, looking concerned. "What's wrong?"

"My hand," I said, holding it out.

"Whoa." Her eyes grew wide. "What happened to it?"

"It went like this in Calculus, and I couldn't control it."

"It went like that and Mr. G didn't send you home?"

"He didn't see it," I explained, "but I can't go to English like this."

"No, you can't."

"Any ideas?"

"Um, let's see. How about this?" Emma said. "I'll go tell Mrs. Baxter my mom wants your help on the production crew like last year. Then we sneak to the auditorium and hide you backstage until school gets out."

"I think that would work. Oh, Em, thank you," I said, throwing my arms around her.

"Hey, it's nothing. You've rescued me lots of times," she mumbled into my shoulder.

I looked down, saw my ghost hand pressed against her back, and pulled away, stumbling against the toilet.

"What?" Emma asked, staring at me.

"I need you to promise me something, okay?" I said, putting my hand behind me. "If my hand starts going weird, you have to get away from me. Don't stay. Don't argue. Don't wait to see what happens. Just run."

"What in the world happened in Calc? Hey, I heard Passion Wainwright fainted and— Oh my God! Did your hand have something to do with *that*?"

"Just promise me," I demanded.

"Fine. I promise. But only if you promise to tell me everything."

"I'll tell you," I said. "Just get me out of English."

"No problem," she said, opening the stall door.

I shut and latched it behind her. Then I sat back down, relief washing over me. Emma was an amazing best friend. I didn't have a clique or a group like most people. I was more of a loner like my dad, who had been a self-proclaimed introvert and artist. Not a wealthy or well-known artist, but a good one with a little studio gallery in our backyard and the occasional big city exhibition. He had actually been one of my best friends and understood me in a way my mother never would. And he had been a buffer between the two of us.

But not anymore.

He'd died of cancer four years ago.

Four years for my relationship with my mom to become what she referred to as "strained", but that was just psycho-babble for the sad fact that we couldn't stand each other. Our relationship had never been peachy, but after my dad died, it had gotten much worse.

Don't get me wrong. I love my mom. But despite the fact that she has a PhD in psychology, she doesn't understand me at all, and that drives her crazy. And then there's the issue of my ghost hand. My dad had always been fascinated by it, but my mother has never been able to hide her disappointment. My parents never came right out and told me, but I know the reason I'm an only child is that my mother didn't want to risk having another baby with PSS.

The restroom door banged opened, and Emma's voice chimed, "It's me. Mrs. Baxter was a piece of cake."

"Thank God." I pulled my backpack over my shoulder and exited the stall. My hand looked almost back to normal if you didn't look too closely.

The halls were pretty empty, and Emma and I made it to the auditorium without any trouble. When we got back stage to the prop room, I collapsed into a ratty, overstuffed chair, while Emma rummaged through a giant chest overflowing with bad wigs, weird hats, and feather boas.

"Here," she said, holding out a long, black, satiny opera glove. "For camouflage, just in case."

"Thanks." I took it and slipped it on, flexing my PSS inside the satin, testing its obedience, molding it to the shape of the glove. My hand seemed completely back to normal. Still, I rested it on my knee where I could keep an eye on it. In the new glove, it looked like someone else's hand, like some villainous overdressed imposter.

"Now," Emma said, flopping into a beanbag, "tell me everything."

4

TELLING EMMA

I was just telling Emma how Marcus had stared at my hand and it had gone all warm, when Mrs. Campbell stuck her head in the prop room door.

"Girls," she said, "I'm desperate for backdrop painters. Come help."

We couldn't exactly refuse, since helping her was sort of my whole cover story. Of course, we weren't the only ones painting, so I couldn't tell Emma anything then. I thought someone might comment on my opera glove, or Mrs. Campbell might ask me to take it off to paint, but everyone was way too occupied speculating about Passion Wainwright to notice anything else. The paint crew had all kinds of theories about why she had fainted. She was pregnant or mentally ill (Thanks Leah and Brittany). She was anemic. She was a vampire. Her dad sexually abused her. She was a lesbian. She was sleeping with Mr. G. (not sure why any of those last four would make someone faint). And the final theory of the day, she was a cutter. I knew Mr. G would blame me for that one, even though I hadn't told a soul. Maybe when he heard he was sleeping with her, he'd understand the true irrepressible nature of the high school rumor mill and cut me some slack.

Anyway, Mrs. Campbell finally figured out what everyone was talking about and put a stop to it.

Usually, I was a pretty good painter. I got that from my dad. But when the final bell rang and Mrs. Campbell came over to take a look at what I'd done, she stared at it in surprise and said, "Olivia, are you all right?"

No, I was not all right. I couldn't stop worrying about Passion. I was terrified my hand was going to impale someone else. I was paranoid about getting caught at school with a backpack full of razor blades. And now I sucked at painting. But I couldn't tell Emma's mom any of that, so I just said, "I'm a little tired."

The rest of the paint crew left to go home, but Emma's mom was our ride, so the three of us stayed and finished repainting my lame backdrop together.

After that, Mrs. Campbell locked up the auditorium, we piled in her mini-van, and she dropped me and Emma off at their place on her way to pick up Mr. Campbell from work. It was their monthly date night, and I always slept over at Emma's on date night.

Finally, Emma and I would be totally alone. Even Grant, Emma's older brother, wouldn't be home. He'd recently left to start his freshman year at Indianapolis University.

Emma opened the back door, tossed her backpack on a kitchen chair, and crossed to the fridge. "Let's get you some food. You're looking kind of pale. And then you can tell me what happened in Calc."

I closed the Campbells' back door and started to toss my backpack too, but then I remembered the blades. I needed to get rid of them, but I couldn't just throw them in Emma's kitchen trash. Someone might see them. I needed someplace no one would find them; maybe I could bury them or something.

"Coke and Cheetos, or Fanta and Funyuns?" Emma asked, her head in the fridge.

"Fanta and Funyuns? That's disgusting." My stomach roiled at the thought. I sat down at the Campbells' kitchen table and set my backpack at my feet.

"Coke and Cheetos it is then," she said, emerging from the fridge with two Cokes clutched in one hand. She snagged a large bag of Cheetos out of the cupboard with the other, kicked the fridge door closed, and sat down next to me. "You okay?" she asked handing me a soda.

"Not really," I said. This was our Friday ritual. Emma's house. Plenty of junk food. Talking about anything and everything that crossed our minds. And it always made me feel better, no matter how bad the week had been, but I was pretty sure it wasn't going to help this time. If I had been in shock, like Marcus had said, it was wearing off and whatever came after it felt an awful lot like needing to cry and hyperventilate at the same time.

"So tell me," Emma said gently, just as a muffled ringing rose from my bag.

We both stared down at it.

"Your phone," Emma said, looking at me expectantly.

It rang again, but I didn't move. What had I been thinking when I'd put my phone in with the blades? That was just the problem; I hadn't been thinking.

The phone rang a third time, insistent, unrelenting.

"Are you going to answer it?" Emma asked.

I reached down and unzipped the bag a little. Thankfully, my phone was resting on top of the blades, so I pulled it out quickly and answered, "Hello?"

"Where are you?" snapped my mother. "I expected you home half an hour ago."

"What? Why? I'm at Emma's. You know I always spend the night at Emma's on the Campbells' date night."

"Yes, I do," she said, "which is why I reminded you three times this morning that I needed you home by four tonight."

"Well, I guess I forgot. Why do you need me home?"

"I want to talk to you," my mother said, her voice backed by a strange, low buzzing.

"Um, okay. Aren't we talking now?" The buzzing was getting louder. I pulled the phone away from my face and looked at it. The battery was almost completely dead. I was losing the connection. "Mom, my phone's about to die," I said, but my mother was talking over me.

"This is not something to discuss over the phone. It's important." My mother's lectures were always important. To my mother. I glanced at Emma, rolling my eyes, but Emma wasn't looking at me. She was staring at my backpack.

"Do you hear that?" she asked, leaning forward and looking down into it.

"Oh, shit!" I said. The buzzing wasn't coming from my phone. It was coming from the blades.

"What did you just say?" my mother demanded.

"Shoot, I said 'shoot'" I lied.

Emma was staring wide-eyed at the blades, now buzzing like a hornet's nest. "What is that?" she asked, looking up at me.

I shook my head, leaned over, tried to zip up the backpack with one hand, and dropped my phone.

"Just a sec—my mom—the phone," I said, picking the phone back up only to find it had hung up.

The blades buzzed, vibrating against my legs through the leather bag.

Emma reached into my pack, grabbed the top of the baggie, and tried to pull it out. It resisted, the zipper of the pack not quite open enough, and then it came away with a tearing sound, razor blades cascading into the depths of my backpack in an avalanche of sharp metallic whispers.

"Sorry," Emma said, the shredded, plastic baggy hanging limply in her hand.

My phone rang again.

"Mom, I dropped my phone," I answered, having to talk loudly over the noise the blades were still making. "And it's almost dead. Can't we talk tomorrow?"

"I have clients tomorrow," she said, her voice clipped and cold. "I expect to see you home in half an hour or there will be consequences."

"But that's not fair. I —"

The phone gave a little chirp, flashed a low battery message, and shut itself off.

I looked over at Emma.

"What are those things in your bag?" she demanded, shaking the torn baggy at me. "And why are they making that noise?"

"They're razor blades," I said.

"Razor blades?" I could see the wheels spinning behind her eyes, making connections, jumping to conclusions.

"They're not mine," I said. "I think my hand pulled them out of Passion. And I have no idea why they're making that noise."

5

THE DARK MAN

"Em, I'm sorry, I really have to go." I was standing under the glow of the Campbells' front porch light. I'd told Emma what I could—a very condensed version of what had happened with my hand and Passion and Marcus and the blades. Of course, she had a lot of questions. Questions I didn't have time or answers for. In the end, she'd offered to keep the blades hidden at her house until we could figure out what to do with them. But as much as they scared me, the thought of leaving them with Emma scared me even more. I didn't know what they were, or why I had them, but I knew I couldn't just dump them in my best friend's lap. And while we talked, they'd grown quiet in the bottom of my pack as if they were listening, as if they were aware and didn't want to be given away.

"You *will* call me," Emma said, "First thing tomorrow we'll get together and figure this out. Are you sure you don't want me to walk you home?"

"Nah. Then you'd just have to walk back by yourself. And my mom is going to be pissed when I get there."

"Okay," she said. "But be careful, and don't do anything stupid." She hugged me and I hugged her back, still careful to keep my ghost hand far away from her.

I stepped off the porch and walked down the Campbells' front walk, looking back at Emma twice and waving.

As I rounded the first corner, the street lights of Greenfield were just flickering on. The wind was whipping up swirls of fallen leaves on the grey, shadowed sidewalks. I loved fall, especially at night. The sharp, crisp, tingle in the air made me feel better, somehow hopeful, even despite the nightmarish events of the day.

I set off down Vine Street. My house was on the other side of town from Emma's, but in Greenfield that was only a fifteen minute walk. The dark wasn't an issue. I'd been walking between my house and Emma's since third grade, day and night.

At the end of Vine, I turned onto Locust Street. At the end of Locust, I veered off the obvious street-course home and headed up Sunset Hill Drive toward the cemetery, the huge oaks that lined it burying me in their darker-than-night shadows. I often cut through the cemetery during the day when the gates were left open for visitors. They were usually locked at dusk, but it was worth a try.

Emma thought the cemetery was creepy, but it was one of my favorite places. Before my dad had died, we'd spent a lot of time there together. He'd liked to take etchings of the tombstones, or sketch stone angels, or tell me bizarre stories of death and woe to match the names and dates on the tombstones. Once, we'd even had a picnic on the top of an old sarcophagus and watched the sunset. And now that my dad was in the cemetery, how could I be afraid of it? Dead people weren't scary. They were just people; mothers, fathers, sisters, brothers, wives and husbands. People someone loved and missed. Emma didn't get that. She'd never lost anyone she loved.

Halfway up Sunset Hill, a car approached, bathing me in the beam of its headlights. I waved as it went by, and the driver waved back. Everyone in Greenfield waved.

At the top of the hill I came to the gates of the Sunset Cemetery, huge, wrought-iron and locked up tight with a chain and hefty padlock. I gripped the bars and rattled them a little. My dad would have known what to do about my hand.

The blades started buzzing again, vibrating against my back. Why were they doing that? It was so random. I slipped off my backpack, set it on the ground, and reached for the zipper with my ghost hand.

Pain shot up my arm into my elbow and I yanked it back. What the—? It had felt like a jolt of electricity. I glanced up and down the street, an instinct born purely of embarrassment. *Did anyone see that?*

And that's when I saw him.

At the bottom of the hill, a dark figure was coming up the sidewalk. His head was bent, looking at something in his hand—a phone or an iPod maybe—so I couldn't see his face. But I knew the moment I saw him that I didn't know him. He wasn't just a tall man in dark clothing taking a brisk stroll through a quiet rural town at night. He was a strange man.

That in itself wasn't so alarming. Out-of-towners did occasionally show up in Greenfield. Relatives. Tourists. People just passing through. This man didn't look particularly threatening. He wasn't even looking my way. But with every step he took, the buzzing of the blades grew sharper and louder and more insistent, as if they were trying to warn me of something.

The Dark Man lifted his head, his face cast in shadows by the overhanging trees, but I felt the moment he noticed me. I felt myself *become seen*.

He quickened his pace.

And I knew he was coming for me.

I threw my backpack over my shoulder. Thankfully, it didn't zap me again. The blades wouldn't shut up though, rattling at my back. I turned to the cemetery gates and pushed my ghost hand through the satin glove, straight into the rusty old padlock. It was a trick I'd used before to help kids open their lockers. My PSS pulsed against the metal workings inside the lock until it clicked and released.

I fumbled to pull the lock off the chain, at the same time looking over my shoulder.

He was halfway up the hill.

The lock came loose in my hand, and I tugged at the hard loops of the chain, hoping for enough slack to make a gap in the gates I could fit through. One more tug and I slammed my shoulder against the right gate, turning by body sideways and jamming my knee against the left gate, widening the gap. I pressed myself between them, ducking my head under the chain, but I only made it halfway. I'd forgotten to factor in the backpack. It was stuck. I was stuck.

I pushed, metal digging into me, not caring if the backpack tore or the blades spilled out. He was coming. I could hear him, the thud of his footfalls contending with the wild thumping of my heart. I pushed again, straps biting into my shoulders, and then the backpack gave way, slipping through the bars, and I was on the other side. Instinct screamed at me to run, but I didn't. I forced myself to reach between the gates, slip the lock back on the chain, and snap it closed with a satisfying click. He wasn't going to make it through that gap; he was way bigger than I was.

If I took off down the narrow, paved road of the cemetery, I'd be out in the open. Instead, I scurried to the side where the gates were hinged into an old stone wall and ducked down, crouching behind a bush. The wall was massive, with tall shrubs and hedges growing so close to it that it was green and frilly with moss. But the cemetery caretaker, Mr. Jackson, worked very hard to make sure nothing grew directly against the wall to dig roots into old mortar and pull away stone. Because of this, there was a thin, dark gap, almost like a deer trail, running along the entire inside perimeter of the wall. I knew I could follow it all the way to the south gate because I'd done it just for fun when I was ten.

I sat, huddled in the dark, the backpack still buzzing angrily between my shoulder blades. Would he be able to hear that from outside the gate? It wasn't that loud. More like a sensation even, than a sound. It just felt loud to me because it was right against my back. Maybe he wasn't even following me. Why would he? Why would anyone? When he'd looked up at me, I'd been so sure. But suddenly, it seemed ridiculous.

If he walked past the gate, if he kept going, I'd know. Just a strange man out for an evening stroll. No reason to get freaked and go tearing through the cemetery. From where I was I couldn't see much outside the gate, but I'd know if he tried to open it.

I waited, the evening breeze brushing my face, the quick intake of my own breath punctuating the night.

Suddenly two pale hands slipped through the gate, gripping it and rattling it exactly the way I had. He rattled it again, harder. He might still give up. Just because he wanted in the cemetery didn't mean he was after me. Maybe he'd come to visit a dead relative. At night. In the dark.

The hands stayed and were joined by a triangular wedge of black jutting between the bars near the ground. It was the toe of his shoe wedged against the bottom bar of the gate. He was going to climb over. Shit! I hadn't thought of that. Time to get moving.

I got up as quietly as I could and took off along the dark little trail that skirted the wall. He wouldn't guess I'd come this way, unless he was some kind of professional tracker. Or he could see in the dark. Or the blades really were calling to him. Any of those and I was screwed. I thought about ditching the blades, but now that they were loose inside my backpack, that would mean tossing the whole thing. There was stuff in there I needed, like my phone and my homework, not to mention that I'd bought the backpack myself, searching long and hard for it on the internet. Besides, how could the blades have anything to do with the guy chasing me if they'd come from inside Passion?

I ran a little further, then stopped and listened. No footfalls behind me. No sound of someone pursuing me through the brush. A feeling of elation came over me. I'd done it. I'd lost him. Let dark creepy stalker-man wander around in the cemetery all night, he wasn't getting what he wanted. Whatever that was.

Following the hidden trail along the wall was not as easy as it had been when I was ten. First, I had been much shorter then. Second, I hadn't remembered it being so snarly and bumpy and annoying. Already, I had almost been brained by low-hanging branches twice, not to mention there was a small rock in my boot, digging painfully into my foot. I had no idea how long it had been since I'd left Emma's, but I probably wasn't going to make my mother's deadline unless I broke out into the clear.

The blades had quieted to a bare tremble. I wasn't even sure I was still hearing them. Maybe it was just the memory of hearing them, an echo in my imagination.

I came around a bend in the path and tripped on a root, flailing forward. I grabbed for the wall with my left hand, skin scraping against stone, and managed to keep myself from falling flat on my face.

"This is stupid," I hissed when I'd regained my balance. My hand was stinging like crazy, and I could see just enough to know it was oozing blood. "That's it," I pushed my way between two bushes and walked out into the dappled moonlight of the open cemetery.

Dark, stumpy silhouettes of tombstone, like sleeping dwarves, rose from the ground all around me. Down the hill toward the cemetery road, several large stone crosses jutted above the rest like King and Queen. Up the hill to my left was the boxy slab of an aboveground sarcophagus, the same one my dad and I had picnicked on. I knew exactly where I was. It was an older part of the cemetery, but just down the hill and across the road was the section where my dad was buried. I could cross that way toward the south gate and home.

I stood, listening. I could see most of the cemetery, and I didn't see any sign of the Dark Man. No moving shadows. No sound but the sigh of the wind and the rustling of the leaves. Even the blades were silent. Still, it would pay to keep out of sight as much as I could.

I made my way down the hill, ducking from shadow to shadow, weaving between gravestones. I crossed the road under the dark canopy of an overhanging elm. Again, I waited and watched. Then I crossed into the grass and limped the few paces to my father's grave so I could remove the rock from my boot. The only thing to sit on, other than wet grass, was Melva Price's headstone, *1938-1999, Beloved Mother and Wife, now in God's hands*. I sat on it. I always sat on Melva; she didn't mind.

My father's grave was just a grassy mound without a marker, and I tried to quell the surge of anger I always felt when I saw it. My mother had refused to buy a tombstone. She hadn't asked my opinion. She'd informed me, "We don't need anything to mark his grave. That's not him." So, all there was to indicate Stephen Black's place of rest, to declare his time and existence on this earth, was a small stone provided by the cemetery that said G42. G for the cemetery section. 42 for the number of the plot. Just a letter and a number so they wouldn't dig him up by accident, or bury someone on top of him. My dad was nothing but a bingo call.

But not for much longer. I'd been saving for two years. Not for a fancy headstone— those ran in the thousands of dollars and dad wouldn't have wanted anything like that anyway. But I had picked out a simple, etched granite headstone for only fifteen hundred dollars, and I was almost there. My mother thought I was saving for a car.

"Hey Dad," I said softly, bending over to unbuckle and loosen my boot. I tried to do it quickly, but they weren't exactly designed for easy removal. "Today pretty much sucked," I told him, still glancing around nervously. "My hand went all weird, reached into

Passion Wainwright, and pulled something out." I yanked my boot off, tipped it upside down, and shook out the rock. "And I think someone was following me, so I have to get moving." I said, pulling my boot back on.

In my backpack, the blades began to tremble. Leaves crunched behind me, and suddenly a hand was on my face, slapped across my mouth, smashing my lips into my teeth. Two muscled arms closed around me, and someone pressed against my back, grinding my pack into my shoulder blades. A warm huff of a voice in my ear said, "I won't hurt y—" and before I could even struggle, I was yanked backwards off Melva Price's headstone.

When I hit the ground, it wasn't ground. Something writhed under me. Not something. Someone. The Dark Man had found me and was gripping me so tightly I could barely breathe, and yet *he* seemed to be the one convulsing and choking, and gasping for air. I tried to roll away, to kick him, to extract myself from his clutches. Instead, we rolled down the slope of Section G, his body smashing mine into the earth numerous times before our momentum was halted by an abrupt crash into something hard and prickly.

The world was dark and spinning. I couldn't breathe. All the air had been pounded from my lungs. I opened my mouth, gulping like a fish. When I opened my eyes I thought for a moment that a tree had somehow fallen and landed on top of me. But it wasn't a tree; it was one of the huge hedges that divided the various sections of the cemetery. And it hadn't fallen on me. I had rolled right under its carefully manicured edge and been stopped by its thick trunk, which was now digging into my side. I was facing the dark, upper interior of the hedge, a lower branch poking my left cheek, grinding into my teeth and gums. I tried to push it away, but I couldn't lift my hand.

My captor's grip had gone slack, the two of us so tightly wedged under the bush I could barely move. It wasn't lumpy ground beneath me. It was him. Pinned under me. But he wasn't moving. He was still, very still, though I could feel the rise and fall of his chest, even with my backpack wedged between us. Maybe he'd been knocked out during our downhill tumble. Whatever. It didn't matter. Now was my chance to get away from him.

I pulled my face back from the branch and turned my head. I could see a small strip of cemetery from under the hedge. There was my dad's grave and the bottom portion of Melva's headstone. Beyond that was home, safety, normalcy.

I tensed my muscles and tried to squirm out from under the bush, but I couldn't find any leverage. Maybe I could position my arms and hands against the trunk and push myself out. I squirmed a little more, trying to clear obstacles from around my hands and arm. A branch snapped, but not a branch I'd been pushing on. The noise had come from out in the cemetery.

I froze as a pair of dark feet and legs appeared in my small strip of vision.

Whoever was out there crouched at the side of my dad's grave, inspecting the ground.

I still couldn't see his face, but I could see enough. There was no doubt in my mind. The Dark Man was out there. The man I'd been running from was still after me.

But if he was out there, who the hell was I lying on top of?

I craned my neck, the placid, unconscious face of my attacker looming at my shoulder.

It was Marcus.

6

CPR IN THE CEMETERY

I lay very still under the hedge watching the Dark Man search my dad's grave and the surrounding area. I couldn't see more than his legs and feet, but he kept returning to Melva's gravestone and circling around it. That must be where he lost my trail. Or he was baffled by the addition of Marcus's. Either way, something was confusing him. Something was confusing me too.

Why in the world had Marcus attacked me? How had he even found me, unless he'd been following me just like the Dark Man? Maybe they had been working together, one flushing me out and the other one grabbing me.

But if that was true, why throw me to the ground and roll me down a hill? Why not just hold me and wait for the Dark Man? Then again, it hadn't felt like Marcus had thrown me as much as it had felt like we'd fallen. Both of us tumbling backwards when he'd locked his arms around me, him gripping me and thrashing like he was having some kind of seizure.

Oh my God! What if it had been the blades? The backpack had been pinned between us. What if the blades had zapped Marcus, just like they'd zapped me, except worse? That might explain his stop midsentence, the contracting of his muscles, the thrashing I'd felt and the choking I'd heard.

Well, it served him right. People should not sneak up behind someone at their father's graveside and grab them from behind. Still, to completely spazz out like that he must have gotten a pretty nasty zap. The blades couldn't be conducting electricity—they had no source of current. But they were definitely conducting something.

I looked down at Marcus. His bangs were tossed back off his forehead and my eyes had adjusted enough to notice strange shadows there. On impulse, I extended the tip of my ghost hand's index finger just beyond the glove. Emma called it my ET finger. Like a penlight, it bathed Marcus's face and forehead in its soft glow, revealing that his skull, just below his hairline, was dented and scarred like something that had been broken and glued back together. The scars were thin, pale and old, very distinct from several new pink scratches on his face, no doubt acquired from our recent tumble. A few of the old scars trailed up into his hair, making it fall in multiple, zigzagging parts. Whatever had broken Marcus's head, it had happened a long time ago.

Out in the cemetery, the Dark Man rose from a crouch behind Melva's tombstone and started walking toward the hedge.

I pulled my finger back into the glove and held my breath. Had he seen the glow? What would he do when he looked under the hedge and saw me stuck there? He'd pull me out, that's what. I could kick and scream and scratch and fight, but he was bigger and stronger than I was. No one was likely to hear my protests from this far inside the cemetery. If he saw me, he was going to get me. And whoever's side Marcus was on, it didn't look like it was going to matter.

I felt adrenaline rushing my body as the Dark Man's feet grew larger and larger, dominating my vision. With my left hand I grabbed the trunk of the hedge as tightly as I could. My ghost hand was on the side toward the opening, so I might be able to use it to distract him, if it came to that. Five minutes before, I had really wanted to get out from under the hedge. Now, I was preparing to fight for my life to stay under it.

The shoes stopped at the edge of the hedge, a mere six inches from Marcus's face. They were expensive shoes, maybe even Italian, with a fine stitched detailing around the edges in a grey thread that stood out in the moonlight. Did killers wear shoes like that? Did rapists? They seemed so normal, like something a lawyer or a stockbroker would wear. Why was this guy after me? Why was I hiding from him? Surely there was some perfectly reasonable explanation, and if I just showed myself, I'd find out what it was.

Something squeezed my right arm, and I barely bit back a yelp. I saw the white flash of Marcus's eyes out of the corner of mine. He was awake, conscious, staring at me; his breath puffing into my hair. I wasn't alone.

But was he on my side?

He looked at me, and his eyes panned to the shoes, then back to me with a little shake of his head; he didn't want to be found by the owner of those shoes any more than I did.

The toes of the shoes turned this way and that. The Dark Man had no idea we were lying at his feet. He turned and walked away, back to Melva's gravestone.

Marcus's body relaxed slightly, but I could still feel the tension in every line of it; the twitch of his well-defined bicep against my shoulder, the flex of his warm thigh under me. When he'd been unconscious, lying on him had felt like lying across a lumpy, human-shaped bag of sand. It had been so passive. But not anymore. Now his body felt hard and warm and defined, the hair of his arm brushing against mine and giving me goose bumps. Marcus felt just as good as he looked.

I realized I was still gripping the trunk of the hedge, and I let go of it.

Back at my dad's graveside, the Dark Man slipped something from his pocket, the same thing he'd been using when I'd first seen him coming up Sunset Hill.

Marcus's entire body tensed under me, and his fingers dug into my arm. "He's going to find us now," he whispered in my ear. "I'm going to distract him.

And you're going to run away. But don't show him your hand or use it on him. No matter what."

The Dark Man switched on the thing in his hands, and it gave off a gentle glow.

The bag of blades in my backpack exploded with an angry buzz, but they were wedged so tightly between Marcus and me that it was quite muffled.

Marcus's deep grunt of pain, however, was not so muffled. It sounded like he had been punched in the gut, and he actually tried to buck me off, slamming me into the bottom of the hedge before he fell back, limp, and unmoving.

My face burned, and I felt a warm trickle of blood drip down my cheek where a branch had gouged it.

The blades had zapped Marcus again, and there was nothing I could do about it. I couldn't move away from him. I couldn't even get off of him.

Surely the Dark Man had heard all that flailing and was coming for us.

His legs had turned toward the hedge again, and he was holding out his device like a Geiger counter.

The blades vibrated against my back, the sound of their edges rubbing together like a whisper just beyond meaning.

The Dark Man took a step toward the hedge, shaking the thing in his hand and jabbing its buttons angrily as if it were a broken remote.

I braced myself again, one hand on the tree trunk, ghost hand out and ready.

A blare of rap music shattered the silence of the cemetery, suddenly cut off when the Dark Man reached in his pocket and pulled out a cell phone. Really? That was his ringtone? I found myself biting back a giggle of hysteria.

The Dark Man raised the phone to his cheek, beyond my field of vision and said, "Where are you? Did you bring a meter?"

His voice was deep and commanding and tinged with a slight accent. Not anything strong or identifiable, just an edge of European strangeness.

"This one is not working," he said, shaking the device in his hand again.

I don't know how I'd ever mistaken it for a phone. It was way too thick and not quite the right shape. It was something else; something Marcus had been convinced would find us. Except, apparently it was malfunctioning. Now, if the Dark Man would just give up and go away.

"No. I'll come to you. Meet me at the gate," the Dark Man said, as if on cue to my wish. He turned off his phone and the meter thing and stuck them both in his pocket. He stood for a moment, facing the hedge, perhaps taking one last look, and then his legs and his feet with their nice expensive shoes turned and headed off in the direction of the cemetery road.

I felt my whole body sink into Marcus's chest. The Dark Man was leaving. He hadn't found us. But he might come back, and we had to get out of that godforsaken bush before he did, which meant I had to get Marcus conscious and moving pronto.

"Marcus," I whispered, wiggling around and trying to create room where there wasn't any. "Wake up." It wasn't like I could slap him or douse him with a bucket of water.

I reached up and broke several small branches so I could turn to my side, forcing my backpack toward the trunk of the hedge so it was no longer between us. I had to dig my shoulder and elbow into him to do it, but that didn't rouse him either. Finally, I was in a position to look down at his face. In the darkness of the hedge, the whites of his eyes stared back at me eerily.

"Marcus?"

His eyes didn't move, didn't look my direction. Was he playing some kind of prank, staring blankly past me like that? Pretending to be unconscious with his eyes open.

"Marcus," I hissed, poking him in the ribs with my elbow purposefully this time.

He didn't respond. His lips were parted, but I didn't feel the huff of his breath on my face like I had before.

Because there wasn't any.

"No. No, no, no, no," I chanted, jabbing him with my elbow even harder. "Don't do this to me." I lay still for a moment, trying to feel the rise and fall of his chest under me. But there was nothing. No, there had to be breathing. He was just breathing lightly, imperceptibly, because my mind couldn't go to the place with no breathing. It veered away from—that word. The word that came after not breathing.

Just a minute ago he'd been barking instructions and promising to save the day. Yes, people stopped breathing sometimes. I knew that. My dad hadn't breathed for a very long time. But the actual end of his breathing had taken two years of hospital visits, and chemo, and radiation, and watching him shrivel as the cancer and the cure raced to see who could kill him first. We'd talked about it. We'd prepared. We'd said goodbye. And I'd sat there listening to his labored breathing for days and days before the final, last, sighing, relieved breath had come and gone. It had still hurt me more than anything had ever hurt when it had come, but at least I had seen it coming from a long way off. But this. This wasn't possible. Alive and warm one minute, cold and breathless the next. Someone's existence couldn't turn on a dime like that.

"You're gonna be fine," I told Marcus. He was my age. He was good-looking and in my Calc class. And I was lying on top of him under a hedge. He wasn't allowed to stop breathing under those circumstances. "We just need to get you out of here. Get some help."

How long had the Dark Man been gone? Who cared? What was he going to do if he came back? Kill us? Maybe he knew CPR.

I wrestled my way out from under the hedge, pushing against Marcus and the trunk for leverage, clutching at branches and grass to pull myself free. Once I rolled off his chest, the rest was pretty easy.

I yanked off my backpack and set it beside me, then reached into the dark under the hedge and felt for Marcus's arm. No wonder the Dark Man hadn't seen us. I wouldn't have believed Marcus was under there if I hadn't just crawled off of him.

What had the blades done? With electrocution, or seizures, there was something about turning people on their sides so they didn't choke on their tongues. Marcus had been on his back with me sitting on his chest and no way to turn any direction. He'd tried to buck me off, but I'd had nowhere to go.

No way was this going to be my fault.

I finally found his arm, and wrapped my hands around it. It wasn't cold yet, or stiff. How long did that take? How long after someone stopped breathing could you still revive them? I had no idea, but I had to try. First though, I had to get him out of there.

I pulled, but he barely budged. I got on my knees and put my back into it. That was enough to get one shoulder and half his head out. After that I was able to grab under his armpits and drag him out so that his whole head and chest were clear of the bush.

Now, I just had to remember the CPR class I'd taken freshman year so my mom would let me babysit the Waverly twins. First, I was supposed to check for breathing. I'd already done that. Next, check for an obstruction. His mouth was hanging open, but all I could see was his tongue. It wasn't black or blue or swollen, and it didn't look like he was choking on it, so I left it alone.

I pinched his nose closed, and bent over his head, terrified that any moment those blank, open eyes were going to focus on me and he was going to laugh in my face. It was psyching me out, so I closed my eyes. I felt my lips touch his face. I had to open my mouth surprisingly wide to span the distance around his mouth, and then I realized I hadn't taken a big enough breath. Shit. I pulled away slightly, gulped in some air and dove back toward his mouth like I was bobbing for apples. Huff. Take a gulp of air. Huff. How many times was I supposed to breathe into him? Just a few more for good measure. His mouth was warm, but not firm. I began to see flashes of light on the inside of my eyelids. Maybe I was huffing a little too much. The last thing we needed was for me to pass out on top of him. I pulled away and turned my head so my cheek was just above his mouth. *Come on. You can do it. Breathe back at me.*

Was that a tickle of breath? I couldn't tell. The next step was to start chest compressions. But how many? There was a ratio, but I couldn't remember it. Three breaths and thirty compressions? That seemed like a lot. *Don't over-analyze this. Just do it.* I was supposed to push down in the middle, right between his pecs.

I laced my fingers together, making sure not to lock my elbows.

As I looked down at him, his body seemed infused with light, like his spirit was suddenly bursting to get out.

"Oh, no you don't," I said, positioning myself over him for the first compression. The phrase "break a rib," flashed through my mind. *Idiot! It's break a leg. And that's for plays.*

But my hands never made it to his chest.

His arms shot up, fingers clamping my wrists in a vice grip. "Don't," he said, pushing me away from him even as he pulled his legs out from under the hedge and sat up. "Where is he?" he demanded, glancing around and scrambling to a crouch.

"You were dead," I said. There. I'd used the word. The one that came after not breathing. Except sometimes, apparently, it didn't.

"No, I wasn't," he said.

"Yes, you were," I insisted.

"Well, I'm not now," he said, as if that settled it. "Where's the camper? The one that was stalking you?"

"The camper?" I asked, confused.

"No, not camper. CAMFer. C A M F E R," he spelled out.

"That guy was a CAMFer?"

"Where did he go?"

"Um, he got a phone call and he left," I said. And you were dead. And now you're not.

"He'll be back," Marcus said, grabbing my arm just like he'd done in the school hallway, "and we have to be gone before he does."

"Let go of me," I said, shaking out of his grip, and standing up. "You don't have to grab me." He was so obnoxious when he was alive.

"Then get down," he said, gesturing for me to crouch like he was.

I crouched, glaring at him.

"I'm sorry I grabbed you," he said. "It's just that we're in a lot of danger. Do you even know what CAMF is?"

"Citizens Against Minus Flesh," I said. "They're a lobbyist group trying to pass dehumanizing laws against people with PSS." That was straight from Wikipedia. "But they're just lobbyists. They don't chase people down in cemeteries. They eat lunch with politicians in Washington."

"Some of them do," he agreed. "But that man is a member of a more militant branch of CAMF. That device he had is called a minus meter, and it can both detect and extract PSS. He's been following you since you left your friend's house, and it wasn't so he could buy you lunch. So, we really need to get out of here right now."

"Well his meter thing was broken. That's what he said on the phone anyway. And someone was bringing another one. Wait. What do you mean by 'extract PSS?'"

"Extract. Remove. Take by force," Marcus said like some cold-hearted thesaurus as he scanned the trees again.

I stared down at my ghost hand. "You mean take my hand?"

"Yes," he turned back to me, his face grim.

7

CLUELESS

"How do you know all this?" I asked, staring at Marcus. "How do you know that guy followed me from Emma's, or who he is, or what that meter thing does?" I ploughed on, my voice growing shriller and shriller as I went.

"Shhhh!" he said, raising his hand in my face and cocking his head as if he heard something.

I hated to be shushed. There was nothing I hated more than being shushed, and I was about to tell him that when I heard it too. Men's voices. Distant, but drifting down to us from the upper cemetery.

"They're coming back," Marcus whispered. "We

need somewhere to hide."

"I know a place." I scrambled on the ground for my backpack, finding it by feel, by the gentle hum of the blades. "But won't they just track us with the new minus meter?"

"Maybe," Marcus said. "Would you rather stay here and find out?"

"No."

He stood up and flourished his hand in a gentlemanly "after you" gesture.

I raised my eyebrows at him and that old smirk from Calculus flitted across his lips.

"This way," I said, slinging my backpack on and leading us deeper into Sunset Hill Cemetery.

It was my fault, what happened next. I thought I knew the cemetery so well. Every rock, every scraggly tree and grave marker. Nothing ever really changes in a cemetery. Well, one thing changes, but only when someone dies, and that doesn't happen all that often in Greenfield.

So, I didn't see the freshly dug grave until I was literally teetering over it, dirt cascaded out from under my feet.

I pumped my arms like reverse propellers and threw myself backwards.

Marcus was following very closely behind me.

I collided with him, the backpack nailing him in the chest, and I knew what was going to happen, even as I hurled myself to the side, spinning away from him and falling to the ground.

He screamed—a really freaky scream—a someone-being-brutally-tortured-scream.

When I looked up he was bending over me, clutching his chest and gasping for air, his eyes staring wildly down at me through his bangs. I was just glad to see he wasn't unconscious. Or dead again. Though it certainly would have been a convenient location for it.

"Oh God. I'm sorry. I'm so sorry." I said, struggling to my feet and reaching out to touch his shoulder.

He flinched away, and I couldn't really blame him.

"What—the hell—is in there?" he asked, wheezing between each phrase. Then, "Don't ever touch me with that bag again," his eyes gleaming dangerously.

Voices. The CAMFers' voices. Louder and closer now.

"Fuck!" Marcus said. "They definitely heard that." He straightened up even though it obviously pained him. "We have to get moving."

"This way," I gestured, carefully skirting the grave.

I led us to a small grouping of maintenance sheds. The biggest one had two padlocked barn-style doors to accommodate the riding lawnmowers. It also had a smaller locked back door we could use to make our escape if we were discovered. Neither of the locks would be a problem for my ghost hand.

While I was picking them, I heard the voices again, not too far behind us. Whether by special device or old-fashioned means, we were definitely being tracked.

Once inside the shed, we both crouched near the door. I reached my ghost hand through and fiddled with the chain and padlock until it was neatly locked up again on the outside. *See, it's still locked. No one in here. Go away and leave us alone.*

"What's that noise?" Marcus whispered in my ear, close enough that I could feel his breath on my cheek.

"The sound of you panting like a Labrador?" I whispered back.

"No, that buzz."

"It's— from my backpack. They won't hear it."

"God, what do you have in there?"

"Shhh," I said. I really didn't want to answer that question.

Maybe he didn't like to be shushed either, because I felt him move away from me. I listened at the door, peeking through the crack, but I couldn't see anything useful. I glanced back, trying to find Marcus in the dark, and I could just make out the vague outline of a riding lawnmower with his shadowy frame perched on the seat. I crawled quietly across the cold cement floor, reached out, and touched his leg. He didn't flinch away this time.

"Quiet," he whispered. "They're close."

And he was right. If the blades hadn't been telling me, the shuffle of feet and the rumble of male voices from outside the shed would have.

"We've lost the trail," one of the voices said.

It was so close and loud I pressed against the lawnmower and Marcus's leg, willing myself imperceivable.

"And both these meters are on the fritz," the same voice said in frustration. No accent, so it wasn't the Dark Man.

"I told you." That was definitely him though. "Something is jamming the signal."

"I thought these things couldn't be jammed."

"So did I," said the Dark Man, not angry, but cold, hard, emotionless. "And I thought this girl knew nothing about us, but it seems we were wrong on both counts."

"She doesn't know anything. No one in this backwater town has any idea what's going on in the real world."

"And yet," the Dark Man countered, "our monitors recorded a major PSS flare in this town just this afternoon. And now the only defective living here has evaded us, and apparently she has something that can jam technology you claim she has no knowledge of."

I did not like that voice. It was not a nice voice. And had he just called me defective?

"She's not jamming them," the other voice argued. "They're just broken. I'm telling you, I've been watching this girl for years, and she's as clueless as they come."

Watching me for years? Did I know that voice? Someone in Greenfield had been watching me for years. What the hell for?

Marcus must have sensed me tensing up because he put a hand on my head and patted me like I was a spastic dog.

The voices were moving away. "She's not in here. It's locked tight. All these buildings are locked." That was the spy's voice. So I was clueless, was I? At least I had enough sense to know someone with a PSS hand could pick a lock and close it up again from the inside.

"It doesn't matter," said the Dark Man's voice, receding. "There are other ways of getting—"

Of getting what? My hand? What perfect timing for them to move out of earshot. I felt myself begin to shake, but I didn't know if it was from fear, or anger, or what.

"The buzzing stopped," Marcus whispered.

"I know," I said. "It's some kind of reaction to those devices. I think it's what's jamming them."

"Wait, you mean the thing you pulled out of that girl in math class zaps the hell out of people *and* jams minus meters?"

"How did you—Did you see me pull it out?" I demanded.

"No," he mumbled. "I heard you say it, here in the cemetery."

"You were listening in on my private conversation with my dead father?"

"I was trying to warn you that a CAMFer was stalking you."

"Right," I snapped. "By falling on me and making my backpack torture you. I almost forgot."

"Oh, give me a break! I just saved you out there."

"You saved me? You have got to be kidding me. You spent most of the time playing dead. If anyone saved anyone, I'm pretty sure I saved you."

"Saving someone you've just killed hardly counts."

"Hey! I had no idea it would do that."

"Exactly! You have no clue about anything. You have no idea what your hand can do, or what it pulled into the world. You're walking around with something in your backpack that can torture people on contact. Something those CAMFers would kill to get their hands on. You need to come with me," Marcus insisted, but he didn't grab me this time, and I knew why. He was afraid of getting zapped again. "I can help you keep that thing from falling into the wrong hands," he said, glancing at my backpack warily.

"Come with you? Come with you where? You're in high school, just like me. How in the hell are you going to keep me safe from militant CAMFers?"

"I just can," he said, stepping off the lawnmower and moving past me toward the door. "Trust me. There's a place in the woods—"

"No," I said. "I can't go with you. Don't you get it? My mom expected me home like an hour ago. She'd going to be seriously pissed, especially after I tell her some guys were following me in the cemetery."

Marcus's silhouette stopped in its tracks halfway to the door and turned toward me. "That is a really bad idea," he said.

"Why is that a bad idea?"

"Because," he sputtered, "she'll probably call the cops. Someone in this town has been watching you for years. Might just be one of your friendly neighborhood officers."

"It could be anyone," I argued, but I didn't believe it. I couldn't wrap my mind around it. Someone in Greenfield, someone I knew, someone I had known and trusted for years, had been spying on me.

"The point is you don't know who you can trust," Marcus was saying.

"No," I said, getting up and moving toward him, "the point is I need answers, and you have them, and you're using them to try and get me to disappear into the woods with you. How am I supposed to trust that?"

"I can't tell you what I know unless you come with me," he said in frustration.

"Why, because you don't trust me?"

"No," he shot back. "Because as long as you're within their reach, they won't give up. And if they take you, they're going to find out whatever you know, and I can't risk that."

"I don't know anything! I'm clueless remember?" I said, struggling to keep my voice down. "And take me?" I blinked at him. "I thought they wanted to take my PSS, not me. Where would they take me?"

He just stared at me, his arms crossed.

"At least tell me how you fixed my hand in Calc today."

"Come with me, and I will," But he couldn't even look at me as he said it. He knew it was a cheap shot.

"Oh. Wow. Thanks for nothing," I said, pushing past him. Out of the corner of my eye, I saw him step back, moving well clear of any contact with my backpack. At the shed door, I slipped my ghost hand through and popped the lock.

"Olivia," he said, half-plea, half-warning.

"What?" I said, looking back at him as I pushed the shed door open a crack.

"That thing in your bag. If it can block their minus meters, keep it close to you. And don't let them get their hands on it."

"I get it. I'll be careful," I said, before I turned and slipped out, heading toward the south gate of the cemetery and home, leaving Marcus alone in the dark, which seemed appropriate, since that was exactly how he'd left me.

8

MY MOTHER

On the way home, I kept looking over my shoulder, but if Marcus or the CAMFers were following me, I didn't see them, and the blades had fallen completely silent, which seemed like a good sign. At the cemetery's south gate, I made quick work of the lock, then jogged up North Elm Street and turned onto Durley. My house was the two-story, second on the left. The lights were on, and my mom's sky blue VW bug was in the drive. Now, all I had to do was face the onslaught of her anger and get to my room where I could hide the blades until I figured out what to do with them.

I walked up the path to my front door and turned the knob. It wasn't locked. No one locked their doors in Greenfield unless they were going out of town. Even then, sometimes they left them unlocked so their neighbors could feed the cat and water the plants. I opened the door and walked into the entryway.

The overhead light was off, but a sconce on the wall illuminated one of my favorite paintings by my dad. He had painted it when I was four, around the time my parents had informed me that I was never going to have a little brother or a little sister to play with. It was an oil-on-canvas of a pale, glowing girl on a deeply black-blue background. The girl was ethereal and ghostly, except for her right hand, which was the most realistic, fleshy hand I had ever seen. It looked like you could reach out and take that hand in yours. Everyone who saw the painting said that. My father had titled it *The Other Olivia,* and I had fought long and hard to keep that painting in the entryway after my father had died. My mother had packed up all his other work and stored it in his old garden studio out back.

I smiled at *The Other Olivia* and pulled the front door closed, making sure to lock it behind me.

"No, she isn't home yet," my mother's voice was saying to someone on the phone, and then, "Olivia, is that you?"

"Hey," I rounded the corner into the room's arched doorway, the brighter lights blinding me for a second.

"I have to go," my mother murmured into the receiver and hung up without even saying goodbye.

"Who was that?" I asked.

"I've been waiting for you for over an hour," she said, staring at the phone, her voice tight and throaty. "I can't believe you'd disrespect me like this." She looked up and her mouth dropped open in surprise. "What on earth!" She jumped up from the brown leather couch. "Olivia, you're bleeding." She didn't sound concerned as much as she sounded annoyed, but I was pretty used to that. My mother wasn't great at personal empathy. She was paid to be professionally empathetic but, apparently, she used it all up on her clients.

"I had a little accident on the way home," I said. "It's just a few scratches." I'd realized that Marcus was at least right about one thing; telling my mother that CAMFers had been chasing me was not a good idea.

"Little accident? You're bleeding and you're filthy," she said, taking my left hand and pulling me further into the light.

I gasped and jerked my hand away.

"What—?" she grabbed my wrist and turned my hand palm up. It was bright red, and oozing blood and dirt. "How did you do all this? It's not that difficult to walk home from Emma's."

"I took the cemetery shortcut," I said, "and I tripped on a tombstone in the dark. I tried to catch myself with this hand, but I ended up landing face-first in a bush." I wasn't a great liar, but I could usually pull one off when I had to.

"The cemetery," my mother said, shaking her head. "This is getting ridiculous, Olivia."

"What is ridiculous about the cemetery?"

"Oh come on. We both know you just go there to be dramatic and get under my skin."

"Really? Because I thought I was going there to visit dad," I said, yanking my hand out of hers.

"For clarification, you visit his grave. You don't visit him. He's gone. But that's not what I was referring to, and you know it."

"What were you referring to then?"

"I was referring to your unhealthy, romanticized attachment to the idea of death."

"The *idea* of death? Don't you mean the reality of death? People die, Mom. Dad is dead. It isn't just some crazy idea I have."

"Yes, death is a reality, but obsessing over it isn't mentally healthy."

"Don't analyze me. I'm not one of your clients. And at least I'm not wallowing in denial."

"We weren't talking about me. We were talking about you. And what you just did is called avoidance. Rather than face your own issues—"

"Oh please, save it for the office! You and I both know I'm not the only one in this family with issues about death." So, we were fighting again. We always fought. It was one of the few things I could count on.

"Again, that's avoidance," she said. "As long as you keep putting your grief and anger back on me, you're never going to be able to deal with it."

"Deal with it? *You* think *I'm* not dealing with it? I visit him. I talk to him. I miss him. And yes, I'm extremely pissed at the universe for taking him away. But that is NOT avoidance. Avoidance is constantly analyzing your daughter's feelings so you never have to face your own. Avoidance is hiding his life's work in a shed in the backyard. Avoidance is refusing to mark your husband's grave and never visiting it because you're afraid if you face that reality you'll end up being the mental patient, instead of the doctor. Oh, believe me mom, I know all about avoidance. I see it every day. I live with it, and eat with it, and talk to it, and fight with it. It's practically my mother!"

Her eyes widened with shock. I saw pain, for a moment, tremble at the corners of her lips. For a split second, I thought she was going to slap me. And I wanted her to. I wanted her to hurt and cry and break into a million pieces with me. I didn't want to be alone anymore, feeling everything for both of us. I wanted it so badly, I could feel it in my face, my throat, my chest, my arms, my hands.

"Olivia!" my mother yelped, looking down at my hand.

"It's fine. I told you. It's just a scrape," I said dismissively, looking down too. But my mother wasn't looking at my injured hand. She was looking at my ghost hand and the PSS that was seeping out of the tattered satin glove in spiraling tendrils.

"What is that?" she asked, backing away a step.

I turned and ran down the hallway into the bathroom, slamming and locking the door behind me.

"Olivia, are you all right?" my mother's voice came through the wooden door. "What is wrong with your hand?"

I leaned against the door, panting and looking down at it. "Um, I'm fine. Yeah, it's fine. I just need to get cleaned up." She wasn't going to buy it. She was majorly paranoid when it came to my hand. How was I going to explain this?

Beyond the door there was a long silence.

"Well, don't make a mess," she said. "And after your shower, we still need to talk."

I heard her walk away, her footsteps receding down the hallway and back to the living room as if nothing had happened.

She had seen my hand wacking-out right before her eyes, and she had just walked away. Something was seriously wrong with me, and she knew it, and all she had said was, "Don't make a mess in the bathroom."

I grabbed at my wrist and ripped off the tattered satin glove, the glow of my hand reflecting off white tile like cold starlight. I could tell it was already on its way back to normal. I was beginning to get a feel for its new weirdness. But this time it hadn't given me any warning of heat or warmness before it had changed, and that was bad.

I crossed to the sink and looked in the mirror. My face was scratched and bloody. I lifted my ghost hand and watched its reflection move and twist, coming back into shape. It almost looked like it was doing sign language, like it was trying to tell me something.

"Why are you doing this?" I asked it. "What do you want?"

But it didn't answer back.

I flipped on the light over the mirror and took a better look at my face. The scratches were long, but not too deep. Blood, now mostly dry, made maroon tear-tracks down my cheeks. One of the tracks curved, running right into the seam between my black lips. Wow. The Manic Black lipstick I'd bought online was really as long-lasting as they said it was. Several other blood trails went all the way under the curve of my chin and down behind my neck because I'd been lying on my back as I bled. Lying on top of Marcus. *Don't think about that. Don't think about him.*

There was a twig, jutting like a single antenna out of my dyed-black hair. I reached up and pulled it out, watching dirt, leaves, and grass rain down into the sink and onto the tile floor. My shirt was torn a little at the shoulder. And my whole body was beginning to ache, but it was nothing compared to the stinging of my injured hand.

I shrugged off my backpack and tossed it in a corner. What I needed was a nice hot shower. After that I could deal with all the other stuff—my mother, my ghost hand, the bag of blades, and the CAMFers. While I waited for the water to get warm, I undressed, more forest debris raining down on the bathroom floor. So much for not making a mess.

Just as I opened the shower and stepped into its warm billowing steam, I heard the distant jingle of the living room phone. It stopped midway through the second ring. My mother must have picked it up.

Hot water pummeled my back and ran down my arms. Wherever it hit, the scratches, scrapes and wounds burned, but in a good way. Until I picked up the soap. That stung like hell, but there was no getting around it.

I hadn't been in the shower five minutes when there was a knock on the door.

"What?" I yelled, hot water cascading down my face and into my mouth.

"I have to go," came my mother's muffled voice. "Client emergency."

"Okay," I sputtered. That was weird. I couldn't remember the last time my mom had been called away at night, even after she'd started working part time at the hospital in addition to her private practice. People in a small town like Greenfield tried very hard not to call one of their neighbors away from home and family after hours.

"Don't wait up," she said. "We'll have to talk later," and shortly after that, I heard her shut the front door on her way out.

I turned off the shower and stood for a moment, listening to the water drip off my body. I was home. Alone. A state I normally reveled in, but it was dawning on me that my mother probably hadn't locked the door on her way out. And there were men out there who wanted to take me, or my PSS, or whatever. And one of them had been watching me for a very long time, which obviously meant he knew where I lived.

9

A SLIGHT BREACH OF SECURITY

I clambered out of the shower, pulled my robe off the door hook, and threw it on. Dripping all the way, I raced down the hall into the entryway and locked the front door, both the handle and the deadbolt. I'd never locked the deadbolt in my life. On the way to the back door, I checked windows, making sure they were locked, but throwing the final bolt in place on the back door didn't make me feel any better. My heart was hammering in my chest. I had to take deep breaths on my way back to the bathroom, telling myself to calm down. I was locked up safe in the house. Besides, the blades would warn me if the CAMFers were coming. I just needed to stay calm.

I grabbed the backpack off the bathroom floor and went to my room, tossing it on my bed while I dug in my dresser for some clothes. As I pulled on my panties, I noticed a nasty looking scratch on my thigh. Something back in the cemetery must have gouged me right through my jeans. I marched back to the bathroom and opened the medicine cabinet, looking for the antibiotic ointment and the Band Aids. There was plenty of ointment, but the box of Band Aids was out of everything except small circular dots. I applied ointment and a line of dots to the scratch, then stuffed the Band Aid box back in the cabinet. Wiping the steam from the mirror, I checked my face now that it was clean. It still looked like a cat had tried to climb it. I swabbed ointment on a few of larger scratches, and frowned at my reflection.

What was the deal with Passion's blades? They just kept getting weirder and weirder. How could something like that even come out of someone? Obviously, they hadn't come out of her body. They had something to do with her cutting—with her psychological issues, and they'd come out of that. A few months ago, when I'd been grounded and dying of boredom, I'd read an article in one of my mom's psych journals about something called burdens. A burden was a negative thought or experience you carried around inside you, almost like a souvenir. I guess the common term for it was "baggage." Anyway, according to this article, the author had developed a new therapy model to get rid of burdens. All you had to do was imagine your negative thought or experience as a physical object, like a heavy chain weighing you down, or an ugly purse, or a tangled ball of string. Once you imagined the object and it felt right, you went somewhere in your mind, like to the edge of a cliff or something, and you threw the thing off of it. And Voila! Problem solved and burden gone.

My mother had hated that article, probably because if people could just throw their problems off make-believe cliffs in their minds, they wouldn't need her. But I'd thought it was a pretty cool idea. What if the blades were Passion's burden, and for some reason my hand had reached in and snatched them out of her? Maybe they'd been in a plastic baggy because she'd wanted someone to see her pain and discover her cutting, and so that's how she'd imagined them. It was an interesting theory, but it certainly didn't explain why the blades could jam the CAMFers' minus meters. Or zap someone unconscious.

And what was I supposed to do with them? Marcus had told me to keep them safe and close to me because they could warn me of the CAMFers. But he had obviously wanted them, even though he couldn't touch them.

At the edge of my vision a shadow fell across the bathroom's frosted window. By the time I turned to look, it was gone. But the feeling wasn't. Someone was outside, in the dark, walking past the windows, looking in. The bathroom and my bedroom were at the back corner of the house which bumped up against the wooded outskirts of Greenfield. No one from the street could see someone lurking in my backyard. I lived in a small Midwestern town. No one was supposed to be lurking there.

I crouched down on the floor. The doors and windows were locked. No one could get in easily. Still, I glanced around the bathroom, looking for some kind of makeshift weapon. A hair straightener. Cosmetics. An eyelash curler. Toilet paper. Not exactly a deadly arsenal, but I grabbed my mother's hairspray from the bathroom cubby. It wasn't mace, but a shot of hairspray to the eyes was nothing to laugh at.

Think, Olivia. Get yourself out of this.

There had been two CAMFers in the cemetery. If they were both out there, they were probably each covering a door. If I made a run for it, they'd be all over me.

If I stayed inside, they might try to come in after me, but that would make some noise.

I needed to get to a phone and call 911 before they got that desperate. My cell phone was dead, and besides, it was in the backpack with the blades. The blades—Oh shit! They were still in my room.

I got down on all fours and tried to crawl down the hall, thinking it would be stealthier. It might have been, if I hadn't been clutching a can of hairspray and wearing a bathrobe. My knees kept catching the edge of the robe and making me fall on my face. So, I stood up, jammed the hairspray in one of the pockets, cinched the tie tightly around my waist, and ran down the hall to my room. I scrambled toward my bed and grabbed hold of my pack. The blades inside were making a noise like a broken lawnmower. They were loud, louder than they'd ever been before. How many CAMFers were out there?

Glass shattered, and a brick came sailing through the window and landed at my feet. My bedroom curtains billowed inward, curling away and smoking strangely at the edges, as something else followed the brick— an orange, blurred blob that landed on the throw rug next to my bed with a muffled thump.

I stared down at it—a flaming, wooden torch, its end wrapped with a burning rag. The overwhelming stench of gasoline hit me like a smack in the face. *A torch. Really?* What kind of anachronistic bastards were these CAMFers?

I reached out my ghost hand, grabbed the flaming end of the torch, and chucked it right back out my window.

10

OUT OF THE FIRE

The torch sailed beautifully, end-over-end, its flame furling in the air as it hit the man standing outside my window. I heard the satisfying thump, his oomph of surprise. The burning end of the torch had smacked him low in the gut, but the momentary glow hadn't reached high enough to illuminate his face. Whoever he was, he wasn't as lean as the Dark Man. He must be the spy, or some new CAMFer sent to ruin my life.

The torch fell to the ground, or went out. I couldn't tell for sure, but it grew dark for a moment just before the man's shirt caught fire.

He tried to beat it out with several quick slaps of his hand, but the impact of the torch must have doused the shirt with gas, or the material was fairly flammable. Whatever the case, it didn't work. The flames flared. The man cried out and dropped like a rock out of sight below the window ledge. That should distract him for a while.

My legs felt prickly, and I glanced down to see the cotton rug I was standing on go up in a blaze. I danced away from it. Apparently, it didn't matter how old-school a torch was; it was as effective as it had ever been. The fire at the window had consumed the curtains and was licking its way up the wall to the ceiling. The flames on the rug greedily climbed to my bedspread. I needed something to beat it out, or douse it, or contain it, before it devoured the whole house. There was a fire extinguisher in the kitchen. I ran for it.

The smoke alarm in the hallway was shrieking in disapproval. When I made it to the kitchen, I tried to yank the extinguisher off the wall but it refused to come out of its metal bracket. I yanked harder, but it still resisted. Finally, I realized that I had to lift it up and out, but once I did, it was way heavier than I'd expected. I hefted it in both arms like a fat baby and ran back to my room.

The far end of my bed was a pyre.

I pulled the extinguisher's pin, aimed it, and squeezed the handle. It sputtered, a white glop of foam dribbling out of the nozzle. I squeezed the handle again and again, shaking the thing, begging it to work. For a moment, I considered lobbing the entire red canister into the fire, but I was afraid it would explode or something. Instead, I set it down, and it rolled away like some giant, sentient hot dog.

Fire crept up the walls now, devouring the wallpaper and quickly changing the decor of my room to monochrome black—a color I'd once wanted to paint it, which had caused a huge fight with my mother that I had obviously lost. Lower down, the flames were licking at my backpack, which I'd left on the floor near the bed when I'd run for the extinguisher. I kicked out my foot and snagged one of the straps, pulling it toward me.

When I had it in my arms, I backed out of the room. Out in the smoke-filled hallway, I slammed my bedroom door shut, as if that might keep the monster at bay a little longer.

I had to get out of the house now, CAMFers or not.

The smoke was getting thick. My lungs were burning. Fire and heat and smoke went up. I needed to get below it.

I got down on my knees, but I couldn't crawl in the damn robe. The air was better though. I took a careful, sipping breath between coughs and tried to think. I had to ditch the robe. It was either that or die of modesty. I undid the belt, threw the thing off and slung the backpack onto my bare back. It hummed between my shoulder blades, warning me what I already knew—the CAMFers were out there.

Wearing just my underwear, I crawled down the hall and into the kitchen. The cold, hard tile felt like soothing water flowing beneath my knees. The back door was so close. It was right there. All I had to do was open it, run out onto the porch and into the backyard, and I'd be safe. Or would I?

The house was beginning to make strange groaning noises. If I could just hold out until the fire department arrived, surely the CAMFers would be gone, but I didn't even hear sirens yet. Hadn't anyone noticed my house was a raging inferno?

The kitchen was filling with smoke. My eyes were a watery blur, and I squeezed them shut. It didn't really matter. I couldn't see anything anyway. I needed to get below the smoke, but I was already sprawled on the floor. What was lower than the floor? *That was it.* There was a place lower than the floor, a place to escape the smoke and possibly get out past the CAMFers unseen.

I felt my way around the butcher block island that my dad had made my mother for their fifteenth anniversary. I crawled until my head hit the wall, then felt along the baseboard to the basement door. Reaching up, I turned the knob and opened it. Cool, fresh air hit me immediately, and I gulped it in. Quickly, I slid onto the cool top step of the basement stairwell and pulled the door shut behind me. I took a few deep breaths, coughing the smoke out of my system, and forced my stinging eyes open. My ghost hand cast a blue glow down the steep stairs.

I stood up, grabbed the railing, and started down. The wooden steps felt worn and smooth under my bare feet. About halfway to the bottom, I hit a distinct line of even cooler air, the point at which the staircase descended below the insulated ground. I was crossing into another world—the underworld—and a chill traveled up my body as I went down, making things perky and alert that didn't need to be.

In the world above, something fell with a thundering crash, rattling the stairwell and raining dust down on my head from the basement ceiling above. I squealed and leapt the last few steps to the frigid cement floor.

Laid out before me, by the glow of my hand, was the strange jumbled landscape of the basement—mountains of crookedly stacked boxes, foothills of carefully labeled storage tubs, and the occasional strange architecture of abandoned, dusty exercise equipment. Somewhere, there were probably boxes of old clothes, but I didn't have time to look for them. Hanging from a nail on one of the support beams was my mother's old rain poncho. I grabbed it and threw it over my head. It was big enough to go right over the backpack and cover most of my important parts, but it was short enough not to impede me if I had to crawl again. And I was pretty sure I'd have to.

Grey moonlight streamed in the basement's side windows, but not through the two at the back. That was because my mom and dad had added the back porch after they'd bought the house, and now those two windows opened to the underporch, a small area now enclosed by the porch's sides.

At the time of the porch addition, I had been ten, and I'd begged my dad to make the underporch into a clubhouse for me and Emma. He had even helped me draw up plans for it, but my mother had vetoed the idea based on the strong opinion that little girls shouldn't be encouraged to crawl around under porches like disobedient dogs or trolls. That hadn't stopped my dad from making a trapdoor into the underporch from the backyard, with a wink in my direction and an explanation to my mom that it was for "maintenance purposes." The trapdoor was barely noticeable from the exterior of the house, unless you knew what to look for. The CAMFers would not be guarding it.

Another groan and crash shook the ceiling over my head. The burning house seemed to be thinking of collapsing straight into the basement, and I really didn't want to be there when it did.

I hurried to the right window on the farthest wall and tried to pull it open. It didn't budge. The wooden frame felt damp against my fingers. Probably swollen shut by moisture. If the other was jammed, I'd be trapped, buried alive under a burning house. *Don't think about it. Solve the problem. Get yourself out.*

Somewhere up above me, in the far-off land of Greenfield, sirens finally began wailing. The cavalry was coming, but I couldn't wait for them. The house was burning down around my ears.

I abandoned the right window and crossed to the other one. It felt dry, and though it didn't open easily, I could feel it give when I pulled. I pulled harder and was rewarded when the window suddenly swung upwards. It had a hook that fit an eyelet in the ceiling so the window could be secured open. I hooked the window, but the opening was too high for me to just crawl through. I shoved a couple boxes in place and stepped up on them.

Shit! There was no way I was going to fit through the narrow window with my backpack on. I yanked off the poncho and the backpack and pitched them both into the dark ahead of me. Then, I wiggled my way through the window headfirst, my cleavage bulldozing a pile of dust in front of me. When I had pulled my legs and feet through, I sat up and looked around.

There was the trapdoor, outlined by a lighter square of cracks. It was big enough. I could get through with the backpack and poncho, so I put them back on, careful not to make too much noise. I crawled over to the trapdoor and laid an eye against one of its cracks. I couldn't see much, just a strip of grass and the dark backdrop of the woods behind the house, a strange orange glow flickering at the tops of the trees—the reflection of my house burning down above me. I tried looking through several more cracks with similar results. I couldn't see anyone out there waiting for me. I couldn't hear anyone either, because the sirens were getting close now, blocking out all the more subtle sounds with their wailing urgency. My backpack was silent and still against my back. When had the blades stopped buzzing? I had no idea. It could mean the CAMFers were gone. Or it could just mean they had turned off their meters. Should I make a run for it, or hide under the porch until the firemen arrived?

The fire decided for me as the peaceful, cool underworld of the basement caved in with a deafening roar. Smoke and dust, and house shrapnel exploded through both the windows leading into the underporch, scouring me like an apocalyptic wind. I was thrown against the trapdoor. It burst open, and I tumbled out onto the grass.

The sirens were at the front of the house. The stars swam above me in their dark lake. I lay panting and hurting, curled in a fetal position as my house crackled and hissed into the night. My mother's poncho was bunched up around my neck. Eventually, I sat up and pulled it down over my chest and lap. Why was my face wet? There was a medium-sized piece of glass embedded in my thigh. I pulled it out and held it in my ghost hand, watching my PSS shine through it.

Men's voices called to one another. I knew I should get up and go to the firemen, but I just didn't have the will or the energy. The heat of the burning house was so intense though, that I did crawl away and lean against my father's old art studio. At least his art was safe. Except for *The Other Olivia*. She'd be gone forever. But all the rest of it had been saved by my mother's refusal to face death. Maybe every cloud really did have a silver lining. I would have given anything for a sip of water. My eyeballs felt swollen. My tongue tasted like charcoal.

"Olivia," called a deep voice as a figure stepped out of the smoke. Mike Palmer, the Fire Chief, strode toward me, his long, thick, fireman's coat billowing out behind him like a superhero's cape. When he crouched next to me, I saw that he hadn't fastened it up all the way in the front, and he wasn't wearing a shirt underneath. He must have gotten geared up in a hurry.

"Olivia, you're okay."

He sounded sure, so that was good.

"I've got the girl over here," he called over his shoulder as he fastened his fireman's jacket closed. Several more firemen rounded the back corner of the house pulling a hose with them. Wayne Ramping, rooky fireman and only two years older than me, rushed over with what looked like a giant tackle box. He crouched at my other side, then froze as he suddenly realized I was half-naked.

"A blanket," Chief Palmer barked, and Wayne opened the tackle box and pulled out what looked like a huge piece of tin foil. He threw it over my legs, wrapping me up like a space-age burrito and started asking me questions as he and the Chief pulled various medical things out of the box and poked me with them.

"Are you injured?" Wayne asked.

I shook my head, though I wasn't sure.

"Can you breathe easily, or does it hurt?"

"Hurts." It hurt to breath. It hurt to talk. It just plain hurt.

"What is today's date?"

"Friday." I knew that was the day, not the date, but it was shorter.

"Was your mother in the house?"

"No," the Chief answered before I could. "She was the only one inside." Had I already told him that?

"Do you know how the fire started?" Wayne went on.

"She needs oxygen," the Chief said, leaning across me to yank an oxygen mask from Wayne's magic box, which must also contain a small oxygen tank.

As Palmer's arm passed over me, I caught a whiff of something familiar. Something muted, but strong enough to break through the smoky air and my singed nostrils. With the smell came a rush of memory. A flying ball of orange light. The torch on my rug. The man at my window trying to beat the fire out of his own shirt.

I looked up at Chief Palmer as he stretched the oxygen mask's band over my head, his hands leaving behind the faint but distinct smell of gasoline.

11

UMLOT MEMORIAL HOSPITAL

I woke up in a sunny hospital room, which immediately annoyed me. I hated hospitals. They smelled like disinfected death, and were populated by curt, smiling nurses who never left you alone, and cold, cocky doctors who were never there when you needed them. This hospital, the Greenfield Umlot Memorial Hospital, I hated particularly well. It was where my dad had died. It was where I had spent months watching him waste away, and I had exerted a lot of effort over the last four years avoiding it, which hadn't been easy because my mom actually worked at UMH three days a week.

I looked around the room. It was a double, not a private, and they'd put me in the bed closest to the door. The other bed, near the window, was made up and its curtain was open which meant no roommate, so that was good. There was a chair pulled up to the other side of my bed. My mother's purse was on the bedside table next to a half empty glass of water with lipstick on the rim.

Seeing the water made me suddenly have to pee, probably thanks to the giant IV bag plugged into my arm. The bathroom door was only a few feet away, but in addition to the IV, I had one of those pinchy things clamped onto the end of my finger, its cord trailing off to a monitor near the head of the bed.

I was still debating whether to push the nurse call button, when the door swung open and Nurse Jane came in, a familiar face from my dad's hospital days. He had always referred to her as "one of the good ones."

"Hey, you're awake," Nurse Jane said, glancing down at the clipboard in her hands. "How are you feeling?"

Right behind her came my mother.

"Olivia," she crossed quickly to the bedside and took my left hand in hers, finger clamp and all. "How are you, sweetheart? I've been so worried."

I opened my mouth to respond and croaked like a frog.

My mother handed me her glass of water and after a healthy swig, I tried again.

"My throat hurts," I said, my voice still husky, "and I sound like a smoker."

My mother gave me a strange look and seemed about to say something, but Nurse Jane interjected, "That's no surprise." She pulled a pen from her shirt pocket, jotting something down. "You're suffering from smoke inhalation, but it isn't too bad. Your chest x-ray came back clear, and your pulse oximetry is good," she rattled off, gesturing at the monitor. "We're just waiting for some blood tests to come back, but Doctor Fineman thinks you can go ho—," Nurse Jane stopped, quickly redirecting her sentence. "He thinks we'll be able to release you tomorrow."

Release me to where? I no longer had a home, which was exactly why Nurse Jane had just corrected herself. My home had been set on fire and burned to the ground by Greenfield's own Fire Chief, who apparently moonlighted as a secret CAMFer spy.

"Where's my backpack?" I asked, scanning the room.

"What backpack?" my mother asked.

"My school pack. The coffin one. I had it with me."

"I don't know," my mother said. "Did you see a backpack, Jane?"

"Nope. Haven't seen one, but I can go check at the nurse's station. And I'll bring you some food while I'm at it, kiddo," she said, slipping out the door.

"Are you sure you had it?" my mother asked doubtfully. "They said the only thing you had on was my old rain poncho. And where did you get that? I thought I'd buried it in the basement."

"You did. It's a long story," I rasped. "Listen, I had my backpack. I need my backpack." Who had been with me in the ambulance? I tried to dredge up that memory, but everything was a blur. Chief Palmer and Wayne Ramping had stayed by my side giving me oxygen until the paramedics had arrived with a gurney. That much I remembered. I remembered knowing I should be afraid of the Chief, that I should guard myself and the bag of blades, and that was pretty much the last thing I remembered.

"For goodness sake, Olivia, calm down. If you'd had a backpack, I'm sure they would have given it to me."

"No, I had it. I grabbed it out of my room when the fire started."

"Did you see how it started?" my mother asked.

"Yes, I—" I stopped. What could I say? *The Fire Chief threw a torch in my room. Mad CAMFers with PSS extracting devices are after me.* My mother was never going to believe any of that unless I had some kind of proof. Which I didn't. Plus, telling her about the CAMFers led right back to the problems with my ghost hand. I looked down at it, resting in my lap, all innocent looking and almost invisible against the white sheet. Everything had gotten so out of control. Maybe I should just tell my mother.

"Honey," she said gently. Too gently. "If you started the fire, even by accident, you need to tell me."

"Oh— my—God! You think *I* started it?"

"The firemen found the remains of a pack of cigarettes in your room," she said, "and they say that's where the fire originated."

"Cigarettes," I said, staring at her. First Mike Palmer had torched my house like some medieval villager, and now he was trying to frame me for it. Unbelievable. "You know I don't smoke, but you think I burned down our house while smoking?"

"What else am I supposed to think?"

"And here we are," Nurse Jane said, bumping the door open and coming in with a hospital tray sheathed in plastic. "I asked around about your backpack. No one remembers seeing it, but I can leave a note for the night shift. They're the ones who were on duty when you came in." She swung the bed table over my lap and placed the tray on it. There was red Jell-O, a juice cup, and something that might have been grits with gravy, or maybe oatmeal.

My mother stood silently, looking out the window.

If Nurse Jane could sense the tension in the air, she ignored it. "Your throat is going to hurt for a while," she explained, "so you're on liquids and soft solids for today. Are you hungry?"

"I don't know," I said, "but I really have to use the bathroom."

"Well, let's take care of that," Nurse Jane said, pulling the table tray away and moving to help me out of bed.

"I can help her," my mother said.

"No. I can do it myself," I said.

"Well, take it slow," Nurse Jane warned. "Let your mother hold your arm until you're steady, and don't lock the door in case you get faint in there." Something began to beep. Nurse Jane looked down at a call receiver on her belt. "I'll be back in a minute," she said, taking the pinchy thing off my finger before she hurried out the door.

My mother took my arm and my IV pole, and we shuffled to the bathroom. I was surprised how weak and out of breath I felt. My mother positioned the IV by the toilet. I shooed her out and closed the door. When I lifted the hospital gown to sit, I gasped at the sight of my legs. They were bruised and scratched and cut. Someone had bandaged my thigh where I'd pulled the glass out.

When I was done peeing, I crossed to the sink and mirror. My face wasn't much worse than before. The dark circles under the bloodshot eyes were new. My hair looked weird on one side. It was shorter and spikier and felt crunchy like plastic. That's how close I'd been to the fire. It had singed my hair. With that thought it all came rushing back—the heat on my face, the garbagy stench of everything I owned going up in smoke, the feeling of it choking me, chasing me, consuming me, licking me. The house beams groaning and crashing over my head.

A loud, sharp noise cracked me out of that waking nightmare. I was standing at the mirror. I was clutching the sink. Someone was knocking on the bathroom door.

"Olivia," said my mother, voice full of concern. "Are you all right in there?"

"Yeah. Fine. I'll be out in a sec." I turned on the faucet and washed my hands, the crisp plastic hospital bracelet sliding down over my left wrist. I let water pool in the palm of my ghost hand, then run through it, then pool again. My ghost hand didn't need washing since nothing ever really touched it, but it was force of habit. Normal people washed their hands, not their hand.

I splashed some water on my face too, because it felt good, and because I felt like I needed to wake up from a bad dream. When everything was dry, I grabbed my IV and went out to face my mother.

She didn't bring up the cigarettes again, but I could tell she thought I had done it—burned down our house. If my mother didn't believe me about that, why would she ever believe me about the rest?

I felt exhausted, but I couldn't sleep. I kept worrying about the missing bag of blades. Did the CAMFers have them? Probably. What would they do with them? Something bad. Maybe they would leave me alone now that they had something else to play with, but Marcus would be pissed. He'd warned me not to let my backpack fall into their hands, and that's exactly what I'd done. There just wasn't a lot I could do about it from a hospital bed. Of course, there probably wasn't a lot I could do about it out of a hospital bed.

Shortly after lunch, Nurse Jane removed my IV, and Emma and Mrs. Campbell showed up for a visit. As soon as Emma came into the room, she rushed to the bed and hugged me.

"Oh my God, I'm so glad you're all right," she said, almost crying. "I can't believe your house burned down. I'm so sorry, Liv."

"We brought you some clothes," Mrs. Campbell said, setting a large bag at the side of the bed. "Just some things you've left at our place."

I eyed the bag skeptically. It was huge. There was no way I'd left that much over at the Campbells'. In fact, the shirt peeking out of the top was definitely Emma's, a shirt I had frequently admired.

"But that's not mi—" I began to protest.

"And if you need anything else," Mrs. Campbell interrupted, "all you have to do is ask. Now Sophie," she said, turning to my mother, "I've compiled a list of possible housing options for you. Of course, you're both welcome to stay with us as long as you want, but I'm sure you'll want a place of your own as soon as possible. You just tell me what you need, and I'll take care of it." She took my mother by the arm and led her to the far side of the room, where they continued to talk in hushed tones.

"Are you really okay?" Emma asked, touching my arm.

"I have smoke inhalation, but they say I'll survive."

"What happened?" Emma's voice dropped to a whisper. "It wasn't the blades, was it?"

"No," I shook my head. "Well, sort of." How much could I tell Emma with my mom and Mrs. Campbell so close? "After I left your place, someone was following me," I whispered. "So I cut through the cemetery to get away, and then Marcus showed up."

"So, it was Marcus following you?" she asked, confused.

"Yes. And some other guy. The blades were making that noise again, but Marcus was just trying to warn me."

"Warn you about what?"

"Time for us to go, I'm afraid," Mrs. Campbell said, crossing back to our side of the room, my mother trailing after her. "We don't want to tire out the patient."

Emma looked at me, and I looked at her. We both knew there was no arguing with her mother when she was in director mode.

Emma leaned over and hugged me goodbye.

"I didn't start the fire," I whispered in her ear.

"I know," she said, squeezing me and then pulling back. "I'll see you tomorrow. We'll talk more then."

After the Campbells left, my mother was scarce. Apparently, when your house burns down under suspicious circumstances, the insurance company has lots of questions. It pissed me off the way that made me feel, like I'd actually done something wrong.

I must have slept until dinner, because the next thing I knew Nurse Jane was coming in with a tray of something mushy. She set it down in front of me, checked my chart and the monitor, and said, "Lookin' good."

"Good enough to get out of here tonight?"

"Not up to me," she said, "but Dr. Fineman should be in any minute to update you. He's taken over Dr. Mac's patients since he retired."

As if on cue, Dr. Fineman came in with my mother and Nurse Jane stepped aside. I'd never met Dr. Fineman. He'd only been at UMH for a year. He looked like he was in his late forties with short brown hair and a hawkish nose. Of course, I had seen him before, around town, at the grocery store, out raking his yard, but I didn't know him. In fact, this was the first time I'd seen him in his doctor garb or been introduced to him, which was kind of weird. Greenfield was a small community, and my mom worked with the guy. Why hadn't I ever met him?

"Hello, Olivia," he said, his eyes wandering to my ghost hand. I had that effect on doctors. "Your lab tests are back and I'm very pleased with them. Your mother and I were pretty worried when you came in, but all things considered—"

Something about the way he said "your mother and I" made me glance at my mother, who oddly, wouldn't meet my eyes. She was standing awkwardly too, as if she didn't know how much space to put between herself and the doctor, or what to do with her hands. What was wrong with her? Why was she looking as if she wanted to run away?

She looked so vulnerable, standing there in her wrinkled clothes from the night before. She looked exhausted and beaten down and on the verge of tears. I had the sudden urge to interrupt Dr. Fineman, jump out of bed, and give her a big hug. But apparently, I wasn't the only one tuned into my mother. As Dr. Fineman rattled on, he reached out his right hand and placed it on my mother's back. Not on her shoulder or her upper back. Not where doctors touch people to express doctorly concern for their well-being. Dr. Fineman put his hand on my mother's lower back. On the place just above a woman's ass where men put their hands on their girlfriends, or wives, or lovers to say, "I am here. You belong to me."

It only lasted a split second, that intimate touch, but during that split second I saw her lean into it. I saw the dark cloud lift from her face and finally noticed the way Dr. Fineman's body and my mother's had been leaning toward one another since the moment they'd entered the room together.

Then she subtly side-stepped away.

Dr. Fineman dropped his hand, stumbled in his medical rant for a moment, then continued on, obviously doing everything he could to avoid looking in my mother's direction.

And that's when I realized that just when you think things can't get any worse, they do.

12

DR. FINEMAN'S HAND

"So, I can leave?" I interrupted Dr. Fineman mid-sentence. "You're saying I'm fine, so why can't I leave tonight?"

"You're doing well," Dr. Fineman paused, "but it's hospital policy to keep you overnight for observation."

"I was here last night."

"Yes, but you were unconscious."

"And your point is?"

"Olivia," came my mother's one word warning for "You're being rude, child of mine. Don't embarrass me."

"We need to keep you overnight as a conscious patient," Dr. Fineman said.

"Why? So you can keep waking me up to see if I'm conscious?"

"Something like that," Dr. Fineman said, smiling patronizingly.

"No!" I blurted, feeling a giant ball of something awful rising in my throat. "I hate hospitals. And I hate doctors," I shot that in the direction of my mother, wishing I could scream it in her face. "I just need to go home, okay?"

They all just stood there looking at me, my mother, Dr. Fineman, even Nurse Jane. And then I re-remembered I had no home. No home. No backpack. No belongings. No mother. My mother belonged to that hand placed gently on her back—the hand she'd leaned into—Dr. Fineman's hand.

I glanced down at my ghost hand and slipped it under the white hospital sheet.

"We should be able to release you first thing in the morning," Dr. Fineman said, shooting a pleadingly apologetic look at my mother before he retreated out the door.

"I'll ask the night shift to go easy on you," Nurse Jane offered. "You aren't on any meds, and your breathing is good, so there's no reason to check you too often. I'll see you in the morning," she finished with a sad smile and left as well, revealing the bustle of the evening shift-change as she slipped out the door.

"Olivia," my mother sighed, sitting heavily in the chair by the bed.

"I'm really tired." I said, turning my face away, "I think I need some rest."

"I tried to tell you," she said weakly.

"Really?" I looked at her, glaring. "When? When *exactly* did you try to tell me?"

"Last night," she glared back.

"Last night?"

"Yes, last night. That was why I wanted you home early. I was going to tell you, and then Ray was going to come over so you two could meet."

"Ray?" I gagged on the name.

"Don't make this more difficult than it already is," she said, taking my left hand in hers again. "He was there for me when I needed him."

I yanked my hand away. "You want to hold my hand?" I asked, my voice breaking on the last word. I slipped my ghost hand from under the sheet and thrust it at her, "Then hold this one."

She recoiled in surprise, fear flashing in her eyes.

"No?" I taunted, reaching out to touch her face, watching her flinch away from it.

"Olivia, don't!" She knocked my arm down with her forearm and pinned it to the bed rail.

We both looked down at my ghost hand, panting, stunned by our own actions.

I tried to yank my arm away because I could feel it happening—my hand beginning to un-form, to bleed, to reach toward my mother. It didn't like being pushed away and pinned down.

She must have felt it too, because she let go of my arm and jumped up from her chair. For a second, I thought she might bolt from the room, but she didn't. She kept her distance though.

"What is wrong with it?" she asked, trying to sound clinical and detached, like a doctor, but it didn't work. Her voice quivered.

"It wants to pull something out of you," I said flatly, knowing it would scare the shit out of her. Tendrils were beginning to form. How far could they reach? Across the room? Down the hall? Out of this godforsaken hospital?

"How long has this been happening?" she demanded.

How long *had* it been happening? Was it only yesterday I'd been in Calculus taking my test. It seemed like years ago. It seemed like a different world ago.

"I don't know," I said, because it felt true. Vines of PSS energy were stretching over the bedrail, writhing in her direction.

"I'm getting the doctor," she said and shot out the hospital room door.

Now I'd done it. She would never let this drop. Her artist husband hadn't been able to "fix" her daughter, but maybe her precious doctor Ray could. When my mother told him what had just happened, there would be tests. They'd keep me in the hospital. Like a guinea pig. Like an experiment. Like a pin cushion. Like my dad. I couldn't let that happen.

I looked down at my hand, willing it to settle down. If I could just get it under control before my mom and her doctor boyfriend came back. But how? Marcus had grabbed my wrist, and it had gone cold. I glanced around the room frantically, looking for something cold.

My eyes fell to the plastic pitcher of water Nurse Jane had brought in. It wasn't ice cold, but it would have to do.

I grabbed the pitcher, set it in my lap, pulled off the lid, and dunked my wrist in, wild PSS energy and all. Water sloshed over the edges of the pitcher, and soaked my lap, but I didn't care because right before my eyes the PSS shrank back like a sea anemone when it's touched. It happened so quickly, my hand forming back to normal fingers and a normal hand, I could barely believe it.

I pulled my ghost hand out and shoved the lid back on, just as my mother came charging through the door with Dr. Fineman.

I looked up innocently, set the pitcher back on the table, and placed my hands in my lap over the wet spot.

My mother's eyes flew to my ghost hand. "It was—something was wrong with it," she said. "Olivia, tell Dr. Fineman what your hand was doing."

"My hand's fine," I said, holding up my flesh hand and giving them a wave.

"Not that hand," she said, almost growling. "Your PSS hand."

"It's fine too," I said, showing them.

"It wasn't fine a minute ago," she insisted, turning to her Dr. Fineman for support. "It was losing form and stretching across the room toward me. She said it wanted to pull something out of me. And this wasn't the first time. It happened at home, earlier last night. When I asked her how long this has been going on, she said she didn't even know."

"Olivia," the doctor said, approaching my bedside, "if your PSS is experiencing some kind of anomaly, we need to know. Your mother and I just want to help you. Can I see your hand?" he asked, holding out his big man hand, palm up.

Your mother and I. There was that phrase again, burning into my brain. He wanted me to put my hand in his. My own mother wouldn't even touch my ghost hand, was reviled by it, but this guy wanted to take it and he didn't even know me. But he didn't want to help me. He wanted to appease his lover, and maybe get an article on PSS for some medical journal out of it. Still, I had to play this smart. I reached out my ghost hand and put it in his.

He grasped my wrist firmly with his fingers, almost like Marcus had, and it made me jump.

"Did that hurt?" he asked, concerned.

I shook my head.

"Can you tell me when the symptoms started?" he asked, turning my wrist this way and that, looking at my PSS closely.

"What symptoms?" I asked.

"The malformation. The stretching. The things your mother described."

"I don't know what she's talking about," I said, giving Ray my best concerned-for-my-mother look. "She's just afraid of my PSS. She always has been. Ask her to come take my hand and you'll see what I mean."

My mother's face went from red to white as she stared at me over her boyfriend's head.

Dr. Fineman set my wrist gently on the bed. "We can run some tests," he said, looking between me and my mother, "and compare them to the PSS readings taken at her birth."

"No," I said at exactly the same time she said, "Yes."

"Don't you need my consent to run tests on me?" I asked.

My mother looked at me like I'd just grown a third arm. "Who is this creature that defies me?" her eyes asked.

"Actually, no," Dr. Fineman said. "PSS screening of a minor is at the parent's discretion. But," he turned to my mother, "I'll need you to sign a waiver, and I have to put the order in for the tests now, if you want them done in the morning."

"Do that then," she said.

"What are you going to have them do, strap me down?" I asked.

"If I have to," she answered, eyes blazing.

"Sophie, can I talk to you in the hall?" Dr. Fineman said, his arm again going to that place on her back as he guided her toward the door. I could hear their low voices talking even after it had closed behind them.

After about five minutes, my mother came back in.

"We'll talk about this tomorrow when we're both less distraught," she said, obviously trying to regain some of her cold professionalism.

"I'm not letting them test me."

"I need to go work on some housing arrangements for us," she said, ignoring the challenge. "I'll be back first thing in the morning."

"I want to stay at Emma's."

"And I want you to have these tests done," she said, turning her back to me and leaving the room.

The implications of that exchange were clear. *You want to stay at Emma's, then agree to the testing. But if you block what I want, I'll block what you want.* That was pretty harsh, even for my mother. Our house had burned to the ground, and she was going to use the only familiar place I had left as a tool to force me to do what she wanted. What did they call that in psychological terms? Oh, yes—emotional blackmail.

I sat alone in my hospital room, fuming. Everyone else must have known. Nurse Jane. All the doctors and staff. The whole town must have known and been laughing at me behind my back. How long had my mother and Dr. Ray been lovers? A month? A year? She hadn't even grieved my dad. It wasn't right, how she'd left me to wallow in loss alone while she'd gone off and found comfort in the arms of some doctor. He was nothing like my dad. He was cold, and sterile and white like the halls he roamed every day pretending he could fix people.

That's what doctors did. They pretended to have power over death. They gave little girls false hope that their father's wouldn't die of cancer. They tortured and poisoned sick people with things like chemotherapy and radiation in the name of science. That's what they'd done to my father, even though he hadn't wanted it. He had wanted to go home and spend his last few good months with his family, to watch sunsets, and picnic in the yard, and tuck his little girl in at night. That is what he had wanted, what he had told the doctors and me and my mother. But she had wanted him to fight. She had wanted him to take every last excruciating measure to eke out more of his painfully tortured existence. And he'd done it for her. With love in his eyes and heart, he had died longer and harder. Even after he'd gone into a coma, he'd fought, refusing to die, unable to live. That had been the longest month of my life.

I looked toward the room's tall floor-to-ceiling windows. The garden-like UMH courtyard was almost dark, the final dredges of sunset casting the trees in shades of orange. I had seen that same effect a hundred times sitting at my father's bedside. We had dubbed it "the backside of the sun."—not the sunset itself, but the way its reflected light changed the hue of everything it touched.

Once, during one of his stronger spells, I'd mentioned how I missed us seeing the real sunset together, the way we'd used to in the cemetery at the top of Sunset Hill.

"I can't climb that hill anymore, Peanut," he'd said. "But I think we should go see the front side of the sunset together, right now."

Then he had detached all his hospital paraphernalia and he'd gotten out of bed. He'd thrown on a robe from home and some slippers, and put his arm around my shoulders. But, instead of walking out the door, past the nurses and doctors who would have stopped us for sure, he'd guided me over to one of the room's big windows and opened it.

Like a pair of kids skipping school, we'd snuck along the inside of the hospital courtyard, hiding behind bushes, giggling, and swearing fellow-patients to secrecy when they saw us. Then, we'd made our way up the hill behind UMH, and sat in the grass to watch the sunset, side by side. Eventually, before it got too dark, a hospital orderly had been sent out with a wheelchair to retrieve us.

When we got back to dad's room, my mother had been waiting, tight-lipped and livid, her eyes accusing me.

"Don't be angry at her, Sophie," he'd said gently. "Don't ever be angry at her for any of this."

But then he'd died, and anger seemed to be the only thing my mother and I had left between us.

The room door opened, startling me out of my reverie, and a nurse from the night shift came in. She checked the chart and asked a few questions. Then she promised not to bother me for a couple of hours, dimmed the lights, and slipped out the door.

A couple of hours. That gave me until about nine.

I threw my legs over the side of the bed, various aches and pains pinging in protest, and padded barefoot across the cool hospital floor over to the windows. It was dark outside, the lights from the rooms on the other side of the courtyard shining yellow and warm. Several had their vertical blinds pulled closed; two had the lights dimmed like mine, while in others I could see nurses tending their patients, televisions on, a family standing around a bed. I reached over and pulled down the handle of the window closest to me, swinging it open and feeling the night air sweep over me like the breath of freedom.

I leaned out the window, looking north up the hill. Beyond it were some woods with a footpath through them leading straight to McKenzie Park. It was only a few blocks from there to the Campbells' house.

If my dad and I had managed to escape UMH in broad daylight when he was terminally ill, then I could certainly do it in the dark with a slight case of smoke inhalation.

I walked back to my bed, retrieved the bag of clothes Mrs. Campbell had brought me, and headed for the bathroom to change.

13

ESCAPE FROM UMLOT

None of the clothes in Mrs. Campbell's bag had ever been mine. There was the shirt on top, which had been Emma's, and the rest of the clothes were blatantly new and obviously hand-picked with my darkly unique fashion sense in mind. The tags had all been cut off, but everything still had its in-store smell and neatly-on-display creases. At the bottom of the bag there was even a pair of new sneakers, some black army-style lace-up boots, and a smaller plastic bag full of panties and several bras.

After the underwear, I slipped on a pair of black skinny jeans and a dark t-shirt. I started to put on the boots, but there was something stuffed inside the right one. I reached in and pulled out a pair of black, elbow-length leather gloves. My eyes prickled with tears as I imagined Emma picking them out for me. The gloves went on, then a black hooded sweatshirt over everything to complete my ensemble. The simple act of getting dressed had revealed how sore my body was, and I was a little out of breath.

I wadded up the hospital gown and crammed it into the bottom of the clothes bag. I couldn't get the bracelet off without a pair of scissors, so I tucked it inside my sweatshirt sleeve. One last look in the mirror to pull the hood up over my head and around my face, and I was ready to go. I turned off the bathroom light, slipped back out to the dim hospital room, and set the bag of clothes next to the bed.

"Going somewhere?" a voice behind me asked softly.

I spun, arms raised, hands out, poised in some instinctual posture of defense.

Marcus sat in the chair near the end of the bed, his legs sprawled out casually in front of him as if he were just another friendly hospital visitor. He was dressed all in black, just like I was.

"How the hell did you get in here?" I demanded. "You scared the shit out of me."

"Calm down," he said, holding his hands out in a gesture of peace. "You're the one who opened the window for me."

"What are you talking about?" I snapped. "I didn't open it for you. I opened it for me."

"Oh," he said, sounding surprised. "I thought you saw me out there. You looked right at me."

"That is really creepy. You've been out there perving me, just waiting for me to open my window so you could climb in?"

"I wasn't perving," he said, indignation in his voice.

"Really? Then what were you doing?"

"Gee, I don't know. Worrying about you. Hoping you were safe. Making sure CAMFers didn't come take you away."

That stopped me in my tracks. He'd been out there worrying about me?

"I like your new gloves," he said, ruining the compliment by adding, "You must go through a lot of them."

"Only recently," I said. Was he trying to charm me?

"You still haven't told me where you're going dressed like some emo ninja," he said, eyeing my outfit again and raising one of his dark eyebrows.

"I always dress like this," I snapped. "And no, I haven't told you where I'm going." Anger suddenly welled up in me. If he'd wanted to keep me safe, he could have told me something useful in the cemetery. "Why should I tell you anything? You didn't bother telling me the CAMFers would burn down my house with me in it!"

"Hey, I tried to warn you."

"Oh my God! You call that warning me? You followed me around, made vague threats, and insisted I come with you to who-knows-where. Why didn't you just say, 'They're going to burn your house down,'? I probably would have paid attention to that."

"I was vague," he said, anger in his voice now too, "because I didn't know what they'd do. I never thought they'd be that aggressive to someone with connections."

"Connections? What is that supposed to mean?"

"Your mom's the town shrink. You go missing and people notice."

"They didn't try to take me," I pointed out. "They tried to burn me alive."

"I doubt it. They were probably just trying to smoke you out, or make it look like you died in the fire," he said this so casually, as if it were an every-day thing. "But you're right. I never should have let you leave the cemetery alone. I saw the smoke, but by the time I got to your house, they were loading you into the ambulance. So, I followed you here, and I've been watching you ever since. I'm just glad you're okay."

"Okay?" I echoed, hearing my voice escalating to something bordering on hysterical. "I'm not okay! My house is gone. Everything I own is gone."

"Keep your voice down," he warned, nodding toward the door. "I know this has been rough. I wish I could change that, but I can't. We've all lost things, important things, to the CAMFers. And I'm sorry your house is gone. I really am. What about the thing in your backpack? You still have it, right?"

"Is that what you came for?" I felt my body go cold.

"It's one of the things I came for," he said, not a hint of apology in his voice.

"Well, it's not here," I said, looking away from him.

"What do you mean, 'it's not here?'"

"I don't have it."

"Yes you do," he insisted, his eyes doing a quick scan of the room. "I saw the Fire Chief load it into the back of the ambulance with you."

"You mean the Fire Chief who set my house on fire?" I asked, watching the words sink in, seeing understanding wash over his face.

Marcus sat back down heavily in the chair, much like my mother had earlier. He voiced a few choice expletives before looking up at me and asking, "He's the CAMFer spy?"

I nodded.

"I should have known," he said, standing up and pacing at the end of the bed. "They always infiltrate positions of power. But I'm surprised he would reveal himself. I mean, if you know who he is, his cover is blown."

"He doesn't know I know," I said.

"Better he doesn't. It tends to make them a little desperate."

"Desperate?" I asked, my voice growing shrill again. "What do they do when they're desperate? He already tried to kill me."

"I told you, he wasn't trying to kill you," Marcus insisted, pausing at the end of the bed and stepping closer to me. "You're no good to them dead. They need you alive to extract your PSS."

"But why do they even want it? I thought CAMFers wanted to get rid of PSS, not collect it."

"I don't know for sure," Marcus said. "But I do know that for the last six months, they've been trying to take kids with PSS so they can extract them."

"How could you possibly know that? It sounds like some kind of urban legend."

"It is not an urban legend," he said, his voice gone low and angry. "I know it's true because one of them escaped and he told us."

"Who's us?'"

"What?"

"You said, 'told *us*.' Who's us?'"

"Just me and some friends."

"Well, where is he now? Did you report it to the police?"

"No," Marcus said, laughing darkly. "The police were in on it."

"Oh come on, that's just paranoid. All the police couldn't have been in on it."

"Not all, no. But one CAMFer in a position of power is usually enough. Take your Fire Chief for example."

"He's not mine," I said, "but yeah, I get your point."

"Are you sure he has your backpack?"

"Well, I don't have it, and you said you saw him with it."

"We have to assume he has it then. I need you to tell me exactly what's in that bag."

I hesitated, but only for a second. The time for secrets was over. "It's a bag of razor blades," I said. "Well, they used to be in a plastic bag, but that pretty much got cut to shreds, so now they're just loose in the bottom of my pack."

"You pulled a bag of razor blades out of some girl in math class?" he asked, but it was almost drowned out by the muffled voices coming from right outside my room.

The door began to swing open.

We threw ourselves at the dark maw of the bathroom. Marcus pulled the door shut behind us, and I locked it. I turned on the light and the faucet. We both stood, sweating and panting.

"Olivia?" a female voice asked from outside the bathroom door. The night shift nurse.

I reached past Marcus and turned off the faucet. "Yes?" I answered, trying to sound groggy instead of wired with adrenaline.

"Are you all right? I thought I heard voices in here."

"Oh, um. I guess I fell asleep with the TV on. Some action movie woke me up. I just turned it off. Sorry about that."

"Well, do you need anything?" the nurse asked.

"No, I'm good," I said, feeling Marcus behind me, panting like a Labrador again. Why did guys breathe so much?

"Well, it's chilly in here. I'll check the thermostat," said the voice, fading away from the door a little. Then, "Who in the world left your window open?"

"I did that," I called out. "I got really warm."

I heard a distant click, the sound of the nurse closing the window, and the pad of her orthopedically correct nursing shoes coming back to the bathroom door.

"Sounds like you might be running a fever," Nurse Nosey said. "Are you almost done in there? I'd like to take your temperature." Crap. This wasn't good. I pushed past Marcus and turned the shower on.

"I'm just getting into the shower. Could you come back later and do it then?"

"If you're sure you feel all right," the voice said rather reluctantly.

"I'm good. Really. Thanks for checking."

"Okay. I'll be back in half an hour," she said.

"Good job," Marcus said when we'd heard the sound of the room door shut behind her. "Quick thinking."

"Thanks," I turned to face him. The bathroom was small, but not so small he had to stand that close to me. We might as well have been slow dancing. He was the perfect height for me too. My head would fit right there under his collar bone. I blinked up at him, and he looked down at me.

"So, what's the plan?" he asked in a husky whisper. For a change he wasn't grabbing my arm and telling me what to do.

"The plan is to get out of here," I said, trying to sound all business, trying to ignore how badly I suddenly wanted to stare at his lips. "Knowing nurses, we probably have less than half an hour. If we leave the shower on and the bathroom door closed, it might stall her a little longer because she'll think I'm still in here."

"And exactly where are we going?" he asked. Was he just humouring me? Just giving me the illusion of control while he manipulated me into doing what he wanted with his overwhelming proximity?

"*I* am going to my friend Emma's," I said. "I have no idea where you're going."

"Okay," he said, hesitating only slightly before gesturing toward the door.

"What?" I couldn't help myself. I knew he was holding something back, some opinion he was dying to share.

"It sounds like your plan," he said carefully, "might result in the CAMFers burning down your friend's house."

My hand hesitated on the doorknob. Would they do that? Probably not. It would be way too obvious. But they might do something else that would put the Campbells in danger.

"Do you have a plan B?" Marcus asked.

I was impressed. I knew his plan B, and A, and all the plans in between. He wanted me to go with him, but here he was holding back, not imposing it on me. Or maybe that wasn't his plan anymore, now that I'd lost the blades.

"I don't know," I said. "Let's get out of this hospital first." I opened the bathroom door a crack, checking the larger room before I slipped out into it.

I could feel Marcus close behind me.

I kept one eye on the door as I crossed to the window, re-opened it, and stepped quickly out into the darkened courtyard. Crouching behind the bush between my room and the next, I waited for Marcus. What was taking him so long? He'd been right behind me. Finally, I heard a rustle as he climbed through the window, hefting something round and shiny in front of him. It was the bag of clothes from Emma.

"What are you doing?" I whispered in frustration.

"I thought you'd want your clothes," he said, pulling the window shut behind him with a click. If he wanted to drag the bag along, who was I to stop him?

He crouched beside me under the bush. We seemed to be developing a habit of hanging out in shrubbery together.

"Now what?" he whispered.

"Now we crawl along this wing and try not to get seen," I said, echoing the words of my dad from years before. It felt weird escaping with Marcus the same way I'd escaped with him—almost like a betrayal. Like I was superimposing someone over my dad the way my mom had. But I wasn't. I wasn't into Marcus. Yes, he was cute. He just wasn't my type.

We started careful and slow. Marcus followed silently behind me, dragging the bag of clothes with him like some dutiful boyfriend at the mall. By the third window, we picked up the pace. Most of the rooms' blinds had been pulled for the night, and we could speed past those, but we still weren't making great time. I was slowing us down. My whole body ached and my throat burned. We'd probably eaten up half our time already, and we weren't even clear of the hospital building.

I stopped in a bush to catch my breath, and took a look at the next room through the branches. It was going to be our first real challenge. Lights blazing. Blinds open. From where I sat I could see straight into it. There was a blonde girl lying in the hospital bed, her wrists and arms heavily wrapped in bandages, an IV tube snaking out from under them. Her eyes were open, but glazed over. Her face was sickly pale. Her mother was sitting at the side of her bed, head bowed, eyes closed, a Bible clutched in her hands, her lips moving in whispered prayer.

The girl in the bed was Passion Wainwright.

14

BREATHE WITH ME

"What is it?" Marcus whispered, crawling into the shadow of the bush and peering over my shoulder.

I felt the moment he recognized Passion, the slight, sharp intake of his breath, followed by a long exhale that fluttered the hair at the back of my neck.

Passion looked bad. Really bad. And my hand had done that.

"Hey," Marcus said, touching my shoulder. "This isn't your fault."

Not my fault? Who was he kidding? A day ago Passion had been a slightly disturbed cutter. Today she was hospitalized, suicidal and catatonic. This must have been the client emergency my mother had run off to last night. Passion Wainwright slitting her wrists. Whatever the blades were, she obviously needed them back, and I had let the CAMFers take them.

"Sometimes people look worse before they get better," Marcus whispered, squeezing my shoulder. What was he, a fucking Hallmark card? Maybe he really believed the bullshit he was shovelling, but I'd learned a long time ago that the worse things are, the more people lie about them.

"We have to get the blades back for her," I said, shaking his hand off my shoulder. Then, I stood up and bolted past the brightly lit window at a full-out sprint.

Marcus let out a muted, "Hey" behind me, but I didn't care. I didn't care if I left him behind or they sent the entire hospital staff after me. By the time they did, I'd be up in the woods, halfway to Chief Palmer's house, on my way to getting Passion's blades back and fixing this mess my hand had made.

I ran past the next window, and the next, the end of the hospital wing streaming by me. I came to the meadow at the bottom of the hill and didn't even slow down. If anything, I picked up speed, revelling in the satisfying thud of my boots against the grass, the frantic beat of my heart, the pain in my body and the night air stinging down my throat and lungs. I deserved some pain.

I came to the bottom of the hill and started pounding up the incline, but it was like hitting a wall. My body suddenly decided enough was enough. I could feel the rush of adrenaline drain away. Part way up the slope I had to stop, bend over, and gasp for breath. My throat felt like someone had scraped it with a cheese grater.

I turned, looking down at UMH. I was almost at the exact spot my dad and I had sat to watch the sunset. Below me was a dark, humpbacked form trudging up the hill, bent over something in its hand. For one weird moment, I thought it was the Dark Man, then realized it was only Marcus.

"What was that about?" he asked, sounding winded and annoyed, as he tucked his cell phone in his pocket. Strange time to be texting someone. Maybe he'd just been checking the time.

"Did anyone see us?" I asked, ignoring his question.

"Don't think so." He came alongside me, the bag of clothes slung over his shoulder like he was evil Santa or something. He turned and looked down at the hospital. "We should probably keep going. Your nurse will be back to check on you any second. Where to now?" he asked, looking up the hill.

"Plan B," I said, turning upwards and putting one foot in front of the other. "I'm going to get the blades back."

"What? Hey, no way!" Marcus objected, catching up with me.

"I know who has them, and I know exactly where he lives."

"No," Marcus said, dropping the bag and grabbing my arm. Old habits die hard.

"Let go," I said, trying to pull away, but he wasn't messing around.

"Don't be an idiot," he said, moving close to me. "This is exactly what they want you to do. It's probably why they took the backpack in the first place, to lure you after it."

"You're hurting me," I said, though it wasn't technically true.

He looked down at his hand on my arm and loosened his grip, but he didn't let go. "Have you completely forgotten what I just told you down there about what they do?"

"No, I haven't. You also said your friend escaped."

"So you think *you* can?" he asked, laughing in disbelief.

"Why not? I escaped them at the cemetery *and* when they tried to burn my house down."

"You have no idea what you're dealing with," he said. "These guys are insane. There's no way I'm going to let you do this."

"And how do you plan to stop me? Pull my arm off?" I yelled in his face.

Down below light flared, and we both turned toward the hospital to see security flood-lamps flashing on all over the grounds.

"Shit," we said in unison. We were standing right out in the open.

"Run for the trees!" I said, yanking my arm from his hand and tearing up the hill. I could hear him, first behind me, then we were running side by side, the damn bag of clothes bumping between us. My lungs were on fire. My legs were going wobbly. Marcus was paces ahead of me. He turned and waited, holding out his hand. I stumbled into him, and he grabbed me, pulling us both into the shadows.

We collapsed at the foot of a gnarly tree, panting and trying to catch our breaths, but I couldn't find mine. I could hear myself gasping. I gulped at the air, but it didn't do any good. The shadows around me were getting darker, like an encroaching tunnel at the edge of my vision.

"Hey," Marcus said, leaning over me. "Take a deep breath."

I can't. I can't. That's what I tried to say, but it just came out as more gasping.

"Seriously, take it easy."

I tried, but the more I tried the more I felt my throat closing up. I flailed in panic, banging the back of my head against the tree. I didn't know if my eyes were closed or open.

"Olivia!" someone barked, sounding just like my father when he was afraid for me. He grabbed me, wrapping me in his arms and pulling me into his chest. "Breathe," he commanded. "Just like this. Breathe with me."

I fought to catch my breath, to remember the unconscious pattern it had always been, but the air shuddered in, choking me.

He took my ghost hand and slipped it inside his jacket, splaying my fingers against his shirt, against the warm rise and fall of his chest. "Like this. Feel this. Breathe with me," he ordered, placing his hand over mine.

Don't do that. My hand is dangerous. It will hurt you. That's what I thought, but it wasn't what I felt. I felt his chest expand under my hand. I felt my body relax into the warmth of him. Inhale. Then exhale. Then inhale again. The dark tunnel was receding. My throat opened and oxygen, like cool water, seeped into my lungs. I took one long wonderful breath, then another.

Twenty, maybe thirty breaths later, I slowly became aware of more than the need for oxygen. I became aware that I was curled in Marcus's lap, his arms firmly around me, his long legs stretched out under me. My head did tuck under his neck perfectly, just as I'd imagined, and his chin was resting on my head. Both my hands were buried inside his jacket, and yes, I could feel the rise and fall of his chest and under it the loud hammer of his heart. Thu-bump. Thu-bump. Thu-bump. It was so loud, as if there was nothing between it and me.

"Your heart is so loud," I whispered, between one Thu-bump and the next.

His arms tensed, pushing me gently but firmly off his lap onto the grass. "You had me really scared there for a minute," he said, brushing something off his pant leg. "You were hyperventilating pretty badly."

"Sorry," I said. I could barely see his face in the shadows under the trees. Hopefully that meant he hadn't seen the look on mine when he'd dumped me out of his lap. At least he hadn't scooted away from me. Our shoulders were still touching.

"No problem," he said. "Catch your breath. I think we have a little time."

I followed his glance down to the hospital below. It was pretty lit up and I could see several security guards shining their flashlights behind bushes in the courtyard. But Marcus was right. It would probably be a while before they expanded the search to the hills and woods beyond.

"I'm ready," I said, "If we stick to the trees, they shouldn't see us."

"I know you don't want to hear this," he said earnestly, "but I have a place we can go. A safe place."

"No," I said. "I have to get my pack."

"Yes, you do," he said, surprising me with his agreement. "But do you really think you're in any condition to do that tonight?"

We both knew I'd just proven I wasn't.

"You have to give yourself some time to recover," he continued. "And you can't just barge in there. We have to have a plan."

"We?"

"Yes, we. I know the CAMFers. And you know the town."

He had a point. Several actually. And then there was the tiny fact that he knew how to snap my hand back to normal, and I wanted him to teach me how to do it. And he was willing to help me get the blades back. Besides, he'd just helped keep me breathing. It was pretty obvious he didn't pose any kind of threat to me.

"So where's this safe place?" I asked, looking at him.

"It's a bit of a walk," he said, his teeth flashing a white grin in the dark. "You up to it?"

"I think so."

He stood and reached down to help me up. The bag of clothes was under the tree, a few items strewn about.

He quickly stuffed them back in and hefted it over his shoulder. This time, he gently took my arm and guided me over a rocky outcrop. Finally, we entered the woods, leaving the glow of the UMH behind us.

15

SOMEPLACE SAFE

We were on Old Delarente Road, a dirt track about two miles south of town that ended at an ancient, abandoned lumber camp deep in the woods. I had been there before, once on a hike with my dad when he'd still been healthy, a second time to take photos when I'd done a sophomore social studies project on Greenfield history.

I shambled along behind Marcus like a pet zombie, a mindless creature no longer connected to my body. I was exhausted, but I didn't have the energy to admit it. I was just thinking about letting my knees bend, about how nice it would feel to curl into a ball in a pile of leaves and sleep, when an awful smell hit my nostrils, black and bitter and cloying. Marcus stopped in front of me, and I stopped too, just barely keeping myself from running into his back.

To our right, next to the road, two round, silver towers rose into the air, a pond of thick, putrid blackness pooling at their base. Under the moonlight, it was like something out of a dark fairy tale. In the light of day, I knew it was just two leaky oil tanks from the lumbering days, long forgotten. I'd written about them in my history paper. I'd even written a letter to the editor of the Greenfield Advocate, the town newspaper, demanding to know who was responsible for the land, and thus the clean-up of the spill. But they hadn't even printed my letter, which probably meant whoever owned the land also sponsored the newspaper. If this was Marcus's safe place, I wasn't impressed.

"This isn't it," he said, "but let's rest."

I limped to the base of an old tree, upwind from the oil pools, and sat in a pile of leaves just like I'd imagined. After removing several acorns from beneath my butt, I was actually comfortable, though painfully thirsty.

There was an old tin shed just off the road and Marcus walked over to it. I knew it was locked. And rusted shut. But I didn't want to waste my breath telling him.

Marcus reached out, pulled the door open, and disappeared into its little box of darkness. Before I could even grunt my surprise, he was back out, still carrying my bag of clothes with something else in his other hand. When he got closer, I could see it was a one of those hydration packs. He must have broken into the shed earlier and stashed it there.

"Here, have a drink," he said, handing me the pack and sitting down next to me. As I sipped luke-warm water from the plastic mouth piece, he removed several acorns of his own from under his backside and pitched them in the road.

"Leave some for me," he said, taking the tube. He didn't even wipe it off before sticking it in his mouth. He had nice teeth. Nice lips.

He gave me another turn to drink, and there was something intimate about it, me watching him sip, him watching me. He was staring at my lips now, his eyes dark and serious. I handed him the tube, but he didn't reach out to take it. He just kept staring at me, and I wanted him to slide his hand to the back of my neck, and pull me to him. I wanted his breath in my mouth. I wanted him to kiss me. And I was terrified he'd kiss me.

But then my stomach growled, and we both laughed, and the moment was gone.

He took the tube and clipped it onto the backpack.

"Got any food in there?" I asked, eyeing a zipper on the outside of the pack. My head was starting to buzz from hunger.

Marcus unzipped the pouch of the backpack, reached in, and handed me a handful of almonds.

My hunger trumped my sore throat, so I popped one in my mouth.

The buzzing was getting louder. Not my head then. Probably the blades.

The blades.

Which meant CAMFers.

Except I didn't have the blades anymore.

I jumped up, finally recognizing the growing sound for what it was. Lights barreled down the road toward us, engines revved, male voices shouted. The CAMFers had found us.

I spun, trying to figure out which way to run.

Marcus stood up and said something, but the noise of the engines drowned him out.

The CAMFers converged on us, three of them, all riding ATVs, all in a dark hodgepodge of leather and motorcycle gear, like hoodlum farmers. They circled up around us, trying to block off our escape. The only way left to run was toward the oil tanks and their pool of poison.

One of the ATVs pulled up, only a few feet from where we stood.

The man seated on it wore a full-face helmet. As he turned off his machine, all the others drivers followed suit, until the forest was silent again, except for the sound of three hot engines ticking in the darkness. The lead driver reached for his visor.

I didn't wait to see what he looked like. I hurled my handful of almonds right into his face, aiming for his eyes, and leapt at the ATV. My right foot hit the back wheel-well just behind the seat, and I pushed off, intending to jump over the ATV and beyond it. With their engines off, I'd have been able to make it into the thick trees before they could start them up again. And it would have worked too. If my foot hadn't slipped. If my right knee hadn't come crashing down on the metal back panel of the ATV with a crescendo of pain. If I hadn't taken a tumble right over it and done a header in the dirt on the other side.

I crumpled into a fetal position, cradling my throbbing head in my arms. Through a fog of pain I could hear the CAMFer swearing at me from up on the ATV.

"Olivia, are you okay?" Marcus asked, kneeling next to me, putting his hand gently on my back.

"What the hell was that about?" yelled the guy on the ATV. "She pepper-sprayed me. My eyes are burning."

"Shut up, you pussy!" Marcus yelled back. "She threw almonds at you. You've got salt in your eyes. I think you'll live."

Marcus was yelling at the CAMFers. He'd just called one of them a pussy. Like he knew them.

"Well, what'd she do that for?" the CAMFer asked.

Marcus just ignored that question. "Olivia?" he said again, tugging at my arms which I was using to shield my broken head. "Can you hear me?"

"Head—hurts—bad," I managed to say between skull-piercing stabs of pain.

I felt Marcus move away. He demanded that the CAMFers produce a first aid kit, which they promptly did. He came back, knelt next to me, and slipped one of his hands between my arms. "Take this," he said, his fingers playing against my lips and shoving a couple pills between them, followed immediately by the hydration tube. I took it between my teeth and sucked, which caused an explosion of pain and stars inside my head. I must have gasped or sucked in a breath, because suddenly water was pouring into my lungs and I was choking, coughing, hacking. For a moment things went black and I didn't even know if I had swallowed the pills or not.

Marcus moved away again, and I wanted him back. Someone threw a blanket over me and slowly peeled my arms away from my head. They flashed a light in my eyes and it hurt, and I turned my head to the side and threw up. There were voices. Marcus talking to the CAMFers. Them answering back. I knew they were talking about me, but the words held no meaning beyond the shape of the pain they made in my head.

"Hey, stay awake." Marcus was back, lifting me in his arms. "You have a concussion, and we still need to get you to that safe place I was telling you about."

"It hurts," I protested, wishing he would just put me down.

"I know. Just a little further. Don't sleep."

Something hard was under us, his arms still around me. I pressed my throbbing head into his chest. Somehow, the Thu-bump of his heart was soothing, throbbing in sync with my pulsing temples. I felt his arm and chest muscles tighten.

A sound like a roar rumbled under me, around me, through me, filling my head with excruciating pain, rattling my teeth and making my eyes water. Another roar joined it, and another, grinding my thoughts into oblivion. I wrapped my arms around the only solid thing left and tried to bury myself against Marcus to escape.

The world jumped backward, and we jumped forward, as the ATV sped through the dark woods toward someplace safe.

I drifted, slipping between dreams and moments of consciousness the way wind slips through the seams of a tent and out again.

The whisper of rippling canvas.

The gentle creak of tent poles.

The tick and hiss of a camp stove.

I was dreaming of camping with my dad at Bluefly Lake when I was seven. But in the dream I wasn't seven. I was older, and I was holed up in our tent with the window flaps and screens and doors all zipped up tight because the lake had turned to PSS. I was afraid (no, terrified) to go outside because the lake was calling to my hand, and I knew, if I went out there, my hand and the lake would become one. And I would become nothing.

But my dad was out there too. I couldn't see him or hear him, but I knew he was standing just outside the tent. I could sense his artistic soul swelling and marveling over the beautiful, swirling, glowing lake, and I knew he wanted me to come out there with him, even though he wasn't saying it. He wanted me to come out there and let my hand join with the lake. He wanted to see it, and paint it, even if it meant his daughter would become nothing, because what was life without risk and art and beauty? *Which was easy for him to say because he was dead.* And I felt angry about that, because I wanted to be safe. But what I wanted more than anything was to have my dad back in the tent with me.

The murmur of voices. *Who was he talking to?*

The crunch of someone's foot just outside. *Was he going to come in?*

The rustle of tent flaps being brushed aside. *He was. He was.*

I opened my eyes to slits and tried to focus on the dingy green blur in front of them. My head was pounding, and the light felt like it was jabbing at my eyeballs. Finally, after a few minutes, whatever I was looking at coalesced into grainy green fabric with a dark stain shaped like a dog's head splashed on it. I blinked, trying to clear my vision, but the image stayed put. There was a soft, rushing sound from outside and the dog's head rippled.

It was a tent. I was staring at the very-up-close inner wall of a canvas tent. Hadn't I been dreaming about tents? About camping with my dad, but our tent hadn't been canvas. It had been bright blue and made of nylon or something. Who even used canvas tents anymore? The military maybe. The military, or the militant.

I suddenly had the sinking feeling I'd just woken up in a CAMFer tent. And then I remembered the confrontation on Old Delarente Road with the CAMFers. Marcus had talked to them, bossed them around like they worked for him. Most of it was a blur in my head. What wasn't didn't make sense.

I glanced down at myself, half expecting to find my arms tied or my hands bound. Instead, I was lying on a cot wrapped in an old quilt, as if someone's grandma had just tucked me in for the night. I started to turn my aching head to look around, but even that slight movement sent pain shooting through my temples to collide in a crescendo of dazzling sparks behind my eyes.

Oh right. Marcus had said something about a concussion. I was just trying to determine the least painful course of action when someone touched my shoulder. I flailed, rearing up and turning on the cot, adrenaline temporarily overriding the explosion of agony that caused.

"Hey, it's just me," Marcus said, looking down at me, his eyes full of concern.

"You," I said. It came out as a groan. There was some bright light shining from behind him, blinding me and making him look like an angel.

"I'm glad you're awake," he said, sounding relieved. "How's the head?"

"It hurts," I said, closing my eyes, but I still saw the outline of him standing there, a blue boy-shaped bruise burned onto the inside of my retinas. "Where are we?"

"A camp in the woods about three miles outside of town."

"What about the CAMFers? The ones on the ATVs?"

"Those weren't CAMFers," he said. "Those were my friends."

"Your friends?" I asked, trying to wrap my aching head around that.

"Yeah, I called them, back on that hill by the hospital, and asked them to meet us at those oil tanks."

"Wait," I said, trying to sit up, and quickly realizing that was a very bad idea. "I thought they were CAMFers. I freakin' dove on my head so you could get away."

"Oh, is that why you did that?" he asked, grinning. "Because it looked like you slipped."

"I thought they were CAMFers," I groaned.

"I told you they were my friends."

"No, you didn't."

"Yes, I did," he insisted. "I yelled, 'Hey, they're friends' right as they pulled up."

"You've got to be kidding me," I said, glaring at him even though it made my head spin.

"Look, I'm sorry," he said, and he even had the decency to look a little sheepish. "It sort of slipped my mind that I hadn't told you until Nose's wheeler was right there."

"Did you just say Nose's wheeler?" The words coming out of his mouth weren't even making sense anymore. Something was seriously wrong with my head.

"Yeah. Nose is his name. And we call the ATVs wheelers."

"You have a friend named Nose?" I just wanted this confusing conversation to end, but I couldn't seem to keep my mouth from asking.

"Sort of. His real name is actually Trey, but he goes by Nose."

"God, my head hurts," I said. It didn't matter whether I closed my eyes or opened them. The pain just kept getting worse. On the bright side, my body seemed to have completely forgotten about my smoke inhalation.

"Oh shit! I was supposed to give you more pain killer," Marcus said, reaching into his pocket and pulling out a tattered bottle of pills. "And I'm going to have to wake you up every hour through the night, just to make sure your symptoms aren't getting worse," he said, opening the bottle, pouring two white tablets into his palm and handing them to me.

"Oh yay," I moaned, wondering why I'd even escaped from the hospital if Marcus was just going to turn into the night shift nurse.

"Take them," he said gently. At least his bedside manner wasn't terrible.

I opened my hand for the pills, and he dropped them in my palm. Then he crossed behind the bright light source somewhere beyond my vision. I heard the sound of water being poured, and he came back with a blue enamel cup full.

He crouched next to the cot and helped me sit up, his arm warm against my back.

I drank the pills down, ignoring how they scraped my throat as they went.

"So we're not in a CAMFer camp?" I asked, lying back. Even with the incessant throbbing in my skull, I was so tired I couldn't keep my eyes open. From outside the canvas walls, I thought I heard the rustle of another tent being opened and someone entering it. *Maybe it was my dad.*

"No," Marcus said softly, tucking the quilt gently back under me where it had come loose when I'd thrashed away from him earlier. "You're safe. I promise."

16

DAVID'S LIST

I woke up slowly, my head still aching, but it was better. Way better.

This time the dog-shaped stain on the tent's interior seemed to greet me, and by the way burnt orange and murky green shadows danced on the canvas walls, I thought it must be dusk.

Marcus had spent all night taking care of me, waking me up at intervals, giving me pain medicine, bringing me water, and tucking me in. By morning we'd both been exhausted, and he'd finally promised I could sleep without interruption. Apparently, I'd taken him up on it and slept all day.

I glanced around. It didn't hurt as much to turn my head. At least I could do it without feeling like I was going to hurl.

The tent wasn't huge, maybe ten feet square. It had a pitched roof about six feet at the peak. Right next to my cot was the orange camp chair Marcus had sat in all night. As I looked at it a memory flashed in my mind—Marcus asleep in that chair pulled up next to me, his long arm stretched over mine, his hand cupped protectively over my ghost hand.

Beyond the camp chair on the far wall was a square flap covering a screened window. Below the window was a small folding table with a laptop on it. Surrounding the computer were neat stacks of papers and what looked like maps weighted down by a compass, a lighter, a Swiss Army knife, and a rock. Pulled up to the table was another orange camp chair.

In one corner of the tent was an old trunk, the sleeve of a shirt and a sock hanging out from under its mostly closed lid. The top of the trunk was doubling as a table as well, sporting a large plastic jug of water, some enamel camp ware, a coil of rope, an old camp lantern, and the hydration pack we had drunk from on Old Delarente Road.

Beyond the foot of my cot were the door flaps, tied shut but billowing a little in the wind. Just inside the door, was a welcome mat that read "GET OUT" in bold black letters.

It was a cozy place. A safe place, just like he'd promised.

Carefully, I sat up, pushed the quilt away, and swung my legs over the side of the cot. The walls of the tent were growing dark, but my ghost hand lit up all but the corners of the interior.

So far so good. My head wasn't spinning or hurting much more than it had when I'd been lying down.

From outside, I could hear the occasional murmur of voices, the clang of pans, the slosh of water, all the sounds of a camp cleaning up after dinner. *Dinner.* At the mere thought of the word, my stomach gave an audible and very unladylike growl. When was the last time I'd eaten?

Marcus had given me something that morning, saltines accompanied by the instructions, "Don't puke in my tent." Before that, there had been the almonds, most of which I'd thrown in someone's face, or thrown up. Before that, mushy hospital food. No wonder I was starving.

I glanced at the door of the tent. I could go out there and look for Marcus, or some food, or both. There were probably leftovers from dinner, and the smells that still hung in the air were enticing. My stomach growled again, but I just couldn't bring myself to leave. Maybe it was the lingering memory of that weird dream of my dad and Bluefly Lake. It wasn't rational, but it was there. Fear. Fear of the unknown. I knew what was in this tent. Knew I was safe. I had absolutely no idea what was out there, *who* was out there. Marcus had claimed them as friends, but what would they be to me?

Maybe there was food stashed in the tent somewhere. I'd seen the way teen boys ate at school—like ravenous, insatiable dogs. Had Marcus gone out to get the crackers last night, or was there a stash in his tent? I couldn't remember, but that was nothing a little snooping couldn't solve.

I began my search. No food on the computer table, probably none in the trunk where he kept his clothes, but beyond the trunk was a stack of several plastic storage tubs with lids which I hadn't been able to see from the cot. I opened the top one, stuck my ghost hand in as a flashlight, and Bingo! The saltines. More almonds. Some dried fruit. A bag of cinnamon and raisin bagels. Several chocolate bars. Yum.

I snagged a bagel out of the bag and devoured it, followed by some dried apricots and a chocolate bar, all of which just barely took the edge off my hunger. Maybe there was something more substantial (like a turkey dinner with walnut stuffing) in the bottom tub.

I set the top tub to the side and removed the lid of the bottom one, again using my ghost hand to light up the contents. This one didn't have food. It was a keepsake box, or at least that's what my mother would have called it—a box full of odds and ends, stuff that looked like junk but was obviously very important to someone. I knew immediately that I should put the lid back on that box.

But I didn't.

I reached inside and pulled out a photo that was lying on top.

It was a snapshot of a boy and a girl, standing side by side, shoulders touching, faces somber, eyes full of something startling I couldn't even name. Determination? Togetherness? Desperation?

Behind them it looked like there was some kind of dilapidated building or shed.

The boy was obviously Marcus, three or four years younger than he was now (maybe fourteen). The girl was probably a little bit younger than that. She looked so much like Marcus—same dark complexion, same dark hair (but longer), same brooding eyes—there was no question in my mind that they were related.

The photo was strangely overexposed, washed out to a blinding white in the lower left corner that obscured the girl's arm and part of her torso.

I turned the photo over to the back, hoping to find some identifying information written there.

"What are you doing?" Marcus demanded from behind me.

"I was just looking for something to eat," I stammered, dropping the photo into the tub and slamming the lid back on.

"There was food in the top one," he said, his voice hard and cold.

"I know," I said, stacking the top tub back onto the bottom one. "I'm sorry. I was just really hungry, and I thought there might be something more than bagels in that one."

"Well, I brought you some dinner," he said, his voice softening.

I looked up to see that he was indeed holding a steaming plate of something that smelled delicious.

"Oh, thank God!" I stood up and took the plate from him. It looked like some kind of goulash, full of beans, noodles, onion, tomatoes, and little bits of bacon.

Marcus pulled a fork wrapped in a paper napkin out of his back jeans pocket and handed it to me.

I crossed to my cot, sat, and began shoveling the amazing substance into my mouth.

"So, I take it you're feeling better," he said as he checked his tubs, making sure the lids were secure. I got the message; I was forgiven this time, but there shouldn't be a next time.

"Not too bad," I mumbled between mouthfuls. "Just a normal headache now, instead of an uber one."

"Good," he said, lighting the lantern on top of the trunk. Its glow started out soft and pale, echoing the tones of my ghost hand and mingling with them.

Could that really be the same spotlight that had been drilling me in the head last night?

Marcus crossed the tent to sit in the camp chair, our knees almost touching. "We have a lot to talk about," he said, leaning forward.

"Yes, we do," I agreed, cramming more goulash into my mouth. "You talk. I'll eat."

"Um. Let's see. Where do I start?"

"My ghost hand," I said, looking at him over the top of the fork being wielded by the very glowy hand I was referring to. "What did you do to fix it back in Calculus?"

"Ever heard of the Vulcan nerve pinch?" he asked, smiling.

"You gave me a Vulcan nerve pinch?"

"Kind of. I pinched the median nerve in your wrist. I wasn't even sure it would work, but it was the only thing I could think of at the time."

"Show me," I said, setting my plate down on the cot and presenting my wrist to him.

"The nerve runs here," he said, reaching out toward my ghost hand without the slightest hesitation. He pinched my wrist, his thumb between the two knobby bones on top, and his index finger underneath. "It's almost like taking someone's pulse but the finger placement is reversed, and you have to press pretty hard, but it can make people drop things."

"And you know this why?" I asked, distracted by the softness of his fingertips, of his warm hand cupped over mine. He could take his hand away, now that he'd shown me. But he didn't.

"Anatomy's kind of a hobby of mine," he said, stroking his finger along the inside of my wrist to the edge of my stump. "Your median nerve stops here, because of your PSS." His touch seemed to run all the way up my arm into my shoulder and back down to the tips of my ghost fingers.

"Anatomy's kind of a hobby of mine." Was that some kind of corny pick-up line? Because if it was, it was sort of working.

"So, if my nerve ends at my wrist, how could that even work?" I asked, forcing the tremble out of my voice. What was wrong with me? It wasn't like I'd never been touched by a guy before. I'd been on dates and held hands and kissed. Still, it had been a while. For years I'd had this huge crush on Emma's brother Grant. When I was in eighth grade and Grant was in ninth, we'd made out in the Campbells' garage, something we'd both agreed never to tell Emma. When I told her a month later, she already knew because Grant had told her the day after the "garage incident." My freshman year, I'd dated this guy, Ryan Mulligan, but that had only lasted a few weeks because he had been a total asshole. After that, my dad had gotten sick and, after he'd died, guys just seemed sort of immature and pointless.

"I don't know," Marcus said, shrugging and letting go of my wrist.

For a second I couldn't even remember what we'd been talking about.

"Amputees sometimes still feel their limbs, even after they're gone," he continued. "They feel pain or tingling or a tickle. They feel things only nerves could translate. Maybe that's why it worked. When I pinched your wrist, some part of your brain told your hand to let go, even without a nerve to deliver the message."

"Phantom limbs," I said. His ghost limb theory made a certain kind of sense. Cold water had worked in the hospital to snap my hand back, perhaps in the same way his pinch had. Still, I couldn't help feeling disappointed. I'd been so sure that Marcus really knew something. Some secret way to keep my hand in check or cure it from going into people. But something still didn't make sense. "So, why weren't you surprised when my hand— did what it did?" I asked. "You weren't freaked out at all."

"I have friends with PSS," he said, shrugging. "I'm used to weird shit like that."

Friends. Plural. He'd just said he had friends with PSS. "The guys on the ATVs." I realized aloud, feeling stunned.

"Yeah," he nodded and grinned at my obvious surprise. "And someone else," he added, his face closing up a little, his eyes growing serious. "You remember that friend I told you about, the one who got captured by the CAMFers, and escaped, and told us what they were doing?"

I nodded.

"His name was David, and he was my best friend."

Was. Past Tense. But hadn't he escaped?

"While they had him," Marcus went on, "he saw a list with his name at the top. A list of eight teenagers with PSS. Teenagers the CAMFers were going to go after, each with a date next to it, a target date for when they'd go after them, though I didn't figure that out until later. Anyway, after David escaped, he wrote down that list, and he gave it to me."

Marcus's best friend had PSS, and he'd been taken by the CAMFers. That certainly explained a lot.

"What about his parents? Did he tell them? I mean, after he came back."

"No," Marcus shook his head. "David's parents were dead. He was a ward of the state. And the police had been in on the whole thing," his voice dripped with contempt. "It was a cop that handed him over to the CAMFers in the first place. I told you, that's how they work. They infiltrate the existing power structure. Cops. Politicians. Fire Chiefs."

"So, what happened to him?"

"I don't know," Marcus looked away. "He gave me the list, and a few days later he disappeared again."

"Oh my God," I said. How would I feel if Emma suddenly disappeared? I couldn't imagine that. Didn't want to imagine that.

"I don't think they got him," he said. "I think he just went underground. He didn't trust people."

"But he trusted you," I said.

"I guess," Marcus said, looking uncomfortable.

"And you had the list. So, what did you do with it?"

"At first, I didn't know what to do. Then I started looking up the names online. Finding their locations, phone numbers, addresses, contacting them through social networks when I could. The second name on the list, the one after David's, was this guy in California. I decided to go down there for spring break and see if I could find him. I didn't know what I would say if I did. I didn't think anyone would believe me."

"And your parents just let you go, no questions asked?"

"It's hard to ask from the grave," Marcus said, looking me full in the eyes.

I didn't look away or apologize, like others had done so often to me. I had known from the beginning that Marcus and I had something in common, some indefinable mark of the soul that some people call loss. All I could do was nod and return his gaze. It was all I had to do. But there were still so many questions to ask.

"So, you went all the way to California from Chicago?"

"No," he shook his head. "From Portland, Oregon."

"I thought you were from Chicago."

"I'm from a lot of places," Marcus said, gesturing at our surroundings. "I live in a tent."

I looked around, the realization slowly dawning on me; this wasn't a tent he camped in temporarily. Marcus wasn't just vacationing in the woods. This was his home, and it had been for a long time. Yes, I had experienced the loss of my father, but I'd always had my mom, and the Campbells, and a roof over my head, and a quaint hometown surrounding me with security.

He must have read the shock on my face.

"It's not that bad," he said, looking around the tent fondly. "It's way better than juvie. Or foster care. At least now that I'm eighteen, I don't have a case worker breathing down my neck."

He'd said David had been a ward of the state. Had they met in juvie or just on the street? I tried to fit that in my brain—Marcus was homeless, and parentless, and he lived in a tent, but that was so out of joint with who I'd thought he was—some cocky city boy—that I just couldn't make it fit.

"So, what happened in California?" I asked, as I picked up my plate and ate some more, but slower this time. I was still hungry, and I felt exhausted, and my head was starting to hurt again, but there was no way I was going to let Marcus see that just when he was starting to open up.

"I met the guy. We hung out for a couple of days. Eventually, I told him about the list. He was pretty skeptical until the CAMFers showed up. They tried to take us both, and we got away, but just barely. It scared the shit out of him though, and he finally believed me, so we decided to get the next guy on the list together. That's what we've been doing for the last few months. Following that list and collecting the people on it before the CAMFers can. That's who my friends are. What this camp is. The guys call it Piss Camp."

"Piss Camp?"

"You know," he said, "P.S.S. Piss Camp."

"Yeah, I get it," I said, "It's just not funny." I was having trouble believing they were out there, these guys with PSS. Psyche Sans Soma was extremely rare and it hadn't been around that long. The first documented case had been in Norway four years before I was born when a baby girl named Thea Frandsen had entered the world with a PSS foot. I was the only recorded case in Illinois, and there were fewer than two hundred in the United States, fewer than a thousand in the world. And every last one of us was under the age of twenty-two.

So, even though, in my head, I had always known there were people like me out there, I had never truly fathomed what it would feel like, what it would mean to meet one. "You keep saying guys," I pointed out to Marcus. "What about girls? Aren't there any girls on this list?"

"Um, yeah," he said, looking at me oddly, "there are."

"There *are*? So what? You haven't gotten to them yet?"

"Well," Marcus said, taking the fork and empty plate out of my hands and giving me one of his weighty stares, "we have now."

It took me a moment to understand.

But only a moment.

He meant me.

I was on the list.

17

EXPLANATIONS IN A TENT

"My name is on the list," I heard myself say it. It wasn't a question. Of course my name was on the list. That was the reason Marcus had showed up in my Calc class out of the blue just before the CAMFers had come after me. And yet, the idea that my name was on that list hadn't even occurred to me the entire time he'd been talking. Everything he'd been telling me had just seemed like a story.

A story about him.

Not about me.

Marcus didn't say anything. He just sat there looking at me.

"You never were a transfer."

"No," he shook his head. "I dropped out of school when I was sixteen, but it's pretty easy to enroll in a small town school and just tell them your transcripts are on the way."

"So, why not tell me all this from the very beginning? Why all the cryptic bullshit?"

"If I'd told you any of this at the beginning, would you have believed me?"

"No," I said. "Probably not." I barely believed him now, and I suddenly felt sick and achy and on the verge of tears.

"Hey, it's going be okay," Marcus said, reaching out and taking my ghost hand in his. He did it so naturally, as if it was something he'd been doing all his life. I had never met anyone so oblivious to my PSS. Even with my dad and Emma, there had always been an underlying awareness that they *noticed* my hand. It was different—different than other hands, different than their own hands, and they loved me, so that difference didn't mean "freakish" or "worse". But there was still no denying that it was different.

But with Marcus there wasn't even a hint of an awareness of that. Like he was blind, unable to physically see it. Or feel it.

"I knew you wouldn't believe me at first," he said, looking down at my hands. "No one does. And I knew it would be even harder to convince a girl that I wasn't just some kind of whack-job. But that isn't your fault. If you want someone to blame, blame me. I should have thrown you over my shoulder in that hallway at school and carried you out of there."

"Why didn't you?"

"Honestly, I was afraid you'd kick my ass."

"Really?" I said, emitting something halfway between a laugh and a sob.

"A little, yeah. But mostly I was worried about blowing my cover before I'd convinced you I wasn't a lunatic. I also didn't want the CAMFers to see us together if they were watching you. I didn't want to panic them into snatching you before I did."

"You didn't snatch me," I protested. "I was already leaving the hospital. You just came along for the ride."

"Fine, you snatched me then," he said, that cocky smile playing at his lips. He was definitely flirting with me and, as if to prove it, his index finger brushed the inside of my wrist, making it hard to think. Still, something was niggling at the back of my mind. Something big that had to do with us leaving the hospital.

"Oh my God!" I said, yanking my hand from his. "What about my mom? She has no idea where I am. And Emma. And her parents. They must be freaking out."

"They think you ran away," he said. "Here, I'll show you," He got up and retrieved his laptop, bringing it back to set it in my lap. He pushed a button, and the inbox of my e-mail account popped up on the screen. I had twenty-three unread messages.

"Hey, how'd you get into my account?"

"Nose is a computer geek," Marcus explained, pointing to an e-mail with the subject line: Olivia, PLEASE answer this. It was from my mom. I clicked on it.

Olivia,

If you are reading this, please come home or contact me so I know you're safe. I am staying at my office. Or, if you are too upset with me, the Campbells are eager to hear from you, and you can stay there until we work this out, as I know we can. I love you.

Your mom.

So, my mom thought I'd run away because of the hand thing or because of Dr. Fineman, or both. Well, that was pretty much what I'd intended to do. It just hadn't exactly gone down the way I'd planned. I stared at the e-mail, trying to figure out how it made me feel. My mother was worried for me. *Or* she was just worried about how it looked for the town psychologist to be the parent of a runaway teen. She was trying to assure me that if I came back we could work things out, but we never worked things out. And now there was the issue of my ghost hand going weird, which she would never drop. If I knew her, I knew that much.

"I know this might sound bad," Marcus said over the top of the laptop, "but this actually plays to our advantage. If she thinks you ran away, maybe the CAMFers do too. It takes a long time to embed someone like a Fire Chief, and they won't throw that away lightly. They'll keep him in place until they're sure you aren't coming back. That may buy us some time."

"Wait, they have to know what you're doing," I said, confused. "I mean, they saw you in California, and now the people on their list keep disappearing.

Why not ditch the list and grab someone else? There are way more than eight people with PSS. It doesn't make sense."

"I've wondered that myself," Marcus said. "Why the list of names and dates? Obviously, it's a specific list for a specific purpose. That might explain why they haven't deviated from it. For some reason they want those people and no one else."

"But they aren't getting them. You are."

"I know," Marcus said, grinning wickedly. "Even if they've figured that out, there isn't a whole lot they can do about it. My biggest fear is that they'll get to someone before I do, but so far that hasn't happened. For whatever reason, they're bound by their list's timeline. But I'm not."

"What about tracking you with the meters?"

"They have a limited range. They might have tracked your PSS leaving town, but they won't know where we are now."

"So, what now? I just ignore my mom's e-mail?"

"No, you'll answer it eventually. Just not yet."

"What does that mean?"

"It means I think we can use your answer to get the blades back."

"How? My mom doesn't know anything about them. She doesn't even know I had them."

"Even better," he said. "Why don't you tell me what you know about them?"

"Well, you already know they can zap you, but I think they only do that when they're buzzing,"

"And they only buzz when they're jamming the meters," he said.

"Right," I said, and then I told him the rest. About Passion's cutting, and my theory about burdens.

"Yeah," Marcus said, leaning back in his chair. "I don't think we want the CAMFers to have something like that. We need to get them back."

"Agreed," I said. "I know where Mike Palmer lives, and they're probably there."

"Good. First, though, you need time to recover. And I need some sleep," he glanced down at his watch. "Which reminds me—you're due for some pain killer." He dug in his pocket and pulled out the familiar bottle of pills.

I took a good look at him over the edge of the enamel cup after I'd downed my drugs. He did look pretty tapped out. His clothes were wrinkled and dirty. His eyes were bloodshot. And he didn't smell like pine and wood smoke anymore.

Then again, I didn't exactly smell like a rose either. I was still wearing the same outfit I'd escaped the hospital in and it was filthy. My boots, which no one had even bothered to take off, were scuffed and caked with dirt. I needed a shower. I needed a change of clothes. I needed to feel human again.

"How did I sleep like this?" I looked at Marcus in horror.

"Didn't seem to bother you until now," he shrugged, "but I guess the fact that you're noticing means you're feeling better. Maybe this will help," he said, reaching under the cot and pulling out the bag of clothes from Emma and her mom.

"Oh, thank God!" I'd completely forgotten he'd brought them. "Can I change? Maybe clean up a little?"

"I can bring you some hot water in a plastic tub, but that's about it. We have a solar shower, but we only set it up when we're sure we're not going to have to break camp in a hurry."

"Some water would be great. And some soap?"

"No problem. I'll be right back," he said, standing up and slipping out of the tent.

While I waited, I opened the clothes bag. There were the leather gloves folded neatly on top. I had no recollection of taking them off, but I must have. Or Marcus had taken them off for me. I dug through the bag and chose something to wear.

Marcus came in carrying a steaming pot of water, and I watched, impressed, as he mixed it with cooler water from the jug into a large plastic basin. Then he produced a washcloth, two towels, soap, shampoo, a hairbrush, and some deodorant, though it was obviously man-deodorant.

"I'll let you get to it," he said, shyly, and he was gone before I could even say thank you.

I crossed to the tent door, and took a quick peek out. Whatever kind of camp they had out there was shrouded in vague, lumpy darkness. I tied the tent flaps snugly closed and went back to the basin. This was Marcus's home. His tent. His room, and I'd just kicked him out to take a sponge bath. How would he know when I was done? What if he came back too soon? He couldn't exactly knock on the door. So, I'd better hurry.

18

JUST A LITTLE AIR RAID

I woke to a tent filled with the pink-orange light of early morning. The air was chilly against my face, but there were blankets piled on top of me, keeping the rest of me toasty.

I peered over the side of my cot, and there was Marcus lying on the floor next to it. The sunlight and shadow made the scars on his forehead stand out. He was on his back, wrapped in a sleeping bag; his lips slightly parted, his face open and relaxed, making him look like a young boy, innocent and vulnerable. My eyes followed the line of his brown neck down to the dark blue t-shirt he was wearing. He'd changed clothes last night, sometime after I'd cleaned up and fallen asleep on the cot waiting for him to come back. Had he changed in the tent, right there next to me? What was with sleeping in his shirt anyway? Grant slept shirtless, bumbling around Emma's house on Saturday mornings bare-chested which was always a treat. I had just assumed all guys slept like that. Maybe Marcus was self-conscious about his body (which he totally shouldn't be). Or maybe he just didn't want the strange girl sleeping in his tent ogling him in the morning. I ogled him for a few more minutes, then reached my hand out and touched the outside of his sleeping bag saying, "Hey, wake up."

His eyes opened to slits, blinking at me. Something about him always reminded me of an anime character, as if he were drawn in dark pensive lines.

"Good morning," I said, smiling.

"Good morning," he mumbled, rolling onto his side to face me.

"You know, I have no idea what day it is."

"It's Monday," he said, looking at his watch. "6:04 am."

"That was a rough weekend," I moaned, lying back in my cot.

"Yes, it was." He sat up in his sleeping bag and it slouched down to his waist, revealing he'd even slept in his jeans. "How's your head?"

"Not bad," I said, pulling my eyes away from him. "Still a bit—"

"Marcus!" someone barked from just outside the tent.

I nearly fell out of my cot, but Marcus stood up and kicked his sleeping bag aside in one fluid motion. "What?" he called, already at the door pulling on his boots. Maybe this kind of thing was exactly why he slept fully clothed.

"We picked up a 'copter on the radio," the disembodied voice said, sounding urgent and calm all at the same time.

"Shit!" Marcus said, lacing up his boots like a mad man, "I should have known Fire Chief wouldn't wait another day to start a search. How soon?"

"Ten minutes tops," said the voice.

"You know what to do," Marcus said." I'll be out in a minute."

I heard the sound of feet hurrying away.

Marcus turned to me. "You heard that. They're coming with a helicopter, and we have to camouflage camp before they get here. I need you to stay in this tent. Don't come out under any circumstances. I'll be back as soon as I can."

Before I could say a word, he was gone.

I sat for a minute, stunned, listening to the sounds outside; muffled voices, the rustle of things being moved, a soft whispering scrape against the side of the tent that made me think of all those scary campfire stories. Suddenly, the light inside the tent went a shade darker, like someone had pulled something over it. A helicopter was coming. The CAMFers were looking for me. And if they found me, they'd find Marcus and his camp and everyone in it.

I stood up and paced to one of the window flaps. It was tied shut. They all were, but I lifted a corner and took a peek through the screen. I couldn't see a thing though. Someone had placed a large evergreen bough against the window.

"Cover up yer god-damned PSS," came a voice full of southern drawl from just outside.

I yanked my ghost hand away from the window and took a step back. Then, I crossed to the cot and pulled on my gloves and my boots. The door flaps were untied, swaying in the breeze. Marcus had said not to leave the tent, so instead I stood just inside the door, trying to catch a glimpse of something. I could hear a faint hum in the distance. If the CAMFers were coming with a helicopter and their minus meters, what good was it going to do to cover the tent?

The hum in the distance grew louder. I parted the door flaps a little and peered between them.

A short man wearing a black ski mask emerged from a stand of trees, looked around, then charged straight toward me. He had a gun. Behind him I could see other forms, crouching, silent, military in their movements, and all headed in my direction. I let go of the door flap and stumbled back, glancing around the tent for something, anything, that I could use as a weapon.

Marcus had left me alone, unarmed and defenseless. I grabbed the rock paperweight and the Swiss army knife from the computer table. With one in each hand, I turned to face the oncoming CAMFers.

Ski Mask barreled in through the flaps, and skidded to a halt in front of me. I raised the knife handle between us, fumbling to release the blade.

"You keep it," Ski Mask said, patting his gun. "I prefer Old Betsy here."

A second guy charged into the tent, tall and Asian, followed quickly by Marcus. Behind them came someone else dragging the trunk of a small tree, a long gun slung over his back. The last guy pulled the tree halfway into the tent and tied the flaps off around it.

"Everyone huddle," Marcus ordered over the loud din of the approaching helicopter.

They all rushed me. Before I even understood what was happening, I found myself crouched in a corner of the tent, surrounded by four musky, panting boys, one with a ski mask and two with guns pointed at the door. My hands were empty. I had no idea what had happened to the rock or the army knife.

Outside, the helicopter's growl grew louder and louder. The tent sides began to whip and strain like they were being battered by a storm. The helicopter must be close to kick up wind like that.

I glanced to my left and caught Ski Mask smiling at me through his mouth slit. Was he actually enjoying this? Marcus was next to him, directly in front of me. To Marcus's right was the lanky, Asian guy, and to his right was the tree dragger, blonde, scruffy and wearing a scowl the size of his gun. All four of them were between me and the door.

As I sat there surrounded by their well-armed chivalry, it suddenly dawned on me that these guys—Ski Mask, Asian Guy, and Tree Dragger—had PSS. They were like me, in the flesh, sitting close enough that I could reach out and touch them. I looked at each one, trying to see some glimmer or hint of their PSS, but they just looked like normal guys. Was that how I looked when I wore a glove? I still felt different, even when people didn't know about my hand. I *was* different, whether someone knew it or not. And so were these guys. But I had always thought I'd recognize someone with PSS, that I would have an instant connection with them, like finding a long lost twin or something.

The sound of the helicopter began to fade, then came back louder than before. Maybe they were circling, looking for a place to land.

Sweat dripped in my eyes, stinging them. My toes were cramping inside my boots. All the weight of my body was riding on my ankles and it was not comfortable. What if I got a leg cramp? *Idiot. Don't think about it.* My headache crept back into my temples, sending slivers of pain behind my eyes. I squeezed them shut, but for some reason that made me feel dizzy. I blinked them open and bit back the bile rising in my throat. The last thing I wanted to do was puke all over the back of Marcus's friends.

The helicopter roared right over our heads. Tree Dragger shifted position, pressing back into my knees, the smell of him wafting up into my nostrils. I could feel the tension in his body, like a mad, coiled spring on the verge of breaking. He was so close that, even over the monster whirl of the helicopter, I heard the soft click as he released the safety on his gun.

He wanted to kill someone. He wanted it bad. I could feel the hate pulsing off of him.

My ankles wobbled, and I thrust my hand out to catch my balance on the most solid thing in front of me.

And my ghost hand went straight into his back.

This was not like the other times with the warning of heat, or my hand melting and stretching away from me. My ghost hand, shaped just like a hand, slipped into him like he was made of thin air. But he didn't feel like thin air. Reaching into him felt like reaching into a meat grinder. Sharp, cold, metallic, squeezing, sharp-edged hatred gripped my hand.

I tried to pull it back, yanking, panicking.

Tree Dragger did not faint like Passion Wainwright. Instead, he spun around, dragging me with him, my hand still imbedded in his back. He grabbed me, pushing me to the floor of the tent, and sat on top of me, gun in my face, eyes like a mad man's, screaming, "Let go of me. Let go of me or I'll kill you!"

As I stared up the barrel of his gun, everything else faded into the background. His yelling. The yelling behind him. The hum of the helicopter behind that. The hands trying to pull him off me. The painful angle of my arm bent up and around him, practically wrenching my shoulder out of its socket. Even the pinch and grind of the hate machine within him that had hold of me. Fear. Darkness. Pain. Death. It all went away, my entire existence converging in the tips of my ghost fingers. I could feel something there, just out of reach, taunting me.

My hand wanted it.

My fingers stretched, reaching for it, grasping something small and smooth, long and thin. I curled my fist around it, and my hand slipped out of Tree Dragger.

He felt it go. He must have, the way he glanced wildly over his shoulder. Then suddenly he was off me, scrambling backwards, his gun still pointed at me.

"Olivia, are you all right?" Marcus moved between us, kneeling over me, blocking my view.

In the background I could hear the others talking Tree Dragger down, superimposed over the sounds of the helicopter receding into the distance, but that hardly seemed to matter anymore. Why was Marcus worried about me? I was the assailant, not the victim.

"I got it," I said, opening my ghost hand to show him what I'd found.

He stared at the bullet I held in my palm for a moment and said softly, "Put that away," placing his hand over mine and gently folding my ghost fingers back over it.

"If she ever touches me again," Tree Dragger said, appearing over Marcus's shoulder, "I *will* kill her." His southern accent was thicker than ever. Someone had taken his gun away. Just like I'd taken his bullet. But it hadn't changed anything. He was still full of killing. "What the fuck was she doing to me?" he demanded.

"Nothing. You're fine," Marcus said. "She doesn't have complete control of her hand yet."

"Well, she better fucking get control of it, or I'm gonna kill her," Tree Dragger reiterated.

"No, you're not," Marcus snapped, "just like none of us are going to kill you for being trigger happy. Now, get out of here and go break camp. Whoever was in that helicopter will be back. We don't have time for this."

"Keep her away from me," Tree Dragger insisted.

"Go break camp," Marcus ordered.

Tree Dragger turned and barged from the tent.

"Can you sit up?" Even as he asked, Marcus was helping me do so.

"You didn't hit your head again, did you?" Asian Guy asked. He was holding Tree Dragger's gun.

"The safety's not on," I told him.

"It is now," he said, clicking it. "I'm Yale, by the way."

"And I'm Nose," said Ski Mask, bowing like a musketeer.

"And the asshole with the temper is Jason," Yale added.

"Um, I'm Olivia," I said, standing up, Marcus's hand still on my arm, lending support.

"And now that everyone's met," he said, "let's get out of here before the CAMFers come back."

"Why didn't they land?" I wondered out loud.

"No open ground close enough," Marcus explained.

"But they know we're here," Nose said. "No doubt about that."

"They know someone with PSS is here," Marcus said. "But they didn't get a read on us individually. We were too close together."

"That's why you had us huddle," I said.

"They'll still come looking though," Yale said.

"Yes, they will," Marcus agreed.

"We'll go help Jase," Yale said, and he and Nose ducked out of the tent.

"I'll be there in a minute," Marcus called after them before turning back to me. "Take these and keep them on you," he said, reaching in his pocket and pulling out the bottle of pain killers wrapped in a folded piece of paper. "This," he said, indicating the paper, "is what I want you to send to your mom. Do it now, because everything in this tent is going to be packed into a trailer in the next fifteen minutes." He shoved the paper and pills at me. "Other than that, just stay out of the way, and be ready to go."

"Where are we going?" I asked.

"A fallback location," he said over his shoulder as he left.

When he was gone, I set the tub down on the floor. I shook out two pain pills and swallowed them dry. Then I unfolded the paper he'd given me and read it.

> Mom,
>
> Don't worry about me. I'm safe. I just needed some time to think. There is something about the fire I need to tell you. Please, meet me at our house tonight at 8:00 pm alone.
>
> Olivia

I read it again, staring at my name signed in Marcus's boyish handwriting. Somehow, this message was supposed to help us get the blades back, but I had no idea how. Did he really expect me to meet my mom at our burnt out house and tell her something about the fire?

I crossed to the laptop table, sat in the camp chair, and pulled up my e-mail account. I typed the message in. Read it over. Read it over again, my cursor hovering over the send button. Did I trust Marcus? Yes. Did I trust him enough to send a message to my mother I didn't understand?

I clicked send and got up to pack my clothes.

19

BOYS WITH GUNS

From up on a shrubby ridge, we watched the four men down below search the ruins of the old lumber mill where we'd so recently camped. It had been clever of Marcus to pitch the smaller tents inside the abandoned buildings. His larger tent had been under an overhanging fir tree, nearly invisible from above unless you knew what to look for. There was no way the CAMFers had seen it from the air. Still, it had been impossible to remove all signs of Piss Camp in fifteen minutes. The men below had already discovered the remains of the campfire and the tramped down path that led to what was obviously a latrine. And of course, there was a tent, a small pup tent Marcus had left pitched in an old tool shed, the tent that Chief Palmer was about to find.

Marcus tapped me on the shoulder and held out his hand. Reluctantly, I handed his binoculars back. I glanced to my right where Yale, Nose (still in his ski mask) and Jason were all hunkered down on the ridge watching, each with their own field glasses. Yale noticed my glance and held out his pair, but I shook my head, looking back down below. Mike Palmer was opening the shed. He looked inside and then ducked in, unnoticed by the other men. After several minutes, he emerged and called the others over. They pulled the tent out and inspected it, obviously having a discussion we were much too far away to hear.

The whole idea had been for them to think the tent belonged to me, a lone runaway hiding out in the lumber camp all by myself. I was beginning to appreciate Marcus's intelligence almost as much as I appreciated his exterior.

After a few minutes, the men down below folded up the tent, took a final look around the lumber camp, and headed into the woods back toward Old Delarente Road.

"So, what does that mean?" I asked, turning toward Marcus.

"I think they bought it," he said, sounding confident.

Yale and Nose joined us in a huddle up against the ridge. Jason kept his distance, moving only close enough to hear the discussion. Maybe I should have felt guilty that he was afraid of me, but I didn't.

"They took it with them," Marcus continued, "and they didn't even look for tracks or a trail. They're hoping you'll get spooked when you come back and find your tent gone. And maybe you'll run back home to your mommy."

"Which would make it easier for them to grab me," I said. Which was why the e-mail wasn't making any sense to me. If the CAMFers thought I was going to run back to my mother, wouldn't that be the worst move we could make? Wouldn't I be running right into a trap?

"There were four down there," Yale said to Marcus. "I thought you said there were only two."

"There were two in the cemetery, but who knows how many there are now," Marcus answered.

"The Dark Man wasn't down there," I pointed out. "The only CAMFer in that group was the Fire Chief. The others were just firehouse rookies."

"How could you know that?" Jason asked, oozing suspicion.

"Because," I explained, "when he saw the tent in the shack, he didn't call them over. He checked it out first, so he could cover up anything he didn't want them to see."

"That doesn't mean shit," Jason argued, but Marcus gave me a look of approval.

"Who cares how many there are?" Nose asked. "We got what we came for," he said, nodding at me. "If she's good enough to travel, why don't we get the hell out of here?"

"We will," Marcus said, "but first we need to retrieve something."

Jason and Nose looked surprised, but Yale didn't. Maybe Marcus had told him earlier.

"Retrieve what?" Jason asked.

"Something the CAMFers took from Olivia," Marcus said. "Something that can block minus meters."

"Where the hell did she get something like that?" Nose asked.

"Yeah, what a coincidence," Jason said sarcastically.

"She found it," Marcus said, ignoring Jason. "I was with her when she did. But when the CAMFers torched her house, they took it. There's a chance they haven't figured out what it does yet. And I want to get it back before they do."

"You still haven't said what it is," Jason pointed out.

"A set of blades," Marcus said.

"Blades?" Nose perked up, a gleam in his eyes. "You mean like swords, daggers, throwing knives, that sort of thing?"

"Not exactly," Marcus said. "They're razor blades."

"Razor blades? Like for shaving?" Nose asked, looking confused.

"Razor blades that block minus meters?" Jason laughed, rolling his eyes. "That makes sense."

"I've seen them do it," Marcus said, staring Jason down, "and there's a chance they can block extraction as well."

"Holy shit!" Yale said. "That would give us a huge advantage."

"If they couldn't track us or extract us, it would change everything," Nose said.

"I don't believe this," Jason said, throwing up his arms. "We find this girl and she just happens to have something that can block CAMFer tech, but *conveniently* the CAMFers steal it right after she tells us about it, and the only way to get it back is to walk right into a CAMFer trap. Come on, it's obvious she's working for them. You're idiots if you trust her. No way. I'm not setting foot in that town for this."

"Good," Marcus said without missing a beat. "Because I want you to hold down camp while we're gone in case anyone comes back looking for us."

Jason opened his mouth, shot me an extra-dirty look, glanced at Marcus, and closed his mouth again. He'd walked right into that one.

"So," Yale said, "how do we get into town without being detected in the first place?"

Suddenly, I knew the answer to that.

"They think she ran away," Marcus said. "They also think they found where she's been hiding. And, if they're monitoring her mom's e-mail like I think they are, they also think Olivia's coming to town to meet her tonight. That's how we get in. As one blip on their meters. The blip they're expecting."

"So you know it's a trap and you're going to walk right into it?" Jason asked in disbelief.

"He's right," I said. "When they catch up to that blip, they've got all of us." This was Marcus's plan?

"They won't catch up to it," Marcus insisted. "When we get close to your house, we split up. Yale and Nose will stay in that general area, but separate, creating two different targets for them to chase. You and I will split off together, and go to the Fire Chief's house to get your pack. He won't be home because he'll be chasing Yale and Nose around in the dark, thinking they're you."

"That's why you put the thing in the message about the fire," I said. "So he'd think I was going to tell my mom about him." It wasn't as bad of a plan as it had first sounded. Except for one thing. "But what about my mom?" I asked, dread creeping over me.

Marcus didn't say anything. He just looked at me that way he did. Resigned. Determined. Like in the picture with the girl and the shed.

"She's just going to stand there in the dark waiting for me." I said, letting it sink in.

"She'll be safe," Marcus said. "The CAMFers don't need her, and they certainly don't want her to suspect you've disappeared under unusual circumstances."

That was his answer; that the CAMFers weren't after my mother? Yes, I was still pissed at her, but that didn't mean I was okay with using her as bait.

"What if they have enough manpower to follow all of us?" Nose asked, "Then we're screwed."

The plan moved on, the boys oblivious to my dilemma. Having grown up in the foster care system, maybe Marcus couldn't understand, but surely the others could. Did they miss their parents and families? Did they even care? Maybe it was different for boys. When Grant had left for college, he'd just smiled, hugged his mom, and gotten in his car and driven away. It hadn't seemed to bother him to leave his family behind for the first time. But later that day, Emma had caught her mom crying in the laundry room holding one of Grant's shirts to her face.

"Not necessarily," Marcus was saying. "The three-way split on their meters will confuse them. There's a good chance they'll think it's a malfunction again. That confusion will buy us time, and that's all we need—time to find the blades. Because once we have them, their meters will be useless."

"Not on Nose and Yale," I pointed out. "You and I will have the blades, but they won't. It's too risky."

"We won't get caught," Yale said.

"We're sneakier than we look," Nose added, which was funny coming from a guy wearing a ski mask.

"What if we don't find the blades fast enough? What if we don't find them at all?" I protested.

"We'll find them," Marcus said, overconfident.

"What if we don't?" I insisted.

Marcus exchanged a look with Nose, who caressed the stock of his gun unconsciously. "We improvise," Marcus said after a long pause.

"You mean shoot people?" I asked, appalled.

They didn't say no, but Yale glanced away from me. The others just looked at me, grim faced, but with some deeper glint of excitement in their eyes. They were talking about shooting people. About shooting people in my home town. What was it with boys and their guns?

"No way," I said. "I'm not doing anything that involves guns or shooting. The blades aren't worth that."

"She's right," Jason said grimly, surprising everyone. "Not about the killing part. But she's right about the risk. It ain't worth it. Once you do this, they'll know she didn't just run away. They'll know there's a group of us, and they'll come after us."

"Not necessarily," Marcus argued. "If they don't see us, they could still think Olivia ran away and just came back for her pack before she left town."

"They could think that," Nose said, "but I doubt it."

"So, by the time they figure it out, we're long gone," Marcus said. "And I think it would still be worth it. Those blades would finally give us the upper hand."

Passion's blades. They were talking about using Passion's blades to help get the rest of the teens on the list. Marcus had wanted those blades from the moment he'd known about them. For this. As a powerful piece in a game of strategy against the CAMFers. What if Passion's blades weren't meant to be thrown off a cliff? What if they were meant for this?

"He's right," I said. "We should do it."

They all looked at me.

"But no guns," I said. "I'll help, but only if we don't take guns." They needed me to pull this off. I knew the town. My mother was the bait, and it was my hometown, and I wasn't going to lead an armed contingent of teenage boys into it, no matter what.

"Fine," Marcus said. "We leave the guns with Jason." He pulled out a map of Greenfield, and spread it out before us. "Here's what we do," he began.

20

JASON'S BULLET

By the time we'd hiked down the ridge to the dry creek bed where the wheelers were parked, the sun was already high in the sky.

Between getting buzzed by the helicopter, tearing down camp, spying on the lumber camp, and mapping out our plan, there'd been no time for breakfast, so Nose unpacked a cooler of sandwich stuff, and we each made our own. He never took off his mask. Of course, I knew why; it was pretty obvious. His nickname was Nose. Maybe mine would be The Hand.

"So where do you get all this stuff?" I asked Yale as I ate my sandwich, glancing at the ATVs and their trailers piled high with camping and survival equipment. "Do you steal it?"

"No, we don't steal it," he said, laughing. "We resupply once a month from the nearest town. Everything you see here was bought and paid for by our infamous leader."

"Marcus?" I asked, looking around for him, but he and Jason were deep in a discussion well out of earshot. "I thought he was—" and suddenly I didn't know how to finish that sentence. Poor. Homeless. An orphan with no resources. Thankfully, Yale rescued me from my own idiocy.

"He has a trust fund," he said, taking the last bite of his PB&J and talking right through it. "Some kind of out-of-court settlement from when he was a kid. I guess by the time he turned eighteen and finally got access, it was a lot of money."

"So, Marcus is rich," I said, "and he lives in a tent."

"Yep," Yale nodded, grinning.

I was leaning against an ATV, polishing off a packaged oatmeal cookie, when Marcus came over and handed me one of the black hydration packs.

"Thanks" I said, slinging it on and taking a long sip.

"Follow me," Marcus said. "We need to talk."

"Oow, it sounds serious," I said, "Are you breaking up with me?"

"I—we aren't—" Marcus stammered, all his cool composure of a moment before completely obliterated.

"Um, that was a joke," I said, rolling my eyes at him. Except it was only partially a joke. It was probably time to admit to myself that I liked Marcus.

"Right. Good," he said, sounding relieved.

"Where are we going?" I asked, trying to sound casual.

"There's a stream just over there," he said, pointing toward the woods. "I like the sound. It helps me think."

And covers the sound of us talking so the others can't hear. The more I got to know Marcus, the more I realized how calculating he was. His motives were never simple. Marcus was not "what you see is what you get." What you saw barely scratched the surface.

"Lead the way," I said.

It didn't take long for us to reach a burbling, shady stream. Marcus sat down on the grassy bank and I sat next to him. He seemed suddenly unsure of himself, which made me feel pleased and worried all at the same time. I looked across the stream, waiting for him to speak.

"So, mainly, I just wanted to, you know, see how you're doing," he said, digging his hands into the grass like it was Berber carpet.

"Oh, I'm great," I said. "Last time I checked I had smoke inhalation, a concussion, and a hand that likes to reach inside people and yank random shit out."

Marcus looked up, startled by the heat in my voice. "You didn't hurt Jason," he said.

"Maybe not," I countered, "but I certainly pissed him off."

"He comes pre-pissed," Marcus said, smiling. He reached out and took my ghost hand in his, tugging at the fingers of the glove.

"Don't," I said, pulling away.

"You know, I honestly don't think your hand is doing anything bad," he said, giving me one of his intense stares. "Unusual, yes. But not bad. And you're obviously gaining control of it. You pulled your hand out of Jase on your own."

"It was different than before," I said. "Like my hand knew exactly what it was doing. And what it was looking for."

"Can I see the bullet?" Marcus asked, almost shyly.

"Sure," I dug in my front jeans pocket and pulled it out, rolling it in my ghost hand. It gleamed like a tiny, golden missile, nestled in a crease of my glove.

"It's live ammo, not just a shell casing," Marcus said, poking it with a finger. "For some kind of hunting gun, I'd guess."

"Hey, it has something etched into it," I said, turning it so he could see.

It was a name, Jason's name, scratched into one side.

"Huh. Did any of the blades have that girl's name on them?" Marcus asked.

"Her *name* is Passion. And I don't think so. Not that I noticed anyway. What does it mean? A bullet with his name on it."

"I don't think you want to know," Marcus said, looking away.

"Yes, I do. If it has something to do with my hand, and what it's doing, and why, of course I want to know."

Marcus sighed, finally looking at me. "We picked Jason up right before we came to Greenfield, about two weeks ago. His dad runs a game preserve outside of Fort Worth, Texas," Marcus paused, as if that should mean something to me.

"And?" I prompted, because it didn't.

"His dad is a CAMFer."

"Jason's dad is a CAMFer?"

"Yes," Marcus nodded.

"But how can that be? His own son has PSS."

"Now maybe you understand why Jason comes pre-pissed."

"Yeah, I do." And here I'd thought I had it bad with my mother. "Where's Jason's PSS?" I asked.

"Right leg below the knee," Marcus said.

"But I still don't understand. What does this have to do with the bullet and the name?"

Marcus inhaled a huge breath, as if it hurt to, and said, "Before we got Jason out, we did a lot of recon. We hid outside the game preserve at first, but eventually, we went inside the grounds. Jason's dad is pretty high up with the CAMFers. His preserve is sort of like a lodge for them. They didn't exactly treat Jason well. Honestly, his dad treats the animals on the preserve better than he treated Jason. Until he shoots them."

Until he shoots them. Jason's dad treated animals he raised for slaughter better than his own son. When I had first felt that bullet, first pulled it out, I'd assumed it was some kind of symbol of Jason's violence and hate. But it wasn't that at all. It was a bullet of fear. A bullet with his name on it, etched there by his father. A bullet of belief that his own father might, at any moment, decide to kill him.

"It ended up being pretty easy to get Jason out," Marcus went on, "because they considered him just another animal. It never occurred to them that he would leave, or that anyone would want to take him."

"But he's on their list," I said, feeling my throat tighten up, rage battling with sorrow.

"For extraction," Marcus said. "Maybe his dad volunteered him for the list. I don't know."

"That's horrible," I said, clenching my fist around the bullet. I didn't want it. I needed to get it away from me, far away from me. How could such a tiny thing hold so much awfulness? I raised my arm, ready to fling the bullet into the woods beyond the stream.

Marcus caught hold of my hand, enfolding it in his.

"I don't want it!" I yelled in his face, struggling against his grip.

"I know," he said, "but you can't throw it away."

"Why not?" I demanded. It came out more like a sob than words.

"Because," he said, pulling my hand down, still holding it gently but firmly. "Your hand doesn't just pull horrible things out of people. It changes them into something else. Something we can use. Think about it. Maybe, inside of Passion, the blades were just some kind of burden, but then you brought them out, and they became exactly what you needed most, something to hide you from the CAMFers."

"I don't care," I said, but I did. Marcus had listened to my crazy theory about my hand and people's burdens, and he'd taken it one step further. And what he was saying actually made sense.

He gently unfolded my fingers from around the bullet. "This," he said, touching it, "used to be Jason fear. But we have to figure out what it is now. What it does. And how we can use it to help rescue the others."

"But what about Passion and Jason? He's still as angry as ever. She's in the hospital. Shouldn't removing their burdens help them?"

"I don't know. Maybe it will in time."

"I think I should give it to him," I said softly, curling my fingers back around the bullet.

"Not a good idea," Marcus said, shaking his head.

"It's not ours though. It's his. And maybe giving it to him is what makes things better."

"I highly doubt it," Marcus frowned at me. "You were there when he stuck a loaded gun in your face, right?"

"Yes," I admitted.

"He's not ready for this. Take my word for it. I think you should keep it for now, until we figure out what it does."

"Okay," I sighed, slipping the bullet back in my pocket. I didn't want to leave the stream. I didn't want to walk back to the ATVs and see Jason and know what I knew. Not yet.

But then Marcus said, "We'd better get back to the others," and he got up, and I didn't have much choice but to follow him.

21

THE BEST LAID PLANS

In the dark we hiked, silent, dressed in black, and full of nervous energy. Marcus led the way, with me behind him. Then came Nose, and Yale brought up the rear. We'd spent the entire afternoon setting up a new camp and going over our plan, refining it, coming up with alternatives in case this or that went wrong. After an early dinner of canned stew heated on a camp stove, it was time to start the long hike into town. The wheelers were too loud and hard to hide, plus they limited our escape routes to wider roads and paths. On foot, Marcus had assured us, we could melt in and out of the landscape.

My head still throbbed a little, but I'd taken some pain killer right before we'd left. It was slow going tramping through thick, uncut underbrush. We'd taken a route far from Old Delarente Road in case the CAMFers were still using it.

Suddenly, in front of me, Marcus made an "oofing" noise and his flashlight went sailing, end over end, through the air. There was a heavy thud, and a lighter one off in the distance as the flashlight landed and flicked out. I crouched in the dark, my own flashlight tucked in toward my body. I couldn't see Marcus in front of me anymore. Were we under attack? Had he been ambushed by waiting CAMFers?

"What was that?" Nose whispered from behind me.

"I don't know," I whispered back.

"I tripped on a log," Marcus groaned from a few feet away. "These damn flashlights are too dim. I didn't even see it."

"So much for melting into the landscape," Nose chuckled softly.

"Are you okay?" I asked, shining my flashlight in Marcus's direction. By the scowl on his face as he sat up from behind a rather large log, I hadn't kept the laughter out of my question.

"Don't shine that in my eyes," he barked, shaking leaves out of his hair.

I lowered the beam.

"We need more light," he said, standing up and stepping carefully back over the log. "If we could see better, we could move faster." He glanced down not-so-subtly at my gloved hand.

"Fine," I said, starting to take off my glove, but then I stopped and looked at Nose. And at Yale behind him. I wasn't the only one with glow-in-the-dark parts anymore. With everything that had happened, I hadn't had a chance to ask Yale and Nose about their PSS, let alone have some show-and-tell. But if Marcus was asking me to whip out my ghost hand, maybe it was time. "Why me?" I asked, turning back to Marcus. "Why not one of them?"

"I will, if you will." Nose smiled, his ski mask wrinkling at his cheeks.

"It's a deal," I said. I was finally going to get to see someone else's PSS.

Nose reached up and pulled off his mask in one quick tug.

I couldn't help but stare. Bright, blue, beautiful PSS shone like a beacon smack out of the middle of his face. It illuminated his ebony skin, and dark brown eyes, bathing his short black hair in shades of blue. But it was also disturbing, the way you felt like you were looking straight into his head. In the depths of his PSS nose, you could see where the small dark tunnels of his sinuses began, making you wonder just how far back it all went. It wasn't gross or anything, not any grosser than my wrist stump. But it wasn't normal either.

Nose turned his head, showing off his profile and the wonderful nose he'd formed for it. As I watched, the nose changed shapes— a Roman nose, a hawkish nose, a bulbous nose, and finally the hooked nose of a witch, complete with a bumpy wart on the end.

"Show off," Yale mumbled under his breath.

"Very nice, but we're kind of in a hurry here," Marcus added.

Nose turned back toward me and said, "Your turn."

I reached down and peeled off my glove. I held up my ghost hand, flexed it, and watched them all stare, the reflection of my PSS glowing in their eyes.

"Sweet," Nose said with admiration, "but no need to show off. We've already seen what that puppy can do."

"Looks like there might be a way to pick your nose after all," Yale said, clapping Nose on the back and laughing.

"Gross," I said, lowering my hand. "How old are you, ten?"

"Sorry," Yale mumbled, looking properly chagrined. I could actually see his expression now. I could see all three guys quite clearly and a good ten to twelve feet in any direction, thanks to the glow of the PSS.

"Won't the CAMFers see us coming from a mile away though?" I asked Marcus.

"Maybe," he said, shrugging. "But if they do it's likely to scare the shit out of them. Besides, we need to see. It's worth the risk."

"What about you, Yale?" I asked. "Three would make it even brighter."

Yale looked suddenly and completely embarrassed.

Nose and Marcus exchanged a glance, both of them grinning from ear to ear.

"Yes, Yale," Nose said. "Help us shed some light on the situation."

"Shut up," Yale said, punching Nose in the shoulder.

Marcus and Nose were practically doubled-over with laughter.

I just stood there, confused. Obviously, they had some kind of a private joke about Yale's PSS. Maybe he was really shy about it.

"Yale's PSS is—" Marcus began.

"Shut up," Yale interrupted. He wouldn't even look at me.

"—located in a rather delicate area," Marcus finished, smirking like a jack-o-lantern.

"Oh. Ohhhh," I said, feeling my face flush with embarrassment. How could I have known Yale's PSS was one of "those" parts? And which of those parts was it?

"It's not what you think," Nose said.

"I'm not thinking anything," I lied.

"Please just shut up," Yale pleaded.

"Let's just say, there's not much of a *moon* out tonight," Nose continued anyway, "*but* if Yale joined us, there would be."

Moon. But. I immediately got the picture, loud and clear. And when I did I had a lot of trouble holding back a laugh. I'd always thought a PSS hand was a pain in the ass. *Pain in the ass. He he.*

"See, it wasn't that bad telling her, Yale," Marcus said, turning to lead us over the fallen log.

I tucked my flashlight into a pocket and followed, holding my ghost hand out ahead of me.

From behind me, Nose began to hum "This Little Light of Mine."

"Shut up, Nose," Yale said.

"It's six after eight." Marcus informed us.

We'd just arrived at the edge of the woods right behind my house—what was left of it anyway.

Nose put his mask back on, and I pulled my glove back over my ghost hand, crouching next to Marcus.

There, just past my dad's studio shed, was a heaping pile of charred remains, the two old brick chimneys of the fireplaces jutted up out of the black debris like alien monoliths, the only real landmarks of what had once been my home.

"So, that was your house?" Nose asked softly.

"Yeah," I said, looking beyond it to the front yard area and the driveway. "But I don't see my mom."

"She may be parked where we can't see her," Marcus said, "or waiting for you to show yourself before she does. But we can't wait. The CAMFers have probably zeroed in on us already."

"So they know where we are, but we have no idea where they are," I pointed out. How had this ever seemed like a good plan?

"Which is why we need to move fast," Marcus said. "Are you ready?"

"As ready as I'll ever be." I was measuring distances in my head. Our position was halfway between the shed and the old maple tree.

"Remember, we're right here if you need us," Marcus promised.

I exhaled, took a deep breath, and stood up. I stepped away from the guys, wading through tangled ivy and rotten leaves to the edge of my backyard. I was tempted to glance back to see if I could pick out the three teenage boys crouched in the shadows, but that might give away their position. And the CAMFers needed to think I was alone, that I had come by myself to meet my mother.

I stepped out on the lawn and realized I was shaking, my body grown suddenly cold and wobbly. This was where I'd barely escaped a fiery death, where the CAMFers had almost killed me, whether they'd been trying to or not. They had done that, and here I was, baiting them. This was stupid. Why had I ever agreed to this?

After a few calming breaths, I walked across the backyard and stood at the edge of the burnt back porch. The underporch was gone, reduced to damp, grey ash. I took a few more steps up the incline toward the front of the house, and stopped. I hadn't expected to get this far. We'd thought the CAMFers would try for me as soon as I showed myself. And I still didn't see my mother anywhere. Maybe she hadn't come.

I walked along the side yard, coming even with the living room chimney, and something caught my eye—color, pattern, a familiar wisp of shape and face, a blue figure on black. It was my dad's painting, *The Other Olivia*, tossed on top of what had once been our leather couch and looking only mildly scorched. My heart leapt with sudden, inexplicable joy. It had survived. I wouldn't have to live in a world where I would never see it again. But why would anyone just leave it there, like trash, like nothing?

I glanced around, scanning the front yard and the street, my neighbor's fences and houses. I strained, listening, but there was no one nearby. Not my mother. Not the CAMFers. Not even a stray cat or two. Nobody. The CAMFers hadn't taken our bait. Maybe they weren't even monitoring my mom's e-mail. In all our planning, we'd considered every possible scenario except this one—the one where the bad guys didn't even show up.

I let myself relax a little. I should go back. The guys were waiting. I knew that. But I couldn't bring myself to leave *The Other Olivia* lying there like a piece of garbage.

I gave a quick, furtive look to the dark spot between the garden shed and the maple. Then I waded through soggy black gunk, stepped over several piles of melted something, and bent over my dad's painting. The canvas was singed a little, but only around the edges. It didn't appear to have any water damage, which was amazing. I could have it cut down and re-stretched over a new frame. It was salvageable. I was sure of it.

I grabbed the edges of the painting, hefting it in my arms.

A few feet to my left, a dark form emerged from behind the living room chimney and reached out for me.

"Got ya," said Mike Palmer, grabbing at me.

I swung the painting out of pure reflex, knocking his hands aside.

He grabbed it, and we grappled, the painting between us. He was trying to rip it from my hands, but I hung on for all I was worth. This was not the plan. The plan had been for me to bolt and run at the merest sign of CAMFers. They would chase me back to the guys in the woods, where Nose and Yale would split off and lead them on a wild goose chase while Marcus and I went to get the blades. The plan had not included my father's painting. I needed to let go of it and get out of there.

Instead, I kicked as hard as I could under the edge of the canvas, feeling my boot connect solidly with some softer part of Mike Palmer.

He bellowed and yanked the painting upward, pulling me off my feet. I didn't let go. I was not going to let go. This was the bastard who had taken everything from me. He'd burned my house to the ground with me in it. He'd stolen the only personal possession I'd had left in the world, while I'd lain unconscious in an ambulance. And now he was trying to take something else, and I'd be damned if I was going to let him do that. I needed my dad's painting. I was not leaving it behind. I was not losing one more thing.

I came back down on my feet, one of my ankles twisting, and I lost hold of the painting. At least that's what I thought happened. One minute the painting was there, the fulcrum between me and Mike Palmer's struggle, and the next minute it was gone.

We both fell backwards.

I crashed into the soggy couch behind me.

Mike stumbled back against the chimney. The painting wasn't in his hands. It wasn't on the ground. It wasn't anywhere in the debris. It was as if it had gotten fed up with being fought over and simply blipped itself out of existence.

"What the—what did you do, you little freak?" The Fire Chief asked, fear in his eyes.

And that's when I saw the handgun tucked in his belt. The gun he was reaching for.

"Olivia," someone called, and I looked up to see Marcus, and Nose, and Yale running across my backyard toward me, running toward us, toward the man with the gun.

"No!" I yelled, rising from the couch. This wasn't the plan. I was supposed to lead the CAMFers to them. They weren't supposed to run to my rescue. I hadn't let them bring their guns. There weren't supposed to be any guns.

Mike Palmer ignored all that, pulled out his weapon, and fired.

22

UNLOCKING THE BULLET

It was strange how things seemed to happen out of order.

Marcus, who was only a few feet away from me, suddenly jerked backwards and crumpled to the ground.

The weapon in Mike Palmer's hand gave a tooth-jarring crack.

Nose let out a guttural yell, and leapt over Marcus, still charging Mike.

Mike took aim at Nose.

Yale fell to his knees beside Marcus.

I saw it all. Saw Marcus lying still and silent where he'd fallen, Yale bending over him. Saw Mike's finger pulling back on the trigger again. Saw Nose coming, relentless, fearless, running straight toward the man who was going to kill him. I saw everything that shouldn't happen. That couldn't happen. That *was* happening. Everything that would be my fault and destroy what little was left to me.

I saw all this in the blink of an eye, and I threw myself at Mike Palmer, clipping him in the shoulder and knocking him off balance even as his gun discharged a second time. Mike tried to right himself, to swing the gun toward me, but he was too slow. I jumped on his back, arms locked around his neck, legs wrapped around his waist; clinging to him, I covered his face with my hands so he couldn't see to shoot again.

He reached up with a meaty arm, knocking my hands away, but I clung to him with my legs.

I knew what to do.

I tugged at the edge of my glove, stripping it from my ghost hand and tossing it away. I grasped at Mike Palmer's nose, his lips, his eyebrows, wherever my ghost fingers could find purchase.

He roared and tried to shake me off, bucking and spinning in a circle like a deranged bull. I could feel his entire body spasm in fear. He was afraid now. Afraid of my PSS touching his face. So afraid that he dropped his gun and reached up with both hands, trying to pry me off.

"Don't move," Nose barked from in front of us, pointing the gun at the Fire Chief's chest.

But Mike Palmer was beyond reason. He charged backwards, ramming me into the chimney, pinning me between unrelenting brick and the hardness of his back. The air whooshed from my lungs. A cascade of cold, crumbling mortar trickled down the inside of my shirt. I was losing my grip on him.

But if I let go, he wasn't going to stop. Nose was going to have to shoot him. That was the only way we were going to get out of here, and it was all because I hadn't let go of my dad's painting. A painting that was now inexplicably gone. If only Mike Palmer had disappeared with it.

And then he did.

One second he was there, as solid as the chimney he was grinding me into, and the next he was gone.

I dropped to the ground like a stone, my butt banging painfully as I landed at the base of the chimney.

"Holy shit!" Nose said, waving the gun back and forth wildly. "Where did he go?"

I just sat, curled in a ball of pain, trying to breathe again.

Nose scrambled over to me. "What the hell did you do?" he asked, awe in his voice.

"Don't know," I managed, sitting up a little and leaning back against the chimney. Police sirens howled in the distance. Someone had called in the gunshots already.

"We have to get out of here," Nose said, grabbing my arm and pulling me up. He still had Mike's gun in his other hand. Together we stumbled away, racing back toward Yale and Marcus. Yale rose up ahead of us, falling to one knee for a minute, then regaining his balance. He had something big slung over his shoulder, and it took me a moment to realize it was Marcus.

The sirens were getting closer. We all made it to the dark edge of the woods at the same time, but we didn't stop there. I led the way, following a faint path by the light of my ghost hand. I could hear Nose and Yale laboring behind me, both carrying Marcus now. I knew where to take them. There was a place I had discovered as a kid, an old cement ice house that had once stored blocks of ice harvested from Bluefly Lake before the age of refrigeration. I had taken Emma there a few times, but mostly it was the place I went to be utterly alone, to hide from the world, to escape and think.

Yale and Nose didn't ask where we were going. They just followed me, even when we began to descend the sharp incline that led down into the gulley where the ice house was. At the bottom I turned, holding up my ghost hand so they could see, gesturing toward the little building behind me.

The icehouse didn't have a door anymore, just a cold cement floor, four walls, and a rusted tin roof. Nose and Yale set Marcus gently on the floor inside, both breathing heavily with exertion.

I crawled in next to Marcus, and looked down at him. His eyes were wide open and staring, just like in the cemetery. There was a bullet hole in the left front panel of his jacket, but there wasn't any blood. I unzipped it and saw the same hole in his t-shirt, but still no blood. I couldn't even see a wound. What the hell? Was he wearing a flak jacket? I tugged at the t-shirt material, pulling it away from his flesh. Then I stuck my fingers into the hole and yanked, tearing the shirt in two and exposing a hole in his chest the size of a beach ball.

I stared down at it, seeing the pebbly expanse of the cement floor right through his chest cavity.

"Oh my God!" I scrambled backwards, straight into Yale's lap. "Oh my God. Oh my God."

"Olivia," Yale voice came from a great distance, "It's all right."

"No!" I shook my head. "No. He's dead. Oh my God, he's dead."

"Calm down" Yale said, wrapping his arms around me, "Marcus is okay."

"Okay?" I echoed hysterically. "He's not okay. There's a huge hole in his chest. He's dead. Dead is not okay."

"Usually, that's true," Yale said, "but not with Marcus."

From across the ice house, Nose voiced his agreement.

They were crazy. They had to be. Marcus was their hero, the one who had saved them from the CAMFers. He was their leader and they looked up to him. They were in shock, unable to admit that he was dead. Very dead. Extremely dead. How could Mike Palmer's handgun make a hole that size in anybody?

And then I saw a spark of blue, like lightning, flash from the hollow of Marcus's chest.

I jerked back even further into Yale's arms, smashing him against the cement wall.

"Just watch," Nose said.

The flash came again, and then again, pulsing almost like a heartbeat, a heartbeat of light and energy. It gained rhythm, flashing faster and faster, strobing the small interior of the ice house until I felt almost nauseous. The flashes began to run together, indistinguishable from one another until, at last, they became one steady PSS glow.

Marcus inhaled a gasping breath and suddenly sat up.

I stared at him—at his chest—his PSS chest, the cavity that I'd mistaken as a bullet hole now filled with it. Marcus had a PSS chest. How was that even possible? What about his vital organs, his heart and lungs? Even as I wondered, I saw them forming out of the swirling storm of PSS, taking shape, his blue heart pumping, his lungs expanding as he inhaled, frosty ribs solidifying around them like sideways icicles. It was like watching some kind of a medical hologram. Internal organs and bones of raw PSS energy. I had never heard of anything like that. My ghost hand didn't have bones. What kind of control would it take to form physiological details like that?

"What happened?" Marcus demanded, scanning his surroundings. His eyes fell on me wrapped in Yale's arms, and he frowned.

Yale dropped his arms to his side and said, "We're safe. For now."

"The CAMFer disappeared," Nose added.

"What do you mean he disappeared?" Marcus asked. "Where'd he go? How do you know he didn't follow us? That they aren't tracking us."

Both Nose and Yale glanced at me.

"She disappeared him," Nose said. "One minute he was there. The next he wasn't."

Marcus looked at me. "You didn't tell me you could do that," he accused.

I lifted my chin and stared back at him. "Because I can't. I didn't. I don't know what happened to him. And how dare you accuse *me* of not telling you something," I finished, glaring pointedly at his chest.

Marcus looked down. "Ah, man! This was my favorite shirt. Who tore it?" he asked, trying to pull the ragged edges together.

"I tore it," I snapped, "and I should have torn a hell of a lot more than that."

By the stifled snickers, Yale and Nose got some enjoyment out of that comment.

"I thought you were dead," I said, still feeling the fresh raw horror of it. "Just like I thought you were dead in the cemetery. Someone shot you in the heart. But you aren't dead. You weren't dead then, and you aren't dead now because you have PSS of the chest, and all this time you've been lying to me."

"I never lied to you," he said.

"What?" I said in disbelief.

"I didn't lie to you," he insisted. "I just didn't mention some things," he ended lamely.

"You are a complete dick! I can't believe I ever trusted you. I tried to give you CPR in the cemetery for Christ's sake, and you didn't even need it."

"You gave me mouth-to-mouth?" he asked, that damn smirk flitting across his lips.

"Don't even try it," I said, glaring at him, hot tears prickling at the edge of my vision. "You've had PSS all this time, and you didn't tell me? When I saw you get shot—when I saw the hole in your chest—" I couldn't go on because the tears were coming, and the last thing I wanted was for him to see me cry over him.

I stood up and ran out of the ice house, the tears coming hard and fast before I'd made it around back. I leaned against the cold exterior wall, letting myself slide to the ground. I thought about just disappearing into the woods, away from Marcus and his band of brothers and his pack of lies. Instead, I just sat there crying, hoping he'd come find me, which made me cry even harder.

What a complete idiot I'd been. Now it seemed so obvious. Of course the leader of Piss Camp had PSS. That was probably how Marcus had met David, why they'd become best friends—two guys trapped in the system with one major thing in common. And it was why the others trusted Marcus so much, followed him so easily. He was one of them. He was like them. He was like me. No wonder he was so passionate about the list—about saving the others.

So, why hadn't he just told me? Obviously, the guys had known, so why not tell me?

I heard him coming, his boots squishing on the soft ground, his arm brushing up against the side of the ice house. A thrill of gladness shot through me, and that pissed me off more. Why couldn't I just hate him? I wiped my face on my sleeve and hoped he couldn't see the tear tracks in the dark.

He sat down next to me, his long legs stretching into the underbrush.

We both stared straight ahead into the dark, ignoring the glow of his chest and my hand coalescing between us.

"The CAMFers could be out here," he said, finally.

"Fuck you," I said. He had been using the CAMFers to scare me. To make me trust him and follow him. He could have used himself, his honesty, but he hadn't.

"You're right," he said, as if he'd read my mind. "I should have told you."

I didn't say anything. I was all out of words.

"I have a hard time trusting people," he said. "It's not an excuse. I still should have told you."

Another long pause while we both just stared into the dark.

"I'm sorry, okay?" he said.

"Sure. Fine," I said, not looking at him.

"Hey, I apologized. What else do you want from me?" he growled in frustration.

"Nothing." It was a lie and we both knew it. A lie in exchange for his. Maybe he could uncover the truth if he tried, but he'd have to work for it.

"I was born with PSS of the chest," he said, as if we'd been having another conversation entirely. He was accepting my terms. He was finally going to tell me something true about himself. "As far as I know I'm the first and only case of internal organ manifestation. You have a hand of PSS. I have a PSS heart and PSS lungs."

"How does that even work?" I asked, my eyes traveling down to his torn shirt and the glow emanating from it. I was still mad at him, but that didn't change the fact that he was absolutely fascinating. *His PSS was fascinating. That's all I was interested in. His PSS.* "I mean, how can something made from energy pump blood or process oxygen?"

"I don't know," Marcus shrugged. "You have theories about your hand. I have theories about my chest. Maybe my body transforms PSS energy into the material and vice versa. When I'm cut, I don't bleed PSS. When I breathe, I breathe air. I don't know exactly how it works. I'm just really glad it does."

"And what? Your PSS just re-forms when you die or get shot in the chest?"

"My PSS is more sensitive than yours. When things pass through it, it gets disrupted. But it regenerates after about ten minutes."

"But I've never heard of PSS organs or regeneration, not in any of the medical studies or anything."

"Neither have I, and I'd really like to keep it that way."

I understood that. Doctors and researchers would have a field day with Marcus and his magical regenerating chest. How had he avoided the media? "What about when you were born?" I asked. "Didn't they test your PSS at the hospital and record all that stuff?"

"I wasn't born in a hospital," Marcus said, his voice gone low and quiet.

I could feel it. We were closing in on something he didn't want to talk about, something that would send him running back to all his protective lies if I pushed him. And I wanted to push him. But another part of me knew I shouldn't. I had to approach him like a deer in the woods, slowly, quietly, ready to stop at the slightest hint of him bolting.

"The guys say you saved us back there," he said, changing the subject. "That you rode that CAMFer like a bull."

"No," I shook my head. "It was my fault we needed saving in the first place. I thought they hadn't shown up, my mother or the CAMFers. And then I saw one of my dad's paintings. It had survived the fire."

"When you moved toward the interior of the house, that chimney was blocking our view. We couldn't see you, but Nose thought he heard a struggle. Why didn't you just run like we'd planned?"

"I wanted the painting," I said, knowing it sounded stupid, "and then he was there, grabbing it, grabbing me."

"We ran for you as soon as we realized. But I never saw a painting."

"It disappeared," I said. Is that really what had happened? Maybe we'd just dropped it. No, one moment it had been there. And the next it hadn't.

"What do you mean disappeared?"

"We were fighting over it," I tried to explain. "I mean, he didn't want it. He wanted me, but I managed to keep it between us. I kicked him. He tried to shake me off of it. And then it was just gone. Poof. No more painting."

"And that's what happened to him too?" Marcus asked, sounding like he actually believed it.

"Pretty much. Ask Nose and Yale. They saw that part."

"When he disappeared, were you touching him?"

"Of course I was touching him. I was clinging to his back, but what does that have to do with—?" I stopped, my mind grinding to a halt on one horrible thought. *Had my ghost hand done this too?*

"What were you thinking?" Marcus pressed. "Did you want something? Did you need something?"

"He wasn't going to stop. Nose was going to shoot him."

"So you needed him gone," Marcus surmised, "and you had the bullet with you."

"Yes," I exhaled, finally understanding what he was getting at. It hadn't been my ghost hand. It had been the bullet. The bullet had manifested an ability in answer to my need, just like the blades had. It had made things disappear. First the painting. Then Mike Palmer. I could feel it in my jeans pocket, digging into my hip, such a tiny thing. "But where did they—?" I started to ask.

"Shhhh!" Marcus hissed. Suddenly, he was in a crouch, back to me, peering around the corner. "Cover your hand," he whispered, and I heard him zipping up his jacket, the glow of his PSS suddenly doused.

My right glove was off—gone—lost back at the house during my struggle with Palmer. I stripped off the left one, put it on my ghost hand inside out, and our little hiding spot grew a shade darker.

Were the CAMFers coming? I didn't hear anything except the wind in the trees and the beating of my own heart. Even Nose and Yale were dead silent in the ice house, the low mumble of their voices gone, which meant they'd probably heard it too—whatever Marcus had heard.

"Follow me," he said, slipping around the corner toward the front.

23

THE CAMFer SPY

Nose and Yale were already on alert and flanking the doorway, Mike Palmer's gun gripped firmly in Nose's hand.

"We heard something," Marcus told them as we slipped back inside.

"Us too," Yale whispered. "Something moving through the brush."

"Could be an animal," Nose said, keeping his voice low, "but it sounded bigger."

The loud snap of a branch broke the silence of the night, followed by the rustle of bushes. It didn't sound like an animal. It sounded like someone walking through the woods toward us.

"Stay here with the gun," Marcus ordered. "I'll try to flank them, and if they get too close, I'll draw them off."

He was gone, out the door and into the dark, before I could protest.

I glanced from Nose to Yale, feeling panic rise in my throat.

"He'll be fine," Nose said, "He's hard to kill."

Hard or impossible? I wanted to ask, but the sounds outside were getting closer. For a second, off to the left, I thought I saw the beam of a flashlight cut through the blackness.

A minute later, from that same direction, there was a loud crashing of brush followed by a yell cut short, followed by more crashing of brush. And then silence.

I stood with Nose and Yale, peering out into the dark woods.

A figure, lumpy and misshapen, stumbled into the clearing.

"I got him," Marcus called, emerging from the bushes as well, his hand locked on the arm of what looked like a headless torso dressed in black.

It took me a moment to realize that Marcus had thrown his jacket over his captive's head and cinched it shut.

Marcus shoved the CAMFer forward and the spy struggled a little, muffled protests coming from inside the jacket. He was a pretty small guy, much shorter than Marcus. He hardly looked threatening.

"That's it?" Nose asked. "That's all they sent?"

"Looks like it," Marcus said. "Let's get him inside and get some answers."

I slipped off my glove to provide some light as Marcus propelled the CAMFer forward, guiding him over the threshold. Marcus pushed him down to a sitting position, and we all stood over him, Nose with the gun ready in his hand.

"You're sure no one else is out there?" Yale asked Marcus. "I doubt he came alone."

"I didn't see anything but this idiot crashing through the brush like a drunken cow with a flashlight."

That comment elicited a muffled protest from under Marcus's jacket. Apparently, this CAMFer didn't appreciate being compared to inebriated bovine.

"Anyway, let's have a look," Marcus said, reaching down and yanking his jacket off the CAMFer with a flourish.

And there sat Emma blinking up at us, the static electricity from the jacket making her red hair float away from her head like some kind of angelic Medusa.

"Emma!" I exclaimed, throwing myself down in front of her.

"Thank God I found you!" she said, hugging me, nearly squeezing the breath out of me.

"Are you okay?" I pulled back, looking her over.

"I've been better," Emma said, rubbing her arm. "One of these guys has a nasty tackle." She looked disapprovingly from Yale to Marcus to Nose, her glance lingering on his ski mask and falling to the gun in his hand, her eyes widening. "What is going on?" she asked, her voice halfway between fear and concern.

"Nose!" I said. "Put that thing away."

He lowered the gun, but he didn't put it away. Yale and Marcus didn't look pleased either. They were eyeing Emma as if they still thought she was a CAMFer spy.

"This is Emma," I explained. "She's my best friend."

"What is your best friend doing out here in the woods at night?" Marcus asked.

"I was looking for her," Emma answered, staring Marcus down, not letting him intimidate her in the least.

"And you just happened to come here, tonight, right now?" he sounded skeptical.

"I've been checking all her hang-outs," Emma said. "I figured her sudden disappearance had something to do with you. Looks like I was right."

"What do you know about me?" Marcus demanded.

"Oh for Christ's sake, would you two just stop it!" I cried. "She is not a CAMFer spy," I said to Marcus, "and he is not a bad guy," I said to Emma. "We're all on the same side."

"A CAMFer spy?" Emma scoffed. "Is that what he thinks I am? I'm not even a Republican. Besides, since when do political lobbyists have spies? That's just ridiculous."

"Actually, it's not," I said. "Mike Palmer is a CAMFer spy. He burned down my house. I saw him do it. And there's at least one more in town."

"Mike Palmer, the Fire Chief, burned down your house?" Emma asked in disbelief.

"Yes."

"Why would he do that?" she asked.

"It's complicated," I said, looking up at the guys.

Yale looked at Emma, sizing her up.

Nose shrugged.

Marcus shook his head.

They didn't want me to tell her anything.

"She might know something," I argued. "She's been in town. She might have seen something that could help us."

"Fine," Marcus said coldly, "then ask her." *But don't tell her*, his eyes said.

"I have a few questions of my own first, thank you very much," Emma countered. "I know who he is," she said, nodding at Marcus, "but who are these other guys?"

"They're my friends, and that's all you need to know," Marcus answered.

He was so melodramatic.

"This is Nose and that's Yale," I said, gesturing at them and ignoring Marcus's glare. "They've all been helping me since I ditched the hospital, and Nose is going to put the gun away, aren't you Nose?"

Nose quickly tucked the gun in his belt, looking apologetic.

"Why don't you two go check outside," Marcus said to the other guys. "Do a perimeter sweep and make sure there's no one else out there."

"Sure," Nose said, but as the two of them exited, I noticed him look back. I could read it on his face; he knew Marcus was sending them out to keep them from hearing what Emma said. There were cracks in the camaraderie of Piss Camp. I wasn't the only one Marcus kept things from.

"Now," Marcus was saying to Emma, "Tell us what's been going on in town."

"I might if you ask nicely," Emma shot back.

"Emma," I said, trying to keep the peace, "please, tell us what's been going on since I left."

"Well," Emma said, addressing me and blatantly ignoring Marcus, "when you disappeared from the hospital, everyone pretty much freaked. Except your mom. The first thing she did was call my mom because she was sure you were at my place. Then, when you weren't, she had a bit of a freak out herself. She told us the two of you had a big fight, and she thought you were hiding out somewhere just to blackmail her."

"Me blackmail her? That's a good one," I said. "She was trying to blackmail me into letting the hospital do a bunch of tests on my hand."

"Tests?" Marcus said. "You never told me that."

"Yes I did."

"No, you didn't," he insisted.

"Well, whatever. I didn't mean not to tell you. In the hospital my hand sort of wacked-out in my mother's general direction, so she convinced her doctor friend to order some tests."

"What kind of tests?" Marcus asked.

"I don't know," I said, annoyed that he was so fixated on some unimportant detail. "Anyway, when I told them no way, they told me they didn't even need my permission."

"That's terrible," Emma said. "So, that's why you left the hospital?"

"Exactly," I said. "And I was planning to come to your place, but then Marcus showed up, and I went with him instead."

"So, what happened after her mom called yours?" Marcus asked, sitting down on the floor instead of standing over us like some kind of Nazi interrogator.

"Well, the hospital and Emergency Services wanted to launch a full scale search," Emma explained. "But your mom nixed that," she said to me. "I mean, it was pretty obvious you hadn't been kidnapped. There were no signs of a struggle, and you'd taken the bag of clothes Mom and I brought you. Your mom thought that once you cooled down, you'd come back. She convinced everyone it would just be best to wait you out."

"How practical of her," I mumbled.

"But I was pretty worried," Emma's said. "I knew even if you were pissed at your mom, you would have called me. But then you didn't, and I knew some strange stuff had been happening with your hand. And with him," she said, glancing at Marcus. "So, last night I snuck out and checked all your places—the cemetery, the old tree house in McKenzie Park, this place. Then today someone found a tent in the old lumber camp," Emma went on, "and they said it must be yours. I was desperate to know you were all right, so I decided to check there tonight, but I figured I'd stop here and check again too, since it was on the way."

"Oh, Em," I said, hugging her. "I'm so sorry you were worried. I should have e-mailed you. But things got really crazy."

"If her mom is so eager for her to come back," Marcus said, "why didn't she meet her tonight like they'd arranged?"

"What are you talking about?" Emma asked, looking confused. "Her mom has been at my house all evening. She's starting to lose it a little, and my mom was worried, so she invited her over for dinner. She's really worried about you, Liv, even though she's trying not to show it."

"What about the e-mail I sent her?" I asked.

"I don't know anything about an e-mail," Emma said.

"The CAMFers probably intercepted it completely," Marcus said. "Anything else strange around town?" he asked Emma. "Any unusual rumors or gossip?"

"No," Emma shook her head, but I could tell there was something. And so could Marcus.

"What is it?" I asked before Marcus could step in and start bullying her.

"It's about Passion Wainwright," Emma said, avoiding my eyes.

"What about her?" I asked, feeling suddenly cold.

"You knew she was in the hospital, right?"

I nodded.

"Well," Emma said, taking a deep breath. "There were rumors flying all over the place that she'd tried to commit suicide, that she had been your mom's patient. And then her parents pulled her from the hospital yesterday and sent her away."

"Sent her away where?" I asked.

"Some religious rehab place," Emma said. "That's what my mom heard."

"Anything else?" Marcus pressed, as if the information about Passion didn't even matter. As if it was nothing.

"There is one more thing," Emma said, looking worriedly at me.

"Just tell me," I said.

"Your mom is staying at Dr. Fineman's house."

"She moved in with him?" I blurted. "She said she was staying at her office."

"She was, at first," Emma explained, "but now she's at his place."

"Who's Dr. Fineman?" Marcus asked, confused.

"Her new boyfriend," I said with disgust. "Well, not exactly new, but I just found out about it. He's the one she convinced to test my hand."

"I see," Marcus said, and it sounded like he really did. "What does this doctor look like?"

"I don't know. He's tall and old and has a big nose," I said. "Why does that even matter?"

Marcus was suddenly standing. "We need to get out of here. Now. And she needs to go home," he said, nodding at Emma.

"No way," Emma said, getting up and crossing her arms over her chest, "I want to help. I'm not going anywhere until I'm sure Olivia is safe."

"Well, then you're going to be living in this shack for a very long time," Marcus said angrily, "but we aren't, because we're not idiots."

"Hey!" I cried. What had gotten into him? He'd been perfectly calm a minute ago, and now he was being a complete ass.

"What's your problem?" Emma snapped, "She's my friend. I just want to help."

"The best way to help is to go home and stay out of this," Marcus said, crossing to the door and calling Nose and Yale back in.

"Where is this shack?" he demanded of Yale as soon as he stepped in the door. "How far are we from town?"

"I don't know," Yale seemed to be trying to calculate. "Half a mile maybe."

"Half a mile," Marcus said, sounding grim.

"We're in meter range," Yale said, going pale. "Shit. I didn't even think about it."

"But we didn't see anyone out there. No signs of CAMFers," Nose said.

"They sent her to distract us," Marcus said, moving toward Emma, "to keep us busy while they set up an ambush."

"No one sent me," Emma insisted, backing away from him. "No one even knows I'm here."

"Stop it," I told Marcus, grabbing his arm. "Stop freaking out. She's my friend. I trust her with my life."

"And with mine?" he asked, whirling on me, scaring me with the wildness in his eyes, "with Nose's and Yale's?"

"Yes," I said, matching his fierceness.

We stood that way, me holding his arm, our eyes locked, oblivious to the others in the room, and I suddenly understood that he was afraid. This was

Marcus afraid, and I didn't like it, and I wanted to comfort him, but I didn't know how.

"Okay," Marcus exhaled, as if we'd just come to some agreement. "We need to get out of here, and she can't come with us."

"I know," I said, dropping my hand from his arm, "but she could spy for us. Be our eyes and ears in town."

"We don't need a spy. We got what we came for. We're leaving."

"But what about the blades?"

"Forget the blades. The CAMFers know we're here now. It's too big of a risk."

I wasn't sure how I felt about leaving Passion's blades in the hands of the CAMFers, but I could see there was no point arguing. "So, we go back to camp," I said, "and Emma goes home. But I need a way to keep in contact with her. I can't just ditch my mom and everything without that. And Emma could tell us when the CAMFers leave. She could tell us if Mike Palmer goes with them or stays in town."

"Hey, I have a phone," Emma said, digging in her pocket. "I meant to give it to you at the hospital, but I forgot. My mom figured you lost yours in the fire, so she bought me a new one and wanted me to give you this," she finished, pulling out her old phone and handing it to me.

"How convenient," Marcus said, grabbing the phone out of my hands.

"I brought it in case I found her," Emma said, as if speaking to a small child. "So we could communicate, even if she didn't want to come back with me."

"Check it," Marcus said, handing it to Nose.

Nose removed the back of the phone, dug out the battery, did a close inspection of the interior and handed it back to Marcus. "No trace on it," he said. "Should be safe enough once I route it through the scrambler."

"Give that to me," I said, snatching it back. "Thank you," I said to Emma, tucking the phone into my jeans pocket.

"Here's your flashlight," Nose said, tossing it to Emma. "We found it outside."

"We have to go," Marcus said, ushering Nose and Yale toward the door.

I turned and hugged Emma. "I'll be okay," I said.

"Are you sure these guys are safe?" she whispered. "You can still come to my place. You don't have to go with them."

"I do though," I said, pulling back. "I'm sorry. I'll keep in touch." We both had tears in our eyes.

"What do I tell your mom?" she asked.

"You don't tell her anything," Marcus interjected. "You don't say anything about Olivia, or us, or the CAMFers. If you do, you put us all in danger. Do you get that?"

"Yeah, I get it," Emma said, glaring at him.

Marcus pulled me away and propelled me out the door.

Nose took the lead through the woods with Marcus and me after him and Yale at the rear, as usual. Yale liked to take up the rear, and at any other time that realization would have made me smile. But not now.

Not when I was leaving my best friend and my town and everything I knew behind me.

I looked back, past Marcus and Yale. I could still see the dark triangle of the ice house, a glint of light in the door.

Emma flicked her flashlight off, then on again.

I raised my ghost hand and waved.

"Let's go," Marcus said gruffly, pulling my hand down as he came alongside me, but he didn't let go of it. He held it gently as we wound our way through the dark woods, and I didn't pull away, even though I was still a little mad at him. Mad for not telling me about his PSS and for the way he'd treated Emma. But then his fingers began to stroke the inside of my wrist, and twine themselves between my ethereal ones, and I could feel my anger ebbing away, and his fear with it. And something else. I'd never felt my ghost hand so solidly as when he held it like that, as if it were a real hand made of flesh. Once, I looked down and thought I saw pale metacarpal bones and thin blue lines of veins forming in my ghost fingers.

But it must have been a trick of the moonlight.

24

BLOOD AND ROMANCE

By the time we reached the ridge beyond the lumber camp, my head hurt. My lungs hurt. My legs hurt. My arms hurt. My ears and my hair and my teeth hurt. The only thing that didn't hurt was my ghost hand, which Marcus wasn't holding anymore. The hand-holding thing had gone from comforting, to helpful, to him clutching my upper arm just to keep me from falling flat on my face.

I was so happy when I saw the open ground of our camp through the trees. I might even have been giddy enough to run forward and give Jason a hug.

But Jason wasn't alone.

"Wait," Marcus said, pulling me back into the shadows.

Nose had already crossed into the open, but he was drawing his gun. He knew something was wrong.

Jason was crouched in the clearing, bent over something large and lumpy. The something was making noises, strange noises, like an injured animal. For some reason the image of a Grizzly Bear in a trap flashed in my mind. There weren't any bears in Illinois. And even if there had been, how would Jason trap one?

Marcus, Yale and I watched as Nose approached Jason. They greeted one another. Nose looked down at the lumpy thing. He asked Jason something as he tucked his gun away. Then he turned back to where the three of us were hiding and waved that the coast was clear.

As tired as I was, I was curious to see what Jason had caught while we were away.

Marcus took my ghost hand again, and we followed Yale into camp.

I could feel the tension in Marcus leaking into me, the angle of his arm making me think he wanted to lead me away. He was still afraid of something, even here in Piss Camp.

Together we walked up to the lump lying at Jason's feet and I looked down.

It took a moment for me to realize what it was. *Who* it was. But finally it registered in my mind that the bloody, bruised, whimpering thing trussed up on the ground was Mike Palmer. Ultimately, the clothing gave it away, because his face was swollen beyond recognition.

"What happened to him?" I blurted, wanting to recoil into Marcus's shoulder but finding myself unable to look away. Last time I'd seen Chief Palmer, right before the bullet had disappeared him, he'd been fine. Is this what it did? Transported people and chewed them to pieces in the process? Had I done this?

"Jason happened to him," Marcus said flatly, wrapping his arm around me.

"He hasn't told me anything yet," Jason said matter-of-factly as he cracked his bloody knuckles, "but he will."

"You—you did this?" I pulled away from Marcus, staring at Jason in horror. "Why? Why would you do this?"

"I didn't kill him," Jason said, as if that explained it. "Well, I nearly did. Almost shot him in the head when he popped out of thin air right in front of me. Lucky for him, that picture came through first and gave me some warning. Damn thing probably saved his life."

I glanced up to see *The Other Olivia* leaning against one of the wheelers.

"Looks like you," Jason said, gesturing at it. "So I figured it had something to do with you when he showed up."

"How long has he been here?" Yale asked.

"Two and a half hours, maybe a little longer," Jason said.

"So the transfer was instant," Marcus noted.

"Somebody want to tell me what the hell is going on?" Jason asked.

"She touched them, and they disappeared," Nose said, glancing at me.

"That was a couple of hours ago," Yale said. "We didn't have a clue where they'd gone until now."

"What the fuck?" Jason said, staring at me, his expression a mixture of fear and awe. "Is that what you were trying to do to me before?" he demanded, stepping over Mike Palmer and coming at me. "Did you try to disappear me?"

"Back off!" Marcus said, stepping between us. "She didn't even know she could do this until tonight. I told you, what happened before was an accident."

On the ground, Mike Palmer groaned loudly.

"Shut up, pig!" Jason yelled, turning and kicking him in the ribs.

"Stop it!" I cried, pushing my way around Marcus and shoving Jason as hard as I could.

"I told you, bitch,—don't ever touch me!" Jason yelled, charging me and grabbing a fistful of my hair.

I wanted to sink my hand into him. I wanted to yank out everything inside of him and make it all disappear.

But before I could, Marcus was on him, clamping Jason in a headlock, pulling him off me, wrenching Jason's hand away with a fistful of my hair in it. I ignored the pain, the stream of vulgarity raining down on me from Jason's mouth, the scuffle going on behind me as Nose and Yale joined the effort to restrain him.

I knelt in the mud next to the bloody blob that was Mike Palmer. It hadn't rained for days. It wasn't mud;

it was blood, soaked into the dust, making it black and wet and sticky.

"Bring me some water and a washcloth," I ordered no one in particular.

They didn't listen at first. I had to say it three times. By the third time, the commotion behind me had died down, and Jason had been escorted away by Nose.

Finally, someone brought me a basin of water and a cloth. Yale and Marcus stood behind me, mumbling, talking, sometimes arguing. I didn't listen, didn't care what they said anymore. I washed Mike Palmer's swollen face, his bloody hair, his neck, his bruised arms, careful to use only my flesh hand. Jason had put duct tape over his mouth, and all the while I cleaned him, he glared at me, hate spilling from eyes swollen to mere slits.

"Get me some bandages," I ordered the hand that took the basin of bloody water from me. The bandages came, but there weren't many. I'd only be able to use them on the worst of his cuts. His head was still bleeding. Head wounds bled a lot.

I'd have to use both hands to apply the bandages.

When my ghost hand neared his head, Mike Palmer rolled his eyes crazily and groaned and rocked, trying to writhe away from it.

"Stop it," I scolded. "I'm trying to help you," but he wouldn't listen.

"Let me try," Marcus said, kneeling beside me and taking some of the bandages, our shoulders touching.

But that only made things worse. Mike Palmer's thrashing grew even wilder. Staring at Marcus, he bucked and whimpered and tried to roll away, making bandaging him completely impossible.

"What's wrong with him?" I asked in frustration.

"He shot me in the chest," Marcus said. "He thinks I've come back from the dead. Or I'm a ghost."

"Oh, right. Well, hold his shoulders then, Ghost Boy."

Marcus circled around to Palmer's bucking shoulders, pinning them with his hands. Quickly and not exactly neatly, I wrapped the bandages around the top of Palmer's head like a mummy, even wrapping them over his eyes. Maybe if he couldn't see us, he wouldn't freak out so much.

I sat back and surveyed my work. He was still tied up, the ropes biting into his skin. He was lying in a puddle of his own blood, this man who had burned down my house, and taken everything from me, and tried to kidnap me, and shot Marcus. But I didn't hate him. I didn't really feel anything; I was too exhausted.

"Is he going to die?" I asked Marcus.

"I doubt it," he replied. "I know it looks bad, but it's all surface stuff. Jason wasn't trying to kill him. He was just interrogating him."

"And that's okay with you?"

"It wasn't my call."

"But we're not letting him go."

"We need what he knows," Marcus said, "but there may be better ways of getting it."

I didn't want to know what he meant by that. "I'm so tired," I said, leaning into him.

"I know, babe," he said, wrapping me in his arms.

I could feel the lively Thu-bump of his PSS heart as he picked me up like a little child and carried me toward the tent. His arms were strong and firm and safe.

And he'd called me babe.

When I woke, *The Other Olivia* was leaning against the nearest tent wall, reaching out her perfect flesh hand to me. Marcus must have brought her in and put her where I'd see her the moment I opened my eyes. Did he know how much that meant to me?

Next to the painting was the cot I usually slept on, folded and leaning against the tent wall too. I turned my head and came face to face with a sleeping Marcus. We were laying side-by-side in sleeping bags on the floor.

One of his arms was slung over me, pinning me down, the weight of it like some unconscious promise. It was so startling that I froze, not knowing if I liked it or not, the way it made me feel trapped and held at the same time.

I suddenly became aware that I was only half-dressed inside my sleeping bag. That realization was followed by a memory of Marcus helping me out of my bloody clothes, out of my sweatshirt, and my boots, and my jeans. Oh God! He'd helped me take off my jeans, and it had not been sexy. Not even close. I'd been completely out of it.

He, on the other hand, had been a complete gentleman.

He'd tried to put me to bed in the cot, but I'd asked him to sleep next to me, to hold me. And that's what he'd done. What he was doing, even as he slept.

I turned, rolling further into the curve of his arm. His eyes, soft with sleep, blinked open, a boyish smile on his lips. Not the smirk this time, but something better, something wholly unguarded.

I didn't even think about it. I went in for a kiss.

His lips quirked in sleepy surprise, but then they were moving against mine. Opening. Tasting. Our lips testing each other. He was a good kisser, and his arm tightened, pulling me against him, reminding me that other parts of him felt nice against other parts of me, even through two thick sleeping bags.

I pulled back, looking at him.

"Good morning to you too," he said, grinning like a pleased cat.

"Good morning," I said, wanting to kiss him again, but feeling suddenly shy.

He raised a hand and brushed a strand of hair away from my face, letting his fingers linger. "How are you?" he asked.

"I'm—okay," I said, the glamour of our kiss suddenly dispelled as I remembered Mike Palmer, and Jason, and the bullet, and all the other horrifying moments of the night before. "Thanks for last night," I said. "I don't know what was wrong with me."

"Nothing was wrong with you," he said gently. "Last night was rough for everyone."

How rough had it been for Mike Palmer? What if he died? What if we'd killed him? He'd lost so much blood.

"Is Mike—?" I didn't even know what to ask.

"He's alive and secure," Marcus said.

"So what now?" I sat up in my sleeping bag. "He needs medical attention. And what if the CAMFers come for him?"

"They don't know where he is," Marcus said, sitting up as well, his bag slipping down to his waist.

He hadn't slept in a shirt this time, just his jeans; he wasn't hiding his PSS from me anymore. I tried not to stare, but his chest was so distracting, his skin so brown and smooth, like mocha ice cream, that I had the sudden urge to lick him.

"Jason checked him for tracking devices last night and smashed his radio," he said, oblivious to my appraisal. "I wish he'd left the radio intact. We might have been able to listen in on them with it. But Jason doesn't always think things through."

"No shit."

"We need the information Palmer has," he said, looking at me.

"If nearly beating him to death didn't get it, I don't know what will."

"There is something he's more afraid of than pain," Marcus said, glancing down. I followed his gaze, saw he was looking at my ghost hand, pale against the darker blue of my sleeping bag.

"No," I said, slipping my hand inside my bag, all my warm feelings for him suddenly gone.

"It would be painless," he said.

"It would still be torture," I argued.

"Is bigoted irrational fear torture? If it is, it's torture of his own making. Was it torture when you cleaned him up and treated his wounds last night? In some war camps, they'd beat the prisoners and then treat their wounds so they could beat them again. So they wouldn't die so soon. So the torture could go on longer."

"That is not what I was doing, and you know it."

"He doesn't," Marcus said, his voice gaining some heat, his eyes boring into mine. "In his mind we are monsters. Nothing is going to change that. We can either let his fear hurt us, or use it to our advantage."

"And those are the only choices? Really? What about staying neutral?"

"After all they've done to you, do you really think there's a neutral?" he asked, throwing his hands up in frustration.

I tried to ignore the way his muscles rippled so nicely when he did that. *You're pissed at him. Don't get distracted.* "Fine. Maybe it is us or them," I said. "But why this? Why me? He's afraid of PSS, so why not unmask Nose in front of him? Or depants Yale? Or better yet, show him your wonderful pecs." *Crap! Had I just said that out loud?*

"My wonderful pecs?" he asked, raising an eyebrow, that familiar smile forming on his lips as he absently scratched a rib, taunting me. His abs were pretty ripped as well.

"They're—well defined," I said, feeling the blush rush to my face, looking anywhere but at his more than adequate physique. "But that's not the point. The point is why does it have to be my PSS?"

"He hasn't seen any of ours," Marcus said, "and the last thing we want is to give him more information about us. Besides, your hand has special properties."

"Special properties," I repeated. Suddenly I felt closed in, stifled, like I couldn't breathe. I unzipped my bag a little, and clutched the zipper, feeling the cold metallic bite of its teeth digging into my flesh. "You don't just want me to scare him with my ghost hand," I said. "You want me to reach into him."

"Yes," Marcus said, his eyes drifting to the zipper, to the black-laced edge of my underwear dark against my pale upper thigh.

I had forgotten I wasn't wearing much inside my sleeping bag. But now I felt it—my nakedness, my vulnerability; the Marcus who had stripped me so gently last night and laid me down and held me safe, now wanted to use my hand to torture someone.

I reached down and zipped the sleeping bag up above my waist. "I'm not going to do that," I said.

"I know you're afraid," he said, gently, comfortingly. Was it comfort? Had any of it ever been genuine, or was it just a way to manipulate me? "But think about it. The blades and the bullet, each one has saved you already. The bullet saved us all. What if we could find something else like that? Something that could help us."

"So, Mike Palmer is one of those vending machines full of toys, and I'm the mechanical claw?"

"How about he's the bastard that burned down your house and shot me and would kill us all in a heartbeat," Marcus said angrily, grabbing his shirt off the tent floor and yanking it over his head. "And maybe you're the one person who can actually do something about it.

The one person who could eliminate the CAMFers as a threat for good, but you're too scared to do it."

I stared at him, hurt welling up in my chest. Yes, I was scared, but how dare he throw it in my face. "That is such a load of superhero crap," I said. "You really believe I'm the *one* person who can stop this? You really want to put that on me?"

He stopped moving, sat staring at me, his eyes anguished, his shirt only pulled down halfway. "No," he said, shaking his head. "You're right. That's not fair."

Something buzzed against my leg, from under my sleeping bag. I rolled aside, revealing my blood encrusted jeans from last night. "It's Emma's phone," I said to Marcus, scrambling in the pockets.

By the time I found the phone and pulled it out, the call had already gone to voicemail. There were two other missed calls.

"Someone called twice last night," I showed Marcus. "Once at 12:35 am. Then at 12:50. Same unknown number. That call just now was Emma's mom."

"Maybe she thinks Emma still has the phone," Marcus said. "Listen to the messages."

I pulled up the first call and put the phone to my ear.

"Olivia," came Emma's voice, muted and hard to hear, as if she was whispering. "I'm scoping out Mike Palmer's place right now. Thought I'd do a little recon before I went back home. There is definitely some action here. I've seen three different guys, none of them Mike and they—" Emma's voice suddenly stopped short.

Then there was a very deep, manly sort of grunt in the background and the phone cut out.

I took the phone from my ear and stared down at it.

"What?" Marcus said. "Who was it?"

"It was Emma," I said, fear climbing the ladder of my ribs straight to my heart. "Calling from her new phone. She went to Palmer's house last night."

"Dammit! I told her to stay out of this."

"The call cuts off," I said, holding the phone out to him, trying to make him understand. Yes, he had told Emma to go home and stay out of it, but I hadn't. I'd suggested she spy for us—that she do the very thing she'd done.

"Maybe she dropped the phone," Marcus said. "The second one is probably her calling back."

Yes, my heart sighed. I'd almost forgotten about the second call. Emma had called back. She must be all right.

I jabbed the button to listen to the second call.

"We have your friend," said the Dark Man's voice in my ear, "but *he* knows what I really want."

That was it. That was all he said before he hung up.

25

LOSING EMMA

"They have her," I said, shoving the phone at Marcus.

He took it from my shaking hands and listened to the message, his eyes growing dark and worried. "Check the last one," he said, handing the phone back to me. "The one from her mom."

I felt a sliver of hope. Maybe Emma had dropped her phone at Palmer's house, and the CAMFers had just found it. Maybe she was safe at home after all, and she'd called us on her mom's phone to tell us not to worry. I selected the last message and put the phone to my ear.

"Emma, where are you?" Mrs. Campbell's voice asked, sounding shaken. "Please call me as soon as you get this. If you're with Olivia, I won't be mad. I tried to call your new phone too, but you didn't answer. Just call so we know you're safe."

"What?" Marcus asked, his eyes scanning my face.

"She didn't make it home," I said, letting my hand and the phone drop to my lap. "Her mom doesn't know where she is."

"I'm so sorry," he said, reaching out and putting his arm around me. He said it like someone had died, like people used to say after my dad passed away.

"Don't be sorry," I said, shrugging out of his embrace. "Do something. We have to do something."

"She took a risk," Marcus said gently, "and it didn't pay off."

"What kind of cold-hearted load of bullshit is that?" I spat at him, pulling away even further. "My best friend has been kidnapped, and that's all you have to say?"

"They won't hurt her," he said. "She doesn't have PSS. She's useless to them."

"Not if they think she can lead them to me. That's what the Dark Man said. They have Emma, but they want me."

"That's not what he said."

But I was already grabbing my clothes. I didn't have time to argue. Emma didn't have time.

"He was talking about me," Marcus went on, "and the list. And that's exactly why we didn't tell Emma anything else. She doesn't know our location. She can't give us away."

"They don't know that," I said, slipping a clean pair of jeans inside the sleeping bag and wrestling them on. "They caught her talking to me on the phone. They're going to assume she knows where I am."

"They'll figure out pretty quickly she doesn't."

"Yes, by hurting her!" I suddenly had a flash of Mike Palmer, tied, swollen and bloody. They might do worse to Emma. She'd said there were three men. Three CAMFer men. What would they do to a teenage girl to make her talk? "We have to get her out of there now," I said, fastening the snap of my jeans and kicking the sleeping bag off. "She did this because I suggested it." I stood, scanning the tent for my boots.

"Olivia, listen to me!" Marcus stood too and tried to grab hold of me, but I dodged away.

"No!" I screamed. "Don't do that. Don't grab me, or touch me, or play my feelings to get me to do what you want."

"Play your feelings?" he asked angrily. "Is that what you think I've been doing? You kissed me this morning, not the other way around."

"Fine. I won't make that mistake again," I snapped, bending to dig the phone out of the folds of the sleeping bag and shoving it in my pocket. "I need to get Emma back," I said, staring him down, "and if you're not going to help me, I'll do it myself, but I am going to do it. You, of all people, should understand that. They had your best friend once, remember?"

"This is not the same," he said, nostrils flaring. "She isn't one of us. She doesn't have PSS. They aren't going to extract her or kill her."

"She isn't one of us?" I looked at him, stunned. "What the fuck does that mean?"

Marcus just stared back at me, saying nothing.

"Oh, I see," I said. "*Them* is anyone without PSS. Is that what you mean? Emma doesn't have PSS, so she doesn't matter? She isn't worth shit if she's not on your little list."

"That's not fair," he said, his voice low and dangerous.

"Then explain what you mean that she isn't one of us," I challenged.

"Okay," he said, stepping close to me. "*Us* are the people I might be able to save, a handful of innocent teenagers who have no idea they're in danger. And *them* is the rest of the world, the people I can't save," his voice broke on the last two words. For a moment, I could see some awful pain welling in his eyes, but then he regained his composure and went on. "And if I try, and I mess up or get caught, then the kids on that list are dead for sure, and I haven't saved anyone."

"I don't even understand why they're doing this. Why take our PSS? What good is it to them?"

"They know how to extract it," Marcus said. "I'm pretty sure they have a way to store it. Now they're working on a way to use it."

"Use it for what?"

"As a renewable energy source would be my guess. That's what the world is clamoring for."

PSS as renewable energy? That was crazy. My hand wasn't a resource; it was my hand. You couldn't farm people's body parts for energy. That was insane. Then again, there was a booming black market for healthy transplant organs, live tissue, babies, and children as sex slaves. The world wasn't exactly picky about where it got what it thought it needed. And PSS might be easier to sell than any of those, once it was removed from its source.

"It's just a theory," Marcus said. "But they've been lobbying against PSS in Washington for years, and they haven't made much progress going that route. Maybe they need to prove something to someone—some big name investor—and the list is a way to conduct some under-the-table experiments until they figure out exactly what they're doing."

"So, we're guinea pigs?"

"Maybe," he shrugged.

"And you actually expect me to leave my best friend with people like that?"

"They can only use Emma if we're still here," he said, taking my ghost hand. "If we'd left when we should have, this wouldn't have happened. And that's my fault. Not yours. I wanted those blades. I thought they could help us, and that blinded me to the risks. But you're right. We can't just leave her at their mercy. So, we call the police, and we leave an anonymous tip. We let the professionals take care of this."

"*You're* advocating calling the police?" I asked, pulling my hand from his. "You're the one who constantly insists that the police force is made entirely of CAMFers."

"Then we text Emma's mom, tell her where Emma is, and let her parents handle it."

"I'm not dragging them into this. The Campbells aren't exactly street wise. They'd probably go running over there and get themselves killed. There's no one else to help her. It has to be us."

"We can't help her without exposing ourselves. You know that."

"So what! We risked that to go after the blades, and it didn't stop you then."

"Yeah, and look how great that went," he pointed out.

"What about David? Do you honestly expect me to believe you wouldn't go after him if they had him again?"

Marcus stared at me long and hard, then looked away. "No, I wouldn't," he said.

"You are a terrible liar."

"Maybe I am," he said, looking down at his hands. "I thought I could keep everyone safe, especially David, but obviously that's not true. But I know he wouldn't want me to risk you for him."

"I didn't ask what David would want," I said. "I asked what you would do."

"You don't know what you're asking," he said, turning away from me. He paced to the far corner of the tent, and stood, his back straight, his fists clenched, battling out some inner struggle.

"She came looking for me," I said to his back. "She went to Palmer's for me. She needs our help." I had been bluffing about doing it on my own. I needed him. Wished I didn't, but I did.

I stepped toward him, put my hand on his back. "We can do this," I promised. "We have the bullet, and we can figure out how to use it. We have Palmer. I can get information from him—Oh my God!"

"What?" Marcus jumped, spinning around as if we were under attack.

"What if they want Palmer back? What if that's what the Dark Man meant?"

"No," Marcus shook his head. "Even if they thought we had him, they'd cut their losses. He botched your capture twice. CAMFers don't treat failure kindly. To them he's expendable."

"How can you be so sure?"

"I just am," he said, reaching out and pulling me to his chest. "It's how they think."

I tucked my head into the curve of his neck, inhaling the scent of him—smoke and woods and sweat and something indefinably him.

"Okay, we'll go get her," he sighed into my hair.

"Really?" I looked up at him, our faces close.

"Yes," he said, smiling down at me. "But only if you promise to keep playing my feelings like this."

"I'm not—I didn't mean to—"

He kissed me this time, his hand finding the back of my neck. His mouth was rough and insistent, the scratch of stubble at the edge of his lips leaving a trail of almost-pain across mine. I opened my mouth wider and our tongues touched, teasing, coaxing. My body melted into his, marveling at the fit of hard against soft, the pressing need, the way we were trying to crawl inside each other. His right arm circled my waist, pulling my hips against his, and I couldn't help myself; I actually moaned into his mouth.

"Did I hurt you?" he asked startled, pulling away.

"No," I said, blushing like crazy, looking anywhere but in those amazing eyes.

"Oh, so you liked it," he said, sounding very pleased with himself. He bent his head again, his mouth kissing its way down my jawline, finding the hollow of my neck. He pulled away, staring at me like he'd never seen me before, and said, "God, you taste good."

"So do you," I said, smiling.

"Olivia," he said, his face gone dark and intense. "This isn't a game to me."

"I know." My eyes strayed back to his lips. "I'm sorry I said that. It's just—I'm not sure what this is."

"Um, I'm pretty sure we're making out."

"Yeah, I know," I said, looking away.

"Hey," he said soberly, touching my cheek and drawing my eyes back to him. "I like you." This time he kissed me gently, brushing his lips across mine. Then kissing me on the nose, and the forehead, like a blessing. Like I was some precious thing.

"I like you too," I said, feeling warm and amazed, but it was followed by a sudden wave of guilt. While I was standing there kissing, Emma was in serious trouble.

He must have seen it in my face, or felt it in my body, because he pulled away and said, "So, we need a plan."

"What are you thinking?"

"If we have any chance of taking the CAMFers down and getting Emma out safely," he said, beginning to pace, "we need to figure out exactly what Jason's bullet does and how to use it. And we need everything we can get from Palmer. You understand what that means, right?"

"I'm going to have to use my hand on him."

"Yes."

I knew it would come to that, even as I'd pleaded with Marcus for help. Palmer would know how many CAMFers there were, how they were armed, where Emma and the blades might be held. Going after Emma was going to come at a cost. I was going to have to do something bad, something that all my convictions were screaming at me not to do. But I was going to do it anyway.

"I'll get the info," I said, praying I'd have the guts to follow through, "but I'm not going to pull anything out of him. Just the information. That's all."

"Fair enough," Marcus agreed, "and one more thing."

"What?"

"The other guys. It has to be their choice to come. I think Nose and Yale will want to. I don't know about Jason. But whoever comes, they come armed."

"Okay," I said, nodding.

"And we should go soon. They weren't anticipating this thing with Emma, which means they're scrambling. We want to get in there before they have a chance to fully set their trap. That means tonight. Are you sure you're up to it?"

"I will be," I said.

26

INTERROGATING MIKE

Mike Palmer didn't look so good in the morning light. He was bruised and swollen, and crusty with dried blood, his body sagging against the ropes the guys had used to tie him to a tree. The bandages I had applied the night before were pushed up on his forehead so he could see, but his eyes were vacant. They didn't track me, didn't even register my existence, as I entered his field of vision. And he smelled bad, really bad. That was when I realized that the dark marks near the crotch of his pants weren't mud or blood.

Yale was sitting guard duty, leaning against a nearby

tree upwind, but he stood when the rest of us entered the small clearing.

The breeze picked up, thrusting the full force of Palmer's stench upon us, and I was afraid we were all going to revisit my breakfast. I took a few deep breaths and thought of Emma instead. Mike Palmer didn't know we'd lost her. He had no idea that she was, at that moment, in the hands of his comrades, a hostage at the mercy of desperate and determined captors just like he was. And the last thing we needed was for him to find out. After all he had done, he deserved what he was about to get. This is what I told myself.

Nose took out Palmer's gun and handed it to Jason.

Jason hefted it in his hand, and the Fire Chief's eyes moved for the first time since we'd approached him, looking at the gun, looking at Jason, then back at the gun.

Jason stepped forward and ripped the duct tape off Palmer's mouth in one savage yank.

"Fuck you," Palmer said, his lips cracked and bleeding.

"Looks like you're the one who's fucked," Jason said, tossing the tape aside. "Went and got yourself caught by a little girl, and now your CAMFer pals don't even give a shit."

"Fuck that bitch too," Palmer said, looking at me with absolute hatred in his eyes. "She's a freak. A mutant that needs to be put down. All you freaks need to die."

I couldn't believe what I was hearing. I had known this man for years, had said hello to him in the supermarket.

I had attended the same backyard barbeques and local sporting events he had. I'd even headed up a fireman's fundraiser in middle school and presented this very man with the proceeds in front of a class of seventh graders, handed it to him with my own ghost hand. And all this time he'd hated me simply because of the way I'd been born, for something completely outside of my control. How many other people felt that way? My teachers? My classmates? The new neighbors who had moved in next door, and then suddenly moved out two weeks later without any explanation?

"You keep your mouth shut," Jason said, striding forward and pressing the gun to Palmer's forehead. "You don't talk unless we ask you something. You don't breathe unless we tell you to. You don't piss yourself till we say so. You got that?"

I glanced at Marcus. Was it really a good idea to start this interrogation with Jason holding a gun to Palmer's head? We needed that head, or at least we needed the information inside of it. But Marcus wasn't looking at me. He was staring at Palmer. *Palmer.* When had I started thinking of him by his last name? Was it easier to dehumanize people when you did that? Probably. It certainly seemed to work for coaches and gym teachers.

"What are you gonna do, kill me?" Palmer asked, looking past Jason and the gun to Marcus; he knew who was really in charge. "Go ahead. Doesn't matter. Whatever you do, I'm not gonna tell you anything."

"Naw, we're not gonna kill you," Jason said, pulling the gun away. "We're gonna do something worse."

Marcus looked at me and nodded.

I could feel all their eyes on me as I stepped forward past Jason, trying not to inhale too deeply. I stared down at Palmer, and everything seemed to recede into the background but him and me. He was my enemy. He had tried to destroy me, end me. He was the door that led to Emma, and I was the key.

I held my gloved ghost hand in front of Palmer's face and saw his eyes flicker with fear. I reached out with my left hand and stripped the glove off, peeling it back, revealing my PSS one slow centimeter at a time, like some kind of uncanny stripper.

Palmer's eyes flashed with uncontrolled panic and dawning understanding.

"My hand goes into people," I said, my voice sounding like someone else's. I raised my ghost hand to his face, almost touching him.

"You're lying," he panted, his very breath belying his confidence. "PSS can't do that."

"You have no idea what I can do," I said, caressing his cheek.

His head recoiled, banging against the tree trunk behind him.

An inexplicable thrill ran through me. He was actually afraid of me. This man who had terrorized me. Now he was afraid.

"Don't touch me, bitch," he said, half-demand, half-plea.

I didn't listen, caressing his face again.

He cringed from my touch, like my mother had in the hospital, thrashing his head back and forth, his wide, white eyes tracking my ghost hand as if he were incapable of looking away. "I'll kill you," he said, spitting at me, the glob of pink phlegm landing on my shoulder.

"And how would you do that?" I asked, white hot rage welling in me. "You're tied to a tree, sitting in your own piss."

"Doesn't matter what you do to me," he said. "They're gonna get you. They're gonna get you all, and make you pay."

"Who's going to make me pay?"

"You don't know?" He laughed.

"So, why don't you tell me?"

"I don't think so," he said, grinning wickedly. "I'll let that part be a special surprise."

Somehow, I'd lost the edge of fear I'd held over him, and I wanted it back. "I'll give you a special surprise," I said, putting my hand back up and touching his face.

This time he resisted the urge to recoil. He was fighting his fear.

"I got somewhere else you can put that hand of yours," he said, leering at me.

My hand began to melt into tendrils, licking at his cheeks, winding in his hair.

His eyes bulged, and he writhed in his cocoon of rope like a giant fly in a spider's web.

Coils of my PSS wound around his neck.

"No, you can't," he choked, squeezing his eyes shut so he wouldn't have to see what I could do to him, so he could pretend it wasn't real.

And I wasn't really choking him, but it didn't matter as long as he thought I was.

"But I can," I said, two of my elongated fingers snaking along his eyelids, peeling them back with the subtle force of my PSS. He was going to watch this. He was going to look at me and know who to fear.

The whites of his eyes rolled in their sockets, frantic, terrified. I wasn't even doing anything to him. He wasn't in physical pain. I'd experienced more discomfort putting my eyeliner on in the morning. But Marcus had been right; fear was more powerful than pain.

I heard murmurs behind me, but I ignored them. They'd asked me to scare Palmer, and that's exactly what I was doing. It wasn't my problem if it scared them too.

Palmer began to thrash as if he were having a seizure. The crotch of his pants grew suddenly darker, the odor of fresh urine spritzing the air even as I heard the trickle down the inside of his pants.

I felt disgusted by him, but I felt something else too. Powerful. This time, I was in control. I was the predator, not the prey. Gone was the insignificant, defective girl. I was some kind of fucking comic book vigilante, and it felt—amazing.

Someone came up to me, touched my upper arm, and I barely bit back the words, "Back off!"

"Olivia," Marcus said.

It was all part of the plan. I was just supposed to scare Palmer. Marcus was going to interrogate him. And while he did, I was supposed stay focused enough to keep my hand from going into anyone. What was wrong with me? I had almost lost control.

Marcus's hand was still on my arm, and I glanced at him, retracting my elongated fingers from the Fire Chief's eyes. I left the tendrils waving around his face and head though, an incentive to cooperate.

"Please. Oh God, please," Palmer whimpered in Marcus's direction.

"Tell us what we need, and I'll keep her off you" Marcus said. "How many CAMFers are in town?"

"Four," Palmer said weakly, his chin falling to his chest. "I told them we didn't need many. She's only a girl. And I didn't know there were more of you. I didn't know."

"Four including you?" Marcus asked.

"Yes."

"Armed with what?"

I saw Palmer hesitate and I sent a tentacle out, tickling his nostril.

"Guns, and minus meters," he blurted, jerking his head away. "But the meters are fucked. They don't work in town. Something is jamming them."

"Can they still extract?" Marcus asked.

"I don't know," Palmer said, avoiding Marcus's gaze. "We didn't test that."

Because they hadn't had anyone to test it on.

"Where's the base of operations? Your house?" Marcus drilled him.

"Yes," Palmer said, looking up at us, comprehension dawning on his face. "You're going in there?" he asked, almost laughing. "You're actually going in there?" Now he *was* laughing, bloody drool running down his chin. "If that's what this is about, if you're just going to walk in there and give yourselves up, I'll tell you anything you want."

"Is that where her backpack is?" Marcus asked, ignoring Palmer's taunt. "Your place?"

"Yes," Palmer answered, but suddenly he wasn't laughing anymore. His eyes looked away. He knew something more about my backpack.

"Do you know what's in it?" Marcus pressed.

Palmer didn't answer. His eyes had gone hard and defiant again.

I wrapped a PSS tendril around his neck and placed the tip just at the opening of his left ear.

He glared at me. He didn't think I had the guts to really hurt him. He thought we were just kids who would lie down, and roll over, and let them kill us.

I made my PSS expand and wind its way into his ear canal. It was a strange sensation. Not at all like any of the times my hand had gone into flesh, but just as intimate, like I was insinuating myself into places no one should go. "I could burst your ear drum right now," I told him, realizing it was true only as I said it. It would be just like picking a lock, except messier.

Palmer squirmed and bucked, yelling something incomprehensible.

"Do you know what's in the backpack?" Marcus demanded again.

I increased the pressure of my PSS by a fraction. What would it feel like to have me in your ear, in your head, probing, pressing?

"Blades," Palmer yelled, shaking his head back and forth as if he could dislodge me.

"And what do they do?"

"I don't know," he cried. "We don't know. He was running tests."

"At your house?"

"Yes. Fuck. Make her stop. She's hurting me." He squeezed his eyes shut.

"I'm not hurting him," I said. "He knows more."

"I don't," Palmer cried. "Get her out of me!"

Marcus looked at me, and I pulled back on the ear penetration, but only a little.

"How do they run guard patrol? What shifts do they take? What frequency is your radio contact?" Marcus fired questions at Palmer.

And he answered without any more encouragement from my hand. Maybe it was only what he'd said, that if the information he gave us led us to walk right into the CAMFers' trap, all the better for him. Whatever the reason for his sudden compliance, I didn't like it. It left me feeling disappointed, my hand itching to go deeper into him.

As I stood there, the interrogation droning in my head, my hand grew warm. I could feel my PSS yearning to do it. There was something in him longing to be brought forth into the light of day. Something I could use. It was calling to me.

It was right there. So close. It would be easy.

But I'd promised myself I wouldn't.

But I wanted to. This was my power. This is what my hand was made to do. What point was there in denying that?

"Olivia!" someone yelled, grabbing my right wrist and pinching it. A flash of cold ran up my arm.

I looked down to see Marcus clutching my wrist, my PSS completely back in hand form. I looked up to see Mike Palmer slumped unconscious in the ropes that bound him to the tree.

"What happened?" I asked, feeling cold and numb and lost. "Did I reach into him?"

"No," Marcus said, "He—he just started screaming, and then he passed out."

"I didn't hear him scream," I said, confused. I was standing mere inches from Palmer. How could I have not heard him scream?

"Well, he was," Nose said, and that's when I realized that they were gathered around me. Yale had a hand on my shoulder. Nose was gripping my left arm. Even Jason was there, leaning slightly into me, his shoulder brushing mine.

"You did good," Jason said with just a hint of grudging admiration. "He told us a lot."

I bent over and vomited my breakfast straight onto his boots.

27

OPERATION ORANGE FRISBEE

Yale checked Palmer's pulse and concluded he wasn't dead.

"Maybe he had a heart attack," Nose suggested.

"He just passed out," Marcus said. "He'll be fine."

"I'm sorry," I said, looking down at Jason's boots. I wasn't feeling so good.

"Is it your head?" Marcus asked, touching my shoulder.

"No, it's just—" Just what? That I suddenly didn't have the stomach for torture, or that I'd found out I actually did? "I'm okay," I said, straightening up.

"Good," he said. "Because I think we got what we

needed. Nose, you keep an eye on Palmer. Yale and Jason, go get the weapons and gear ready."

"Does he really need to be watched?" Nose asked.

"Probably not," Marcus said, checking the security of the ropes. "We can't afford to leave someone behind with him tonight anyway. We have the numbers on them, and I want to keep it that way. Still, check him every half hour until we leave."

Back at camp, Marcus led me to the tent, and the first thing he did when we got inside was sit me down at the laptop table and hand me a cup of water.

"Drink," he said, sitting down next to me. "I know that was tough." He took my hands, holding them in his. "Are you sure you're all right? You look really pale."

"Yeah, I'm better," I said, and drank, which actually did make me feel better, at least physically. I tried not to think about what I'd just done. It had been for Emma, I told myself. Now we could go get her. And Marcus said Palmer would be fine.

"Good. I hate to cut right to it, but do you have the bullet?" Marcus asked.

"Oh, yeah." I started rifling through my pockets. But it wasn't there. "It's in my jeans from last night," I realized, glancing around the tent.

After a short search, we found my jeans, and I pulled Jason's bullet from the front pocket, the cold metal kissing my palm. Immediately, it began to thrum, resonating in my bones, vibrating almost like the blades.

"Give me your hand," I said to Marcus and deposited it in his palm. "Do you feel anything?"

"Nope," Marcus said, looking at me. "Why, do you?"

"Yeah. A vibration. I didn't notice it before, but it's there now."

"Maybe because you used it," Marcus said. "Like it's tuned to you or something."

"Maybe," I took the bullet back, rolling it between my fingers. All we had were a whole lot of maybes. "We have no idea how it works. Or how the blades work. We don't even know how our PSS works. How are we ever going to pull this off?" I was starting to panic and realize that my bravado about rescuing Emma had been just that. Bravado.

"Let's start with what we do know," Marcus said calmly.

"We know it disappears things," I said, cupping the bullet in my ghost palm.

"More like it transports them," Marcus said. "It moves them from one place to another instantly."

"I had to touch Palmer and the painting to make them transport," I said. "So, it takes physical contact for it to work."

"But are we sure of that?" Marcus asked.

"Good point," I said, looking around the tent for something to experiment on.

"Wait," Marcus said, holding up his hand. "Let's think this through first. Last time both things you sent nearly landed on Jason. Why Jason?"

"Jason is the anchor," I said. "The bullet came from him so that's where it sends things." I didn't know how I knew that, but I did.

Marcus didn't argue. "Let's assume that's true," he said. "If he's the anchor, what does that make you? Are you the only one who can use the bullet, or could I?"

"I don't know," I said.

"There's only one way to find out." Marcus crossed to one of his plastic tubs and rummaged through it. "We need to test it," he said, turning back to me with a stack of bright orange Frisbees in his hand.

"By playing Frisbee?" I asked, raising an eyebrow at him.

"We're not going to throw them." He smiled wickedly. "We're going to bullet them."

"We're going to bullet orange Frisbees at Jason?" I asked, trying not to smile too. "You did see what he did to Palmer, right?"

"I'll protect you," Marcus teased, setting all but one of the Frisbees down on the table.

"I don't need you to protect me. I'm just saying, he's your friend."

"Here, hand me the bullet. I'll try first." Marcus held out his other hand, and I put the bullet in it. "Now what?" he asked.

"Now you wish it gone, or safe, or whatever."

Marcus's face took on a look of concentration.

Nothing happened.

He closed his eyes, and rolled his shoulders, and wrinkled his forehead, but still nothing happened. The Frisbee stayed right there in his hand.

"I can't do it." He opened his eyes and looked at me. "Your turn," he said, holding the Frisbee and the bullet out to me.

I curled my fingers around the thrumming bullet, gripped the Frisbee with my ghost hand, and wished it gone.

And it disappeared.

"What the—?" shouted Jason from somewhere across camp, the last words drowned out by a blast of gunfire that made me jump toward Marcus.

"Holy shit!" I said, laughing and tumbling into his arms. "He shot it."

Marcus was laughing too, both of us holding our sides and trying to keep quiet because somewhere out there was a pissed off Jason with a loaded gun.

"What the hell is going on?" Jason's voice boomed, getting closer to the tent.

"I'll take care of him," Marcus said, crossing to the door. "You keep experimenting, and I'll watch what happens on the other end. See if you can send a Frisbee somewhere else. See if you can send more than one at a time," and then he was gone, leaving me alone with a stack of Frisbees and Jason's bullet.

After an hour of Frisbee bulleting, we'd learned this: The bullet only sent things to Jason, not to anyone else, or to any other thing or landmark. No matter how hard I tried, or what I thought of, the Frisbees went to Jason every time, landing about two or three feet directly in front of him. Marcus had even tried standing where the Frisbee usually appeared, and it had simply appeared directly beside him.

I could send more than one. In fact, I could send as many as I could hold, as long as I was touching them, or touching one that was touching the rest. I could hold them with my flesh hand, or my ghost hand, or hold the bullet in either. It didn't make a difference.

And the bullet only worked if it was on my person. If it was in my pocket, or boot, or bra, that was fine, as long as it was touching something that was touching my skin. But any further away from me than that, and nothing happened. I thought that might have something to do with the vibrations—that it had to feel me, and I had to feel it, in order for it to work.

When Marcus finally returned to the tent, arms full of Frisbees, I had to ask him, "So what did Jason think of that? And the other guys? Did it freak them out?"

"It's something we can use, an advantage," he said. "It doesn't matter what they think."

"But they still think it's my hand doing it? Shouldn't we tell them about the bullet?"

"Not yet," he said. "I need them focused on this rescue. Even though we can't use the bullet to zap Emma out of there from a distance, we may still be able to make it work for us."

"What if we kept Jason back, somewhere a safe distance away? If I could get close enough to Emma, I could bullet her out to him."

"It's too risky," Marcus said. "Besides, Jason is our best marksman. He grew up around guns, carrying them, loading them, cleaning them. If it comes down to firepower, we'll need him close."

"What about Nose? He has a gun."

"I think it would be more accurate to say Nose *carries* a gun. He barely knows how to use it. We got both our guns out of a pick-up truck as we were leaving the CAMFer game preserve. We've all been practicing since, and Nose is a better shot than I am, but that isn't saying much."

"Yale's no good?"

"He doesn't like guns," Marcus said. "But I have him working up a homemade tazer as we speak. It's not lethal, and it only works at close range, but it's better than nothing. He can make you one, if you want, or we have a couple of knives.

"No," I said. I didn't think I could ever shoot someone, let alone stab them. And I'd seen videos of tazing on the internet. "I don't want a weapon."

"Well, you'll have the bullet and your hand," he said.

I came armed and dangerous. That's what he meant. Whatever I'd done to Mike Palmer hadn't exactly been the work of a committed pacifist. But I wouldn't do anything like that again. I couldn't.

"They won't shoot to kill," Marcus said, as if that was comforting.

"You mean like Palmer didn't."

"He was an idiot. And it wasn't fatal," he pointed out, that old smirk playing around his lips.

"Easy for you to say," I glared at him "You can't die."

"Actually, the exact opposite," he protested. "You might have noticed I have this annoying habit of dying on a regular basis."

"How many times have you died and come back?"

He stared at me, blinking.

"Come on, how many times?"

"Since you've known me?" he asked, stalling.

"No, not since I've know you. Since you were born. How many times have you died in your lifetime?"

"A lot," he said, rushing on, "but that doesn't make me immortal. I'm hard to kill, especially if you go for my major organs, but I can still be killed."

"Is that supposed to be comforting?" I asked, feeling the panic rise in me once again. What were we doing? What were we thinking? We were just a bunch of teenagers who barely knew how to use guns. I couldn't ask them to do this.

"We're going to get Emma out," Marcus said, cradling my hands in his, boring into me with those wonderful brown eyes. "And no one is going to die."

"You promise?"

"Yes," he said, his voice rough with conviction. "I promise."

"So how do we do it?" I asked, taking a deep breath.

"First, you show me Palmer's house," he said, turning and unfolding his map of Greenfield across the table. "And then we figure that out."

The hike into town was almost too easy. Apparently, not only had I recovered from my injuries, I was also getting in shape.

Palmer's house sat directly across the street from Webster Park, an overgrown, undeveloped piece of land Gregory Webster had donated to the Greenfield Town Council the year before. There couldn't have been a better location for us to hide and recon the house if we'd designed it ourselves.

At the edge of park, Jason scouted out a sycamore tree that still had most of its leaves, its stair-step branches making it easy for us to climb, and we each picked a solid branch to sit on.

Jason took the highest perch, one branch above me, his rifle strapped to his back. He got out his binoculars to scan Palmer's house.

Marcus sat on a branch across from mine, level with me, Palmer's gun at his hip, and when I caught his eye, he winked, smiling.

Yale and Nose were silent a few branches below. Nose hefted the third gun and Yale had his homemade tazer tucked away somewhere.

Then we just sat there, waiting, the autumn sun sinking down between the branches of our tree like a very slow clock.

After about twenty minutes, my butt fell asleep, and the rest of me was not far behind it. I kept nodding off, my body jerking away from the falling edge of sleep every few minutes.

Marcus dug a pen and some scraps of paper out of his pack and started passing me notes. Just little stupid things like, "You're a cute narcoleptic." or "I want to have your babies." They were keeping me awake, but they were also making me giggle. Jason kept frowning at us like a study hall teacher, so after I'd written back, "Babies are evil," Marcus grinned and nodded, but he didn't send anymore.

I was just repositioning myself on my oh-so-comfy branch when Emma's phone began vibrating in my pocket.

Marcus stared at me.

I frantically dug it out while trying to maintain my balance. I looked down at the screen.

The call was from Emma's new number.

It buzzed again.

I looked across at Marcus.

"Give it to me," he said, holding out his hand.

Instead, I jabbed the answer button and put the phone to my ear. "Hello?"

"If you want to see your friend alive again," said the Dark Man in his strangely accented voice, "I'll need to speak to David."

28

THIS IS DAVID

"What?—David isn't here," I stammered.

"Let me talk to David," the Dark Man insisted, as if he hadn't heard me.

"Let me talk to Emma," I demanded back, cold realization flooding my body. Somehow the Dark Man thought I was with David. He was expecting to talk to David.

"Hand me the phone," Marcus said, next to me. He'd moved to my branch, and I hadn't even been aware of it.

"Let me talk to Emma so I know she's alive," I said into the phone.

"You have two minutes to put David on, or she won't be," the Dark Man replied.

"No. Listen. David isn't here. I've never even met him."

"Olivia, let me have the phone," Marcus ordered, trying to pull it from my ear.

"Let go of me," I shoved his hands away. "Please," I begged the Dark Man, "don't hurt her. She doesn't know anything."

"You have one minute remaining," the Dark Man said.

"Olivia," Marcus insisted, this time actually prying the phone out of my hand. He put it to his ear, looking at me, his eyes pleading for something. I had no idea what.

"This is David," he said.

This is David.

I stared at him, watched the lines of his face change as he listened to whatever the Dark Man was saying. The truth was written in his eyes like it had never been before. This was not some lie to save Emma or buy us time. *This is David.* Not Marcus. *David.* He was David. Had always been David, the one who'd been captured by the CAMFers and barely escaped with his life. He'd seen the list with his own name on it. It was my Marcus who'd grown up in the foster care system, and been turned over to the CAMFers by the police, and didn't trust anyone. David hadn't disappeared again; he'd just become someone else.

I glanced up at Jason and saw the weird mixture of hurt and resignation melding in his eyes. He hadn't known either. Nose looked stunned too, but not Yale. When I looked at him he looked away. He had been with Marcus—or did I call him David now?—from almost the beginning. Yale had known Marcus was lying to the rest of us all this time. And if Marcus had lied about his PSS and his identity, what else had he lied about?

"No, that's not—" Marcus-now-David said into the phone, his voice strained.

He listened for a moment, his face tense, and I was close enough to hear the sinuous rise and fall of the Dark Man's voice, though I couldn't make out the words.

"You don't need or want her," Marcus said calmly, firmly, "and we both know it."

I couldn't think of him as David. He was Marcus to me, and I couldn't just suddenly turn that off. "Let her go," he was saying into the phone. "She's useless to you."

More listening. Pain flickering across his face, then pure fury. "Fuck you!" he screamed into the phone, a vein bulging in his forehead.

I tried to reach out and take the phone back, but he turned, blocking my grab. He was losing it. He was going to get Emma killed.

"No!" he said, more calmly, though barely. "You don't need them. This is between you and me. No one else."

Another short pause, while I sat numbly next to him in a tree.

"That's not going to happen, and you know it," he said.

The Dark Man replied. Short. One sentence.

"No, don't—" Marcus said, pulling the phone from his ear and raising it in his fist as if he was going to smash it against the sycamore's trunk.

I caught hold of his hand, restraining him.

"He hung up," he said, releasing the phone back to me.

"What about Emma?" I asked, staring down at it. "What did he say about Emma?"

"She's—alive. For now." Marcus seemed stunned.

"For now? What does that mean? What did he want? What did he ask for?"

"He said we have two hours to turn ourselves in or he kills her." Marcus looked around, as if he'd just realized where he was and what he'd said.

"Nooo," I heard myself moan. He'd promised me this wouldn't happen, that they wouldn't hurt Emma. I wanted to scream it at him, throw his words back in his face, but what good would that do? Obviously, he lied about everything.

"So, he knows about all of us?" Nose asked.

Marcus nodded.

"And he knows we're out here?" Jason asked.

"No," Marcus said, a glimmer of hope flickering in his eyes. "If he'd known that, he wouldn't have given us so much time. And he would have gloated about it. Tried to use it to psych us out. He must think we're still back at camp."

"You know this guy." Nose said. It wasn't a question.

"Yeah," Marcus answered, "I know him. He's the bastard that killed my sister."

"What?" The word came from all directions.

"My sister, Danielle." Marcus said. "We grew up in the system together. No one wanted one PSS kid, let alone a pair, so they split us up. And every time they did, we'd run away, and find each other, and get caught by the cops. The last time they nailed us, the cop didn't take us back to the station, or to our case worker, or to the group home. He took us to this CAMFer compound out in the woods. Sold us out for a wad of cash, and handed us over to that psycho in there for extraction. And then he killed her."

"The Dark Man killed your sister," I said. I had almost forgotten the picture I'd found in Marcus's keepsake box that first day at camp. The picture of him and his sister.

"Yes," Marcus said, "but he was calling himself Dr. Julian then. And he had a different accent. He changes identities the way other people change clothes."

If the Dark Man had killed his sister, how could Marcus have believed that Emma would be safe? He hadn't, I reminded myself. He'd been lying. About everything. He'd lied with his words. With his hands. With his lips. What had he said? *This isn't a game to me.* Lies. All lies.

"If this CAMFer killed your sister," Jason said calmly, "then I say we go in there right now and finish this."

"We'd still have the element of surprise," Yale pointed out. "He thinks he has a couple hours, and he just hung up that phone feeling very pleased with himself."

"I don't believe this," I blurted. "He lied to us," I said, gesturing at Marcus. "He's been lying to us this entire time, and you're all just going to act like nothing's changed? You're still going to follow him in there?" I looked at Jason, then Nose, then my gaze landed on Yale.

"So what?" Yale said, "What difference does it make? Now that you know he's David, you don't want his help to get your friend out alive?"

That pulled me up short. "No, I—" I didn't know what to say. I couldn't trust any of them. Especially Marcus. But that didn't change the fact that I needed them. I didn't have a chance of saving Emma by myself. I looked away from Yale, slipping the phone back into my pocket. I had to make this work.

"So you know this guy," Yale said, turning to Marcus. "You know how he thinks. What he's capable of. How do we get Emma out?"

"I want you all to understand something first," Marcus said, looking at each of us. When his eyes came to me I stared back, hating him, wanting him to see how hurt I was, hoping he would look very very sorry. But he only looked away and continued, "If we go in there, and we fail, he's going to torture you. He's going to extract your PSS until you beg him to kill you. Until your body shrinks and caves in on itself, and your skin turns yellow and your hair turns white. And even then, you won't be dead, and he won't kill you. After he's sucked you dry, he'll simply toss you aside, and leave you to die one excruciating breath at a time."

There was stony silence in the tree. It was dark enough that I could barely see their expressions anymore, but I could tell that the guys thought Marcus was being melodramatic. They thought he was exaggerating to make them cautious, but I didn't think he was. I'd seen the very thing Marcus had just described happen to my dad, not from being drained of PSS, but from being slowly consumed by cancer. A description like that only came from firsthand experience, from having to watch someone you loved die. No one had killed my father. There was no one to blame or punish for his death. But someone had done that to Marcus's sister. They had killed her slowly, cruelly and intentionally. And they had made him watch.

Yes, he was a liar who obviously didn't trust anyone. But maybe I was beginning to understand why.

"Hasn't that always been what's at stake?" I asked.

The other guys murmured agreement.

"Okay then," Marcus said. If he was surprised I'd come around so quickly, he didn't show it. "This doesn't really change the plan," he said, staring at the guys, some silent message passing between the four of them. He avoided looking at me altogether, which was ironic because it was my plan. "We don't know if the meters can extract, but don't let them point one at you. Keep your PSS covered. If they don't know where it is, they won't know where to aim. Gunfire will bring down the cops, so don't shoot unless you have to. The main goal is to get Emma out, and the rest of you with her. Don't worry about the backpack, or the blades. I don't want anyone risking themselves for that," he finished, finally looking at me.

"Let's fucking do this," Jason said, checking the sites of his gun.

"Let's go," Marcus said, and Yale and Nose began to descend quietly, making sure the park was clear below us.

Before Marcus could move away from me, I touched his arm. "Your sister," I said. "She had a ghost hand."

He turned and looked at me, his face even more guarded than usual, but he answered. "Left hand and arm, up to the elbow." Then he jumped down to the branch below, leaving me staring after him.

His sister had been like me. The overexposure marring that picture hadn't been overexposure at all; it had been the flare of her PSS. That was why he'd been so comfortable with my ghost hand. When he'd intertwined his fingers with mine, he'd been remembering the hand of a dead girl.

It was like a bad war movie. The guys crouched, and hid, and pointed their guns, using hand gestures to signal changes of position as we advanced through the park. The street was empty, everyone tucked away in their houses for dinner, and we crossed it easily, moving silently into Mike Palmer's front yard. After that, Nose, Yale and I held our position, while Jason and Marcus did a quick recon around the outside of the house.

When they came back, they reported seeing signs of activity in the kitchen, one of the bedrooms, and the living room.

"She's probably in the front bedroom," Marcus said, "with someone guarding her."

"They tried to black out that window," Jason said, "but they didn't do a very good job. We could still see some light."

"There's a sliding glass door at the back of the house that goes right into the kitchen," Marcus said. "It's the easiest access point."

"But if we go in the back, they could get past us out the front and take Emma with them," Yale pointed out.

"So, we need an approach from the front as well," Marcus said, scanning the open yard, the bright porch light, and the fireman red front door.

"We could just walk up and ring the doorbell," I suggested.

"Get down," Jason barked.

Someone grabbed me and shoved me to the ground. As I was being crushed into the dirt under a bush with what felt like several boys piled on top of me, I could hear the sound of a car pull up along the curb just outside Palmer's house. God! This was getting ridiculous. I was going to have to start staying away from bushes. Or guys. Or both. A slight turn of my head and I could see the bald tires and rear end of a rusty white Toyota. I knew that car. I also knew why it was here.

"Get off me," I hissed, pushing against the body on top of me.

"Just a little payback," Marcus whispered in my ear as he moved away.

"Not funny," I growled, rising to my hands and knees.

"Be quiet," came a hushed command from Jason as the Toyota's door opened and slammed shut. "Could be more CAMFers."

All four guys were crouched in the shadows around me, Jason and Nose both with their guns ready.

"Well, it's not," I whispered. "It's Jay, the Merlin's Pizza guy." The CAMFers had ordered Pizza while they held Emma hostage. Wouldn't want to torture anyone on an empty stomach. Their cockiness was really starting to piss me off.

"I have an idea," I said. Jay's worn sneakers were already padding their way up Palmer's driveway. I crawled out of the bushes and brushed myself off. I could hear the muffled protests of the guys behind me, but I ignored them.

"Hey Jay," I called, striding across the yard and intercepting him near the front of the garage where we couldn't be seen, or hopefully heard, from inside the house.

"Shit girl!" Jay said, almost dropping the three large pizzas he was carrying. "Where the hell'd you come from?"

"I've been waiting for you, actually," I smiled. "The adults in there," I gestured at Palmer's house, "are boring me to tears with their fancy finger food and dry martinis. My mom made me come. You know how it is," I said, reaching for the pizza boxes. "But this will make everything better."

"Oh, a parent party," Jay nodded. "It sucks to be you," he said sympathetically, handing the pizzas to me, the receipt and credit card charge neatly stapled to the top. Jay always forgot to have people sign. I knew this because Emma and I ordered Merlin's Pizza almost every Friday night using Mrs. Campbell's credit card.

"Nice and warm," I said, the boxes radiating heat into my arms. "Thanks," I added, willing Jay to hurry off to his next delivery.

He smiled, and turned to go. Then he hesitated and turned back. "Hey, didn't I hear something about you the other day?"

"Probably. You know this town," I said. "The rumors have rumors."

"Ain't that the truth? But this was weirder than usual. Something about you going missing from the hospital."

"I snuck out," I said. "I hate doctors. Got tired of them poking and prodding me. Besides, there wasn't any Merlin's."

"I know, right? Those nurses are like prison guards. Sick people need pizza. That's what I say. Anyway, I'm glad you got found. Enjoy your pizza," Jay said, walking back down the path to his Toyota.

As soon as he pulled away, I headed back to the bushes and smiled down at the gawking boys over the top of the pizza boxes.

"Now we have our way in the front," I said.

29

PIZZA WITH A SIDE OF TAZER

Yale stood at the front door, looking as pizza-delivery-boyish as we could make him on such short notice. We'd found a navy blue cap in one of the guy's packs, and he was wearing it slightly askew. He was also holding the three pizzas in one hand, and his fully-charged tazer in the other, hidden beneath the pizza boxes.

Jason and I were plastered against the outer wall of the house to Yale's right, Jason's gun out and ready. On the other side of the porch, Marcus and Nose were in a similar pose, both their guns out. This was it. This was the first move in our plan to rescue Emma. It either worked or it didn't, but there was no going back once we rang that door bell.

Marcus looked at us, one by one, then gave the thumbs-up signal.

Jason darted forward, in front of Yale, and pressed the doorbell, then darted back to his position in front of me.

From inside the house, the bell chimed, sounding sweet and homey.

I could hear the pounding of heavy footsteps coming toward the front of the house.

Palmer's front door snicked open.

"You're late," said a deep voice. "Those pizzas better be hot."

"Oh, they are," Yale said, putting the three boxes in the CAMFer's waiting arms and sinking the tazer into his belly.

I heard a loud, sharp crackle. There was a burning smell in the air accompanied by a clicking, and then a heavy thump as the CAMFer went down. He fell across the threshold—a large, overweight man, flopping like a fish, the boxes bouncing on his chest, slices of pizza flying in all directions. His face was discolored, his mouth making some awful gurgling noise. As he convulsed, his shirt rode up revealing a glimpse of the gun that was holstered to his barrel-like chest. Yale pulled the tazer away, surveyed the room beyond the doorway, and said, "She's not in here."

There was yelling from the back of the house, followed by the sound of more footsteps. The other CAMFers had heard their friend go down, and they were coming to see what all the commotion was about.

That was the signal for phase two of the plan.

Jason, Yale and I turned and ran to the far end of the garage. Once we were around the corner of the house, Jason crouched down, gun trained on the porch. His job was to keep anyone from escaping out the front.

"Don't shoot Emma," I couldn't help whispering at him, but he ignored me, his full attention focused on the open front door.

I could hear the other CAMFers there now.

"Frank! What happened? Can you hear me?" said one voice, but it wasn't the Dark Man.

"I think he had a fucking heart attack," said a second voice. Not the Dark Man either. "Look at his face. It's blue."

"Oh man, I think you're right. We should call 911."

"Are you crazy? We can't call the cops. Besides, he's still breathing."

"I may have set this thing too high," Yale whispered, fumbling with his tazer and replacing the batteries in case he needed it again.

"Hey, it worked," I said, "and he's still alive."

"Come on," Yale said when he was done. We didn't have time to stick around and find out Frank's fate. We needed to get Emma out of the house while the CAMFers were still distracted.

The two of us ran along the side of the house, between the wall and the neighbor's fence all the way to the backyard. Nose and Marcus were already waiting for us on the patio just outside the kitchen.

"What took you so long?" Marcus hissed.

I ignored him and stepped up to the sliding glass doors. I extended my ghost hand beyond my glove, through the glass and the vertical blinds, found the locking mechanism, and released it with a satisfying click. I pulled my hand back, smoothed my glove in place, and slid the door open quietly, then stood back for Marcus to enter first.

He moved past me, setting the blinds gently swaying as he pushed them aside with Palmer's handgun. I followed, and Yale and Nose came after me.

The kitchen was bright, empty, and smelled strongly of cigarette smoke. There was an overflowing ashtray on the table, a butt still smoldering in it. To our left was a pantry, door wide open. The other doorway out of the kitchen led down a short dark hall with doors on either side, two on the left and one in the middle on the right.

Marcus started down the hallway, gun out in front of him.

I followed with Yale and Nose behind me. I could still hear the CAMFers' voices, now drifting down the hall from the front of the house.

"Help me get him in this chair," one said.

"We aren't supposed to move him," the other argued.

Marcus moved just past the first door on the left and paused, crouching. I came even with the door and leaned into it, straining to hear anything beyond it, but there was no sound, at least nothing I could hear over the noise of the straining and grunting coming from the front room. Apparently, they had decided to move Frank into the chair after all.

Without even looking back, his eyes still trained on the end of the hallway, Marcus gestured Nose forward.

Nose slipped past Yale and joined me at the door.

I turned the doorknob, looked at Nose, and pulled the door open. Immediately, he was around the doorframe, gun before him. The room was dark, the only light a meager glow from the curtained window. I saw the dim shape of a bed, a dresser, and a chair.

Nose checked the closet. "It's empty," he whispered, coming back to me at the doorway, his ski mask looking more appropriate than ever.

I nodded and stepped back as he pulled the door closed behind him. The click of the latch sounded so loud to me, but the CAMFers didn't hear it. They were still arguing about what to do with Frank.

Marcus led the way down the hall. The door on the right was next. He put his hand on it, gun ready, and opened it himself. I had just enough time to glimpse the edge of a vanity and a toilet before he pulled it shut again. They weren't keeping Emma in the bathroom.

The only door remaining was the one at the end of the hall on our left, the bright light from the dining room slanting onto it. Emma had to be in there. But we were close enough to the end of the hall for me to see that the dining room and the living room were wide open to each other. There was no doorway between them. If the CAMFers looked our direction when we were at the end of the hall, they would see us.

Marcus inched forward, staying in the shadows on the right side of the hallway.

I followed, keeping to the left.

This time, Nose and I huddled next to the wall outside the door.

I reached out and tried to open it, but it was locked. The knob had a keyhole, not a button lock, which meant it would be a little trickier to pick. It also meant we'd probably just found Emma's prison.

"Hey, he's starting to come to. Frank can you hear me?" one of the CAMFers was saying.

"We should get him some water," the other said, his voice growing suddenly louder. He was turning toward us. The door was locked. He was going to see us.

I sank my ghost hand into the doorknob, wrenched the lock, and yanked the door open. I felt someone moving with me, our bodies colliding as we slipped into the dark room, and I pulled the door closed behind us.

I couldn't see a thing. The room was pitch black. I didn't even know for sure who was with me. I could feel a shoulder touching mine, could hear someone breathing, but I didn't dare say anything. Had we all made it in? Nose had been right behind me. He was probably the one I'd run into at the door, the one standing next to me. But what about the others? What about Marcus and Yale? They weren't in the room. I was pretty sure of that.

Outside the door, the CAMFer's footsteps approached and padded down the hall past us to the kitchen, followed by the clinking of glasses.

"Nose?" I dared to whisper.

"Yeah," the dark entity next to me exhaled.

"Where are the others?"

"Not sure," Nose whispered. "Yale was still back by the other bedroom. Marcus was—I don't know."

I heard the swoosh of the kitchen faucet being turned on, then off. The CAMFer seemed to be taking his own sweet time. It sounded like he was getting himself a drink before getting one for poor old Frank. And was that gargling I heard? Whatever it was, it was accompanied by several other odd noises. A sizzle maybe? And a scuffling thud. What was the guy doing?

After a long silence, the CAMFer's footsteps padded back into the hallway, softer and slower this time. Maybe he was being careful not to spill Frank's water. He came closer and closer, then suddenly stopped just outside the door Nose and I were standing behind.

Everything in my body screamed for me to scramble and hide, but I didn't. I stood stock still. I felt Nose raise his gun in front of us, aiming it at the doorway.

The doorknob turned.

The door swung open, light slanting across the figure standing there.

Yale darted into the room, spun, and shut the door silently behind him, enfolding us all in darkness once again.

I stood, stunned, sweaty and panting.

"Is that the muzzle of your gun, or are you just happy to see me?" Yale whispered.

"What the fuck!" Nose said, and I felt him pull the gun back "I almost shot you."

"I got the CAMFer. The one in the kitchen," Yale said. "I was hiding in the pantry, and I took him out with the tazer."

"Then there's only one left," Nose said.

"No," I said, "We haven't seen the Dark Man yet. Plus, Frank is coming to."

"Still, good job," Nose said to Yale. "But next time don't celebrate by making me almost kill you."

"Where's Marcus," I asked Yale.

"Don't know," Yale said. "He might have slipped into the bathroom. I'm not sure. So, your friend's not in here?" he asked, peering into the dark behind us.

I could see his outline and Nose's now. My eyes had at least adjusted that much.

"I seriously doubt it," Nose said, "but let's make sure."

"You've got the gun so watch the door," I said. "Yale and I will look."

"Yes, ma'am," Nose said, and it didn't even sound that sarcastic.

I pulled the glove off my ghost hand, scanning the room by its glow.

Emma wasn't there, but it looked like she might have been recently.

The bed was rumpled, covers pulled back, and there was something small and dark lying in the middle of it.

I walked over and picked it up.

"What is it?" Yale asked, coming up beside me.

"My backpack," I said, shaking it a little. "But it's empty." They'd taken the blades. Maybe they'd taken Emma and the blades somewhere together. Shit! She wasn't here. The CAMFers had set their trap, but where was the bait?

I strode to the window and pulled back the curtains. Someone had taped a black garbage bag over the glass with duct tape and I yanked it off.

"What are you doing?" Yale squawked.

I slid the window open and punched the screen with my fist, sending it flying into the flower beds along the fence. I stuck my head out the window and looked down the wall to where Jason was still crouched. The plan had been to find Emma, bullet her out to Jason if we had to, and all escape out the backyard and over the fence. That had been the plan. Except there was no Emma.

"She's not in here," I called to Jason. "We're coming out."

Jason looked at me, his face hidden in shadow. Then he suddenly stood up and disappeared around the corner of the house, his gun raised.

"Shit!" I pulled my head back in the window. "Jason is charging the front," I said to Nose and Yale. "We have to get out there and help him." Where the hell was Marcus? He was the leader of this little army. Not me.

"My tazer is out of juice," Yale said as I pushed past him and pulled the bedroom door open.

Nose looked up at me, his gun ready, and slipped out into the hall, pressing against the far wall.

"Then stay here," I said to Yale as I moved out into the hallway.

By the time we reached the living room, it was all over. Jason had taken out the CAMFer tending to Frank, snuck up behind him through the front door and brained him with the butt of his gun.

"You didn't shoot him," I breathed a sigh of relief, looking down at the unconscious man.

"Waste of a good bullet," Jason said, dragging groggy Frank out of the recliner he was slumped in, and positioning him next to his friend. Jason pulled a coil of rope out of his pack and starting tying the two of them together. Frank struggled a little, but only until Jason threatened to cut certain key parts of him off and stuff them in his mouth.

"Where's Marcus?" I asked.

"Thought he was with you," Jason said without looking up.

"He was, but we got split up when CAMFer number three went back to the kitchen for a drink of water."

"I tazed him," Yale said. "And I'd better go secure him before he wakes up." He backed away and disappeared down the hall.

I glanced at Nose and he looked down, fiddling with his gun. Why were they all acting so weird? This wasn't over. We hadn't found the Dark Man, or Emma, or the blades. All we'd done was knock out a bunch of CAMFer peons. And now Marcus was missing in action, and they were acting like they didn't even care.

No, they were acting like they didn't *need* to care.

"Where is he?" I asked again.

Jason looked up at me. He looked back down and cinched the final knot on the CAMFer twins.

"Tell me where he is," I demanded.

"He's getting your friend," Jason said. "That's all you need to know."

"What are you talking about?" I felt my chest go numb. "She's not here. We checked the whole house."

"Not quite," Jason said, his eyes glancing past me.

I turned and stared at the interior door tucked between the living room and the dining room. The door to the garage. I'd forgotten about the garage. But it would be the perfect place to hold a prisoner. Marcus had figured that out—somehow gotten in there while the rest of us were pinned down by the CAMFers. It was possible he was confronting the Dark Man alone even as we stood there doing nothing.

I stepped forward, charging toward the garage door.

30

LOSING MARCUS

Just as my hand closed on the doorknob, Nose grabbed me from behind, wrapping his arms around me and pinning me against him.

"Calm down," he said in my ear. "Marcus knows what he's doing. He'll bring your friend back, but our orders are to stay here."

I stopped struggling and relaxed into his hold. When he relaxed in response, I slammed my head back as hard as I could, feeling it connect solidly with his chin.

Pain blossomed in my skull, but it worked; Nose let go of me. I lunged forward and yanked the garage door open.

And stood there staring at a perfectly normal garage—dark and jumbled with dusty hobby crap and garden stuff crammed on metal shelves lining the walls. I could see the outline of a mower near the far wall, and next to it an old chest freezer huddled in the corner.

I reached to my right and found a light switch, flicking it on, but it didn't reveal much more. There was an oil spot in the middle of the garage, and Palmer's Ford Bronco was gone, probably still parked wherever he'd left it when he'd tried to grab me from my burnt house.

And that was it. No Emma. No Marcus. No Dark Man.

Just your typical garage.

"Thit! You may me bi my thung," Nose said from behind me.

This time Jason grabbed me, pinning my arms behind me roughly.

"Let go of me," I said. "He's not here."

"Never said he was," Jason shoved me into the garage. "But I figured you'd throw a fit once you knew he was gone, and this will do for a holding cell until he gets back."

"What's going on?" Yale asked, coming up behind Jason and Nose where they stood in the garage doorway.

"She's giving us trouble," Jason said.

"Thee heh-budded ne," Nose said, still nursing his bloody tongue.

"Where is Marcus?" I asked Yale. I was getting really tired of asking that question.

"He knew where they were holding Emma," he said, "but it was too risky for all of us to go in."

That was when I began to understand; Marcus wasn't in Palmer's house. At all.

"Tell me where they are, and get the hell out of my way," I said, moving toward the door.

"You ain't going anywhere," Jason said. He didn't move. If anything, all three of them just stood there being bulkier and more obstinate than before.

"What is wrong with you?" I asked. "He saved you. All three of you. So, when he says he's going on a suicide mission, you just nod and agree and follow orders? What kind of idiots are you?"

"Not a suicide mission," Jason said, his cheek twitching, so, at least I knew I'd touched a nerve. "He's hard to kill. He'll be fine. He can take this guy down."

"*This guy* murdered his sister in front of him," I pointed out, "and got inside his head in a two-minute phone conversation. We're dealing with a psychopath here, and you let Marcus go face him alone." I didn't know who I was more pissed at—Marcus for lying to me once again and going off to be the hero or these morons for letting him do it.

"He'll be fine," Jason insisted.

"Even if he got caught and they tried to extract him," Yale added, "he'd just reboot and escape like he did last time."

And that was when it all came together in my mind, cascading like a line of dominos, each one tapping down the one next to it.

"Oh fuck!" I said, looking at the guys.

"What?" Yale said, stepping forward.

"He's not coming back," I said, shaking my head. "He didn't go to rescue Emma from the Dark Man. He went to trade himself in for her."

"Wha thee tawking abou?" Nose asked.

"Don't listen to her," Jason said. "She's full of shit."

"All they need is him," I said. I had to make them understand. "That's what he was saying to the Dark Man on the phone. He was offering himself. Not just for Emma. For all of us."

Yale was looking at me, listening to me.

"He told me," I said, my eyes drilling into his, "that the CAMFers were looking for a renewable energy source." If I could convince any of them, it would be Yale. "That's why they want our PSS. The only problem is when they extract it, we die, and that's not very renewable."

Yale's eyes were filling with dawning realization.

"But then they found David," I heard my voice break on the name. "This one special guy who's PSS comes back, even after it's been extracted. Even after he dies. He's an endless supply of PSS."

Yale groaned under his breath. He'd known David the longest. He would understand the next part.

Even Jason and Nose were listening intently, their eyes locked on me.

"That's why he has to save the kids on the list," I said. "Or maybe he lied about that too and there never was a list. It doesn't matter. The point is he came after us because he feels responsible. Because he thinks he could end this. He's probably thought that since his sister died." I took a deep breath, "He thinks if they'd extracted him first, they never would have killed her. That if they have him, they don't need any of us."

"Very nice," Jason said, clapping his free hand against the stock of his gun in mock applause. "That was an amazing load of bullshit."

Nose just looked confused.

But I could see it on Yale's face. He knew I was right.

"Marcus told me he knew what they wanted," I told Yale. "I *convinced* him to do this without even knowing it," I finished, tears running down my face. I wasn't crying. They were leaking out. "He's not coming back."

It was possible I was wrong, but I knew with every fiber of my being that I wasn't.

"We have to go after him," I said, looking from Yale to Jason to Nose.

"We have no idea where he is," Yale said. "I don't even know how he got out of here. He didn't go out the back past me."

"He didn't go out the front past me," Jason said, stepping into the garage, his hand on his gun.

I glanced around. The only other way out was the automatic garage door, but surely Jason would have seen or heard that open.

"We have to find him then," I said, trying to sidle past Jason toward the inner door.

"Don't even think about it," he said, raising his gun to my chest.

"What the fuck are you doing?" Yale yelled at him.

"People don't just disappear," Jason said, "unless someone disappears them."

"Are you crazy?" I looked at him in disbelief. "I didn't disappear Marcus. Have you listened to a word I've said? Besides, when would I have done that? I've been with one of you this entire time."

"Jason, put the gun down," Yale said.

"Not gonna happen," Jason said, clicking the safety off instead. "How could she know all that shit? About the CAMFers. About Marcus. Unless she was one of them."

"For Christ's sake, I'm not a CAMFer," I protested. Were we really back to that?

"Put your hands up. Especially that one," Jason said, gesturing at my ghost hand with the barrel of his gun.

"Yes, I'm a CAMFer with PSS," I said, raising my hands.

"You think they don't have people like us with them?" Jason asked, scowling. "I know they do. I've seen them with my own eyes. Nose, tie her up."

"We're not tying anyone up," Yale said.

"Yes, we are," Jason said. "It ain't gonna hurt her. It's just gonna keep her out of trouble until Marcus gets back."

Nose stepped forward, a coil of rope in his hands from his pack. He didn't look at me and he kept his head down, chin tucked in.

"Tie them behind her back," Jason instructed. "Not in front."

As Nose pulled my arms behind me, I glanced up at Yale. He was behind Jason, his eyes on the gun, on Jason's finger on the trigger. Then he looked at me and shook his head, only a little, but I got the message. He didn't have a gun. His tazer was out of batteries. There was nothing he could do for me at the moment against two armed idiots.

Rope bit into my wrists and Jason said, "Get down on your knees."

Nose helped me down, holding me by my elbows so I wouldn't bang my knee caps on the hard cement floor. "Marcus said to keep you safe," he mumbled as he lowered me. "To not let you come after him no matter what."

"Nose," I pleaded in a whisper. "Come on. You know I'm not—"

"Shut up!" Jason screamed, jamming the barrel of his gun against my cheek. "I knew you was one of them the second I saw you. And so did Marcus. Why else would he keep you so close, and lie to you about everything? He never trusted you."

"Take it easy," Yale said, putting his hand on Jason's shoulder.

Jason pulled the barrel back, but he didn't take his eyes off of me.

I decided it might be a good time to keep my mouth shut.

Nose wrapped rope around my ankles and cinched the end to my wrists. When he was done, he let go of my elbows. I flopped to the floor, landing on my right side, Emma's phone digging into my hip.

"So what now?" Yale asked Jason.

Was he seriously going to let Jason do this? Maybe he was just biding his time until he could get the upper hand. God, I hoped so.

"We secure the CAMFers in separate rooms," Jason said. "And then we wait. If Marcus doesn't come back by midnight, we head back to camp."

"You think it's safe to stay here?" Yale asked.

"I wouldn't have said it if I didn't think it was safe," Jason said. "You got a problem with that?"

"Its juss that he toll us —", Nose began.

"Shut up!" Jason yelled. "You want her to know everything?"

Nose stood, stark still, his hands clenching to fists. Jason's regime was falling apart. I could see it happening. Yale was already on my side. Nose was not happy with the way Jason was treating him. Marcus was the glue that held these three together, and that glue was gone. I couldn't resist prying at that crack a little.

"He told you to go back to camp, didn't he?" I said. "Because he knew he wasn't coming back."

"I said shut up!" Jason yelled, driving the tip of his boot into my side.

Pain jumped up and down my ribs. I couldn't breathe. I squeezed my eyes shut and tried to curl my body in against the next blow. I'd seen what Jason had done to Palmer. Stupid! I was stupid! Jason probably wouldn't shoot me, but he would certainly enjoy beating the shit out of me.

"Stop it!" I heard Yale say, his voice like I'd never heard it before.

I opened my eyes to see him standing between me and Jason.

"He thaid to keep her safe," Nose said, joining Yale. "Thath the only reason I thied her up. But we're naw gonna hur her."

"She's one of them," Jason insisted, but he lowered his gun. He was at least smart enough to recognize when he was outnumbered.

"I highly doubt that," Yale said. "But either way, she can't do anything tied up and locked in a garage."

"You saw what that hand can do," Jason pointed out. "You don't think she can use it to untie those ropes, and break outta here? Maybe she'll even stick it into one of us on her way out. So, we take shifts watching her until Marcus comes back."

I had hoped Yale would pull first shift guarding me, but he didn't.

Jason knew better, so he left Nose in the garage, armed, with instructions to duct tape my mouth if I tried to talk to him. I could hear Yale and Jason arguing in the living room. Yale was working on it, trying to make Jason see reason. I wasn't going to hold my breath for that.

I tried to use my hand on Nose as soon as Jason and Yale left. I willed it to reach out and skewer him, but it refused to cooperate. Maybe it was the cool cement, sucking the warmth out of my body. Maybe it was exhaustion. Or maybe it was just my ghost hand's stubborn determination to only do things that screwed up my life. Whatever the reason, no matter how hard

I tried, it wouldn't take any form but a useless tied-up hand. I had the bullet in my pocket, but that was a joke. Sure, I could disappear my ropes, or maybe even myself, right out of the garage and straight into the paranoid lap of Jason The Wonder Thug. The universe had a sick sense of humor.

I craned my neck, looking at Nose, who was now sitting in an old lawn chair he'd pulled off one of the shelves, his gun in his lap. I couldn't hear Yale and Jason arguing any more. They were probably securing the CAMFers. Would Nose really gag me if I talked to him? I had thought he was my friend. I had liked him. Trusted him. And he had tied me up. I had trusted all of them, Marcus most of all. And he had lied to me and used me. Had the kissing and flirting all been a part of that too? No. He felt something for me. That was why he'd gone off to save Emma. I'd talked him into it. I'd begged him to save my friend and tapped into his guilt over his sister without even knowing it.

I lay my head down, my hair splaying over the oil spot on the floor. I had to find a way out of this. The CAMFers weren't just going to let Emma go once they had Marcus. She knew who they were, and they had no qualms about killing people. I had to get help. I had to get Marcus and Emma back. But how?

How had Marcus known where Emma was? He must have been in contact with the Dark Man, probably through my e-mail account. *Dear Dark Man, meet me at the blah blah blah. I'll give myself up in exchange for the girl.* He knew the CAMFers would intercept the message. It would have been that simple. But then the Dark Man had called Emma's phone. He'd decided he wanted us all, and Marcus's web of lies had begun to unravel. But he'd still gone ahead with the plan to give himself up.

It was possible I was wrong about the whole thing. Maybe Marcus really was going to come back in a few hours with the Dark Man trussed up like a pig and Emma safe and sound. I wanted to believe that pretty badly. And even then, I couldn't.

Something began to niggle at me, something at the edge of my awareness, like a feeling of déjà vu or familiarity. A tremble. A subtle vibration. A sound that, at first, I thought must be coming from outside. A passing car maybe. Or a helicopter flying overhead. No, not a helicopter because it was coming from the floor. Then suddenly I knew what it was. It was the blades. I could feel the buzzing of Passion's blades.

I lifted my head, glancing around the garage frantically, straining my neck.

The blades were nearby. Somewhere in the garage. And they were reacting to the use of a minus meter.

"Whas the madder?" Nose asked, leaning forward in his lawn chair.

"Do you hear that?"

"Hear wha?" he asked, cocking his head.

"That buzzing."

"I don hear nuddin," he said, looking at me suspiciously.

"No, listen. It's the blades. They're here somewhere. In the garage."

"The blaves?"

"Yes, the blades. Follow the sound. Look for them. Maybe they're on one of these shelves."

"Maybe they are," Nose said, getting up and looking on the shelf behind him. "Maybe they are wight here next to the tape," he said, picking it up and walking toward me.

"No!" I begged, tears swimming at the corners of my eyes. "I'm telling you they're here. And someone is using a minus meter nearby. That's what makes them buzz."

"Come on now. I'm nah falling for tha," Nose said, crouching down and setting his gun right in front of my face. "You wan me to look around on these shelves so you can Houdini your way out of here behind my back. I don't thing so." He found the end of the tape and began pulling a piece loose.

"Nose, listen to me."

He tore at the tape, ripping a long strip off.

"Don't do this."

He stretched the strip over my mouth, patting it down tightly.

A tear of frustration rolled down my cheek, catching and welling at the sticky edge of the tape.

Nose started to move away, to go back to his chair, but before he could a new sound rose from below us, from the very earth under the garage. It was muffled and faint through the thick slab of cement, but there was no mistaking it.

It was the sound of someone screaming.

31

FREEZERS DON'T SCREAM

"Wha—is—tha?" Nose said, his eyes filling the holes of his ski mask.

The screaming went on, faint but rising and falling. Then it suddenly cut out.

The garage filled up with silence. The buzzing was gone. The blades had stopped just when the screaming had.

"Hmm. Mm Mmmfph," I said, lips straining against the duct tape.

Nose looked at me. He glanced at the garage door. He looked down at me again, reached over, and ripped off the tape.

"Untie me," I said, even though my lips and cheeks were burning with pain. "They're under us. It came from right under us."

Nose looked toward the garage door again.

"Nose," I said, calling his eyes back to me. "We don't have time to argue with Jason. You know I'm not a CAMFer. Untie me!" I rolled over and shoved my bound hands at him.

"We only hab one gun," he said as he untied me. He was scared. So was I. But we couldn't risk bringing Jason or Yale into this. Obviously, they hadn't heard the buzzing or the screaming—and probably wouldn't believe Nose and I had.

"There must be a basement," I said, pulling my hands free, and then my arms, "Or a cellar under the garage." I sat up and began helping him untie my legs.

"Yeah, bu how do we geh down there?" Nose said, glancing around.

"There has to be an entrance in here," I scanned the garage like I never had before. "If Marcus didn't go out the back of the house, or the front, then the only place he could have come was in here." I got up and started moving around the garage, desperate, looking, shifting things aside as quietly as I could.

Nose joined me. We didn't have much time. His turn guarding me would be over soon.

We searched systematically, silently, moving things off the shelves, feeling along the walls, inspecting the floor for any signs of a trap door.

After about five minutes Nose said, "There's nudding here."

"There has to be. Keep looking." I pulled the mower aside and looked at the chest freezer. Maybe it was covering a trap door. I shoved my hip against it, but it didn't budge. It was damn heavy and wedged in the corner. I put my hand on it, feeling the hum of its motor. Maybe that's what I'd felt before —not the blades—just the vibration of the freezer on the cement floor. But freezers don't scream. Maybe if I unplugged it, Nose and I could move it together and look underneath.

I went around to the freezer's end and found the power cord trailing away behind the nearest shelf. I moved some stuff and found the plug sitting on the shelf. It wasn't plugged in. If the freezer wasn't plugged in, how could the motor be humming?

I threw myself down on the floor next to the freezer, pressing my face to the cement, spreading my hands.

"What are you doing?" Nose asked, standing over me.

"It's happening again," I said, feeling the buzz of the blades rising up from the floor. I hadn't been able to feel them when I was standing up.

Just as Nose knelt down next to me, the screaming started again.

I knew what it was. Could see it in my mind's eye; Marcus on a cold metal slab, his mouth open making that sound. The Dark Man standing over him, extracting his PSS again and again.

The freezer wasn't on, so it was probably empty. And yet I hadn't been able to move it at all.

I jumped up and went back to it, grabbing the door handle, ready to yank it open. There was no doubt the screaming was coming from inside of it. Then, like before, the sound suddenly stopped. The garage was silent. My hand on the freezer felt nothing. No buzzing.

"This is it," I said, feeling Nose come up behind me.

I lifted the freezer door.

The freezer had no bottom. Instead, metal stairs descended into its deep insides, leading down into unknown darkness.

Cool air wafted up at us, fluttering my bangs against my forehead.

"Get your gun," I said to Nose.

For a second, I was afraid he'd chicken out. He stared at the steps leading down into the dark hole under the freezer. If he made the wrong move, I was going to have to reach my ghost hand into him. I was pretty sure I could do it, now that my hand and arm weren't pinned on the cold cement. Just like Jason, I told myself. In and out with no prep or weirdness. Except this time I wouldn't let go until Nose was out cold like Passion had been. I didn't want to do that. Yes, I was still pissed at him for listening to Jason and tying me up, but despite all that, I couldn't help liking Nose. But it didn't matter. I could not risk anyone trying to stop me.

"I'll go first," I said, taking the lead, hoping Nose would follow.

He nodded and went over to the shelf were he'd left his gun. He picked it up and came back to me.

I hiked my leg over the freezer's edge, and slid down onto the top step. I descended to the next, and the next, bending my head a little when I came even with the freezer's lower edge. I heard Nose climb in behind me, his shadow falling across the stairs and blocking out most of the light from above. And there was no light coming from below.

"What's down there?" Nose asked. It sounded like his tongue was doing a lot better.

"I don't know. I can't see. Don't close the lid yet," I whispered, pulling my glove off and jamming it in my pocket. Marcus had warned us not to reveal our PSS, not to use it, but there was no way I was going to walk blindly into a dark room under Mike Palmer's garage.

I took the last step down and held out my ghost hand.

Light sparkled back at me, hundreds of spots of light, my PSS ricocheting around the big empty room I was standing in. The light danced, strobing off the tiny metallic rectangles hanging from the ceiling, looking like some long abandoned rave. The effect was almost enchanting, if you could ignore the fact that the things hanging from the ceiling doing all the twinkling were the razor blades I'd pulled out of Passion Wainwright. But there hadn't been that many, had there?

"It's an empty room," I told Nose, which wasn't totally a lie. He was still at the top of the steps holding the freezer door open a crack.

I couldn't tell what the razor blades were hanging from, maybe just dark-colored wire. They were strung at various heights and distances across the entire room, and it looked like they got closer together in the middle of it. The Dark Man had been doing some nasty little arts and crafts project, it seemed. Palmer had said he was experimenting.

On the far side of the room there was a door, a thin line of yellow light seeping under its threshold.

"Come down," I called up to Nose.

"Okay," he said, pulling the freezer closed, the rubber seal making an odd sucking noise like some strange monster smacking its lips. Nose's descent wasn't exactly quiet. His boots scraped loudly on the stairs. At one point his gun clanged against the metal railing. Even his breathing was loud. Then, when he finally made it to the bottom, he reached out and groped at my chest.

"Hey, watch it," I said, redirecting his hand into mine.

"Sorry," he whispered, looking up. "Oh, whoa, what is this place?" he said like a little kid.

"Those are the blades, the ones that jam minus meters. At least, some of them are. There weren't this many."

"What the hell are they doing up there?"

"I have no idea," I said. But I could guess. "Come on," I said, pulling Nose forward before he had time to guess too. "Just don't touch them, and hurry, and we should be okay." Nose didn't know about the zapping, and I was hoping to keep it that way.

"Where are we going?" Nose protested as I dragged him along, weaving between dangling blades.

"The door across the room."

As we worked our way forward, the blades grew thicker and it was harder to dodge them. Some hung at eye level, some at chest level, some as low as our knees, and now I could see they were hanging from hair-thin transparent cord, its ends glowing wherever it was laced through the razors. In a few places we had to get down and crawl. It was like running a maze or a hanging labyrinth. When we got to the middle of the room there was a thick wall of razors, like one of those beaded door curtains. I was trying to see a way through, thinking maybe we were going to have to backtrack and find a different route when a sound came from behind the door we were heading toward. A voice calling out "No!" A voice I knew, begging for mercy. Marcus's voice.

I didn't even have time to warn Nose.

The air exploded with sound, with a buzzing so loud it rattled my teeth in their sockets and made me clutch at my ears.

The blades rose up, coming alive, whipping this way and that, slicing at my clothes, my skin, my hair, my face. One bit into my cheek and I yanked it out, raising my arms to defend my head and eyes, but I could still feel them battering at my forearms, tearing into my shirt sleeves like mad hummingbirds.

And then the screaming started. And the Pain. The pain in my ghost hand was so excruciating that I suddenly found myself on the floor, curling my body around it. I didn't know where Nose was, and I didn't care. Didn't care where I was, or what I was, or who I was. Barely noticed that someone was kicking me in the head because it was nothing compared to the piercing, cutting, fiery, agony of my hand. Even the screaming. I was screaming. Someone else was screaming. Everyone was screaming. If I could have cut my own hand off, I would have. If it would make it go away. I'd do anything. Just stop. Just make it stop. Please, make it stop.

And then it stopped.

The sound.

The pain.

The screaming.

I was lying on the floor curled in a fetal position.

Someone was moaning near me, up by my head.

Someone was whimpering.

No, that was me. I was making those sounds.

I rolled onto my back and looked up at the twinkling blades against their black ceiling, blinking like so many happy stars in the universe.

I raised my ghost hand and looked at it, surprised that it was still there and intact. I'd expected to find it mangled. Severed. Black. Dead.

From my new angle, the soft blue glow of my PSS illuminated the hanging wires, and I could see that each wire ran from its blade up to the ceiling, those wires connected to more wires imbedded in the ceiling and spiraled across it like some giant glowing spider web.

The blade swaying just above me dripped something wet onto my face.

I reached up and wiped the drop away with my flesh hand, looking at my fingers.

They were covered in gashing cuts and slick with blood.

My forearm was drenched in blood too, ribbons of my shirt and flesh falling away together.

The pain hadn't kicked in yet, but it would.

How much blood had I lost?

Quite a few of the blades I could see were slick and dark with it.

Of course, some of it was probably Nose's.

"Nose," I said, scrambling up to my hands and knees. "We have to get out of here."

He was lying on his back a few feet away from me. His mask was shredded and soaked with blood, and the PSS from his nose was shining through the slits making him look like some radiant, fissured, monster.

"Nose," I said, crawling to him, grabbing him by the shoulders and shaking him. "Do you hear me? We have to get out of this room."

"Yeah," he said, vacant eyes looking past me. He was conscious. Barely. The pain in my hand had been almost unbearable. Nose had felt that same torture in his head, and he wasn't recovering as fast as I had.

"Can you crawl? I think we should crawl." I helped him up on his hands and knees.

We crawled toward the door, hands slipping in our own blood, avoiding blades when we could, plowing through them with our heads down when we couldn't. It wasn't like a few more cuts were going to make a difference. The door was no longer just a slit of light. It was the way out of a living nightmare.

When we got to it, I helped Nose stand up. The blades were more spaced out at the periphery of the room, and there were none right near the door.

I looked back across the room, to the shadowy stairs leading back up to the garage, trying to catch my breath. My eyes flicked to something on the floor near the middle of the room where the blades were thickest.

Nose's gun.

There was no way in hell I was crawling back to get it.

I turned to the door.

"We're going in," I said to Nose and opened it.

32

THE DARK MAN'S LAIR

Whatever I had expected, it wasn't the room laid out before me.

Marcus was lying in a hospital bed near the far wall, handsome but strangely pale, his eyes closed, white sheet carefully folded at the top and tucked across his bare chest. The only thing that distinguished the scene from every soap opera hospital tableau ever filmed was the gaping hole in the patient's chest peeking out above the top of the sheet.

Beyond Marcus were two more hospital beds.

Emma was in the closer one, clearly unconscious as well, with a tube trailing from under her sheet to an IV stand next to her bed.

And in the third bed was Passion Wainwright.

She had an IV too. But she was awake.

Passion looked past the tall, lean man standing at her bedside in a white coat. As her eyes caught mine, a small smile of recognition flitted across her lips. She raised one hand, her wrist crisscrossed with angry, welted, barely-healed cuts, and gave a little wave.

The doctor turned.

Dr. Fineman turned and smiled at me.

"You made it," he said with the Dark Man's accent. "I'm so relieved. We were beginning to worry."

"She's hurt," Passion slurred, sounding drunkenly concerned. And then more perkily, "but she brought a visitor."

"I told you she would," Dr. Dark Man said.

"You said there would be more," Passion pouted, flopping her arms a little. She wasn't drunk. She was drugged.

"Yes, well. It can't be helped," the doctor said. "I'm sure the rest will be coming along shortly. We'll just have to make do with these two, for now."

"You!" I blurted, my brain finally grasping onto that one word. This could not be real. It had to be a nightmare. Maybe Nose and I were still knocked out, lying in pools of our own blood in the razor room, and this was the terror my unconscious mind had decided to run with—all my personal fears rolled into one horrible scenario. Emma and Marcus helpless. In a hospital. With an evil doctor who just happened to be the Dark Man. And dating my mother. And, of course, throw in Passion, scarred and smiling at me. This was way too twisted to be real.

"Olivia, I know you're upset. This must be very confusing," Dr. Dark Man said. "But you're bleeding quite heavily. And so is your friend. Why don't you let me tend to those wounds, and then we can all have a nice, calm chat."

"Chatty, chat, chat," Passion said, her head lolling against her pillow as she closed her eyes.

Dr. Dark Man moved in my direction, past the end of Emma's bed, his empty hands held out to show he was unarmed.

"Stay away from us!" I screamed, holding my ghost hand out in front of me like a gun. Behind me, I heard a noise—Nose sliding down the doorframe, his body coming to rest gently against the heels of my boots. Couldn't anyone stay conscious long enough to help me even a little? It was like I was living in a world of narcoleptics.

"He needs my help," Dr. Dark Man said, the picture of concern.

"Fuck that!" I yelled. "Fuck you!" My whole body seemed to be shaking, blood dripping onto the floor. "These wounds," I said, holding out my ravaged hand and arm, "are because of you, you sick motherfuck." That word had never seemed more appropriate. "This is all because of you."

"Really?" he said, crossing his arms over his chest like a disgruntled parent. "This is all because of me? That's odd. I thought it was all because of you," His voice ground hard on the "you." He was losing his phony bedside manner. "After all, I'm not the one who stuck my hand into poor innocent Passion here and pulled out her insides. I've been trying to clean up that little mess of yours ever since you made it."

"I—what—how?

"Oh yes, I know all the mischief you've been up to, my dear. First there was the huge PSS spike on our meters, which I traced back to your school. Then Passion came to the emergency room and shared with me, her physician, some very strange "memories" associated with that incident. Sadly, she hadn't felt she could share them with her therapist—conflict of interest—you understand. And then, lo and behold, your Fire Chief brought me your backpack full of very odd razor blades. Blades that amplify PSS resonance, among other things. It didn't take a genius, though I am one, to put two and two together. After that, it was only natural that Passion should fall under my specialized care. Her parents seemed quite relieved to have her taken off their hands."

"Who the hell *are* you?" I said, my head spinning a little.

"I am Dr. Salvador Julian, the world's premiere PSS research specialist. I'm also the only one who can help you with your hand."

"Help me by killing me? No thanks." My bleeding was slowing, and I was feeling a little less lightheaded.

"Kill you?" He seemed startled by the idea. "Why would I want to kill you?"

"You tell me. Why did you want to kill Marc—David's sister?"

"Danielle?" he asked, sounding almost pained. "I didn't want to kill her. Nor did I do any such thing. But she died, yes. Leukemia is a truly tragic illness, especially when it strikes the young."

"Leukemia?" I repeated, glancing at Marcus lying in the hospital bed. What he'd described out there in the sycamore tree, the slow death of his sister; it had sounded just like my dad's death. Was this another one of Marcus's well-fabricated lies? Could his sister have died under the care of Dr. Julian, not of PSS extraction, but of leukemia? It was possible; Marcus had lied about everything else.

From behind Dr. Julian, a flash of light caught my eye. In the bed, under Marcus's sheet, a pulse of blue light flared and went out. He was rebooting. Maybe when he came back to life, he'd tell me the truth for a change.

"She didn't die of leukemia," I said, moving a step toward Dr. Julian to keep his attention on me. "You killed her by sucking out her PSS. And you burned down my house," I reminded him. "I know you tried to kill *me*. I was there."

"Yes, well, that was unfortunate, but I wasn't trying to kill you," he said, dismissively. "I simply arranged for you to end up in the hospital under my care."

"Arranged?" I choked on the word. "By burning my house down with me in it?"

"That was your overzealous fireman, not me. How was I supposed to know you small town Americans are so barbaric? Still, in the end, it was effective, if not efficient. And everything would have ended there, if you'd only done what was asked of you. If you'd let me run those tests and take my sample."

"Take a sample?" I didn't believe that. It certainly wasn't how Marcus had described PSS extraction, but I asked because I wanted to keep the doctor's evil rant going a little longer. Out of the corner of my eye, I could see the strobe of Marcus's PSS flashing faster and faster.

"Yes, a sample. This is what I do. My life's work. I sample and categorize PSS signatures for research purposes."

"You just take samples?" I asked, trying not to look at Marcus. "That's why you came to my town, and got a job, and dated my mom, and kidnapped my best friend, and made a fucking pain machine out of razor blades in a room under Mike Palmer's garage. Just to get a sample. What kind of idiot do you think I am?"

"I don't think you are an idiot, my dear girl, but I do think you are a very difficult patient. I had hoped we could come to an understanding, especially after you provided me with those wonderful blades. Truly remarkable. I've only just begun to understand what they can do. I thought perhaps I could persuade you to extract more such items for me. But it seems, as usual, that you insist on doing things the hard way." He reached into his coat pocket, pulled out a minus meter, and pointed it at my hand.

Of course, I had known it was coming, but I hadn't counted on my body being so sluggish when I tried to jump aside. My boots slid in the blood at my feet, and I flew backwards, landing on my back with a wet smack. The hard cement floor knocked the wind right out of me, my ghost hand flailing in the air. At least my head landed on Nose's back, instead of hitting the floor.

A noise like a bug-zapper filled the air.

A stream of light shot out of the minus meter toward me.

Pain erupted in my ghost hand, just like in the razor room, cutting me, killing me, ending me, except this time one thing was different. The pain wasn't trapped inside my hand. It was moving away, being pulled out my fingertips, leeching out of my wrist as my ghost hand elongated and stretched toward Dr. Julian. The pain hung in the air between us as my PSS unwound away from me. Away from me. Away from me. Take the pain away from me. If he took my hand away from me, maybe the pain would go with it.

Through that wall of pain, I saw Marcus and his beautiful PSS chest rise up behind Dr. Julian and grab him around the throat.

The bug-zapper sound sputtered and stalled.

Something let go of my ghost hand, and the pain receded.

Dr. Julian and Marcus wrestled on the floor, Marcus's muscles rippling, his PSS a steady blue glow. Dr. Julian was trying to get the minus meter between them. Marcus pried back Dr. Julian's arm, pushing it away from his chest. They rolled, knocking over a tray of medical instruments that went crashing to the floor.

Passion Wainwright sat up in bed and blurted out, "What would Jesus do?"

I scrambled upright, slipping in my own blood again, leveraging myself against Nose and finally getting up.

Dr. Julian was grabbing one of the sharp medical instruments in his left hand. Marcus didn't see. He was focused on protecting himself from the minus meter.

I rushed forward.

With my flesh hand, I grabbed Dr. Julian's wrist, giving him my best estimation of the radial nerve pinch.

Metal clattered on the floor.

I sank my ghost hand into Dr. Julian's back.

He went stiff.

I followed my hand into emptiness, into a landscape of nothingness. How could someone be so empty? If Jason's insides had been a machine of anger and madness, Dr. Julian's were the opposite. He was a void. An open space my hand needed to fill, but I could find nothing to grab hold of.

"Olivia," someone said, shaking me.

"Don't help me," I said. I had something to do. Something to find. It was there, hiding from me. I could feel it.

My hand groped, fumbled, reached, then closed over something hard, solid and square.

I grabbed it, yanking it out.

Dr. Julian slumped to the floor between Marcus and me.

"I got it," I said, holding up a smooth silver box the size of a Rubik's cube.

I don't know how long it was. A few seconds? A few minutes? Half an hour? I just know that Marcus was holding me when Jason and Yale crashed into the room. They practically tripped over Nose.

Marcus got up and left me. He took something out of Yale's backpack and held it to Nose's nose, Yale and Jason looking on.

"It's not working," Jason said. "Are you sure he can even smell?"

"I don't know," Marcus said. "There's a sink over there. Get some water and splash his face with it. Yale, take the smelling salts and work on the girls. Pull out their IVs first. They're drugged, but we need them coherent enough to walk out of here."

Yale went to work unplugging IVs.

Marcus came back and crouched next to me. "Are you okay?" he asked.

In the background, Passion began softly humming, "Nobody Knows the Trouble I've Seen."

"No," I said, looking down at the silver cube clutched in my hand.

Jason doused Nose with a hospital pitcher full of water. Nose sputtered awake but still seemed out of it. Jason propped him up against the door frame and patted him on the chest. Then he turned and strode toward us, stopping to stand over Dr. Julian. "He dead?" he asked, gesturing with his gun.

"He's still breathing," Marcus observed.

I looked over at the man lying next to me. He was bleeding from the nose.

"Then we should take care of that," Jason said, pointing his gun at the doctor's head.

"Wait!" Marcus said, taking a step toward Jason. "Hand me your flashlight."

Without moving his gun, Jason reached in his pocket and handed his flashlight to Marcus.

Marcus knelt down and pulled Dr. Julian's eyelids back one at a time, flashing the light into them.

"No pupil dilation," Marcus said, looking up at Jason, "which means he's alive, but not by much."

"So?" Jason said.

"He's not waking up any time soon," Marcus stood back up. "I'm not saying you can't kill him, but first we get the girls to safety."

"She fuck him up like that?" Jason asked, nodding toward me as he lowered his gun and took his flashlight back.

Had I done it? I'd been trying to save Marcus, and Emma, and Passion, and myself. I'd been trying to—reach the cube.

"Go help Yale," Marcus said, ignoring the question. "I want us all out of here before any more CAMFers show up."

"But I get to kill him? You promise?" Jason asked.

"I don't care what you do to him once we're out," Marcus replied.

"What about that thing?" Jason asked, gesturing his gun muzzle at the minus meter lying a few feet from Dr. Julian. "We takin' it?"

Marcus walked over and picked it up. "That's strange," he said. "It's flashing like it's still on."

"That's flashing too," I said, pointing above us where something that looked very much like a giant minus meter was fixed to the center of the ceiling, wires trailing away from it in all directions.

Just as Marcus and Jason looked up, the lights in the room flicked off, then flickered back on in exact time with the pulsing of the minus meter in Marcus's hand. And the one on the ceiling. Off. On. Off. On. Like a slow strobe.

"What the fuck?" Jason said.

"What the hell is going on?" Yale called, flashing in and out of view from across the room where he was helping Emma out of bed.

Marcus looked around the room. I saw his face, one frozen frame after another as his eyes traced the wires running across the ceiling toward the exit door, toward the room of blades.

"Shit," he said softly. Then he was screaming, "Go! Go!" He shoved Jason toward the door. "Get the hell out. The room is rigged."

Jason didn't hesitate. He didn't even question. He turned and ran toward the door.

Marcus grabbed me, yanking me up off the floor.

"Get the girls out!" he bellowed. "Get them out."

I saw it all in still life. Shots frozen in time, like old photographs.

Jason, like some war hero, lifting Nose over his shoulders.

Yale, a slouched girl on each arm, dragging them along like a pair of rag dolls.

Jason and Nose, half-swallowed by the darkness of the razor room.

Yale and the girls leaning against the door frame.

Then Marcus was propelling us toward the razor room too.

"No," I said, struggling to escape his grasp. I didn't want to go in that room ever again.

"It's the only way out," he said, shoving me forward.

As soon as we stepped across the threshold, the PSS glow of my hand and his chest filled the room, refracting off the dangling razors, twinkling, sparkling, winking at us like a hundred sharp-eyed conspirators.

In front of us somewhere, Passion said, "Oooh, so pretty."

We moved out into the room, weaving carefully back and forth, crawling and ducking to avoid the touch of the blades, but I thought I could hear them trembling in anticipation. They were already buzzing in my head. Whispering pain. Promising pain.

In the middle of the room, at the curtain of blades, Marcus stopped and grabbed at my hip, tugging something away from me. He'd pulled my glove from my pocket, and he was wrapping it around his right hand.

Before I could even protest, he reached up, clutching at the nearest razor blade.

"No," I said, trying to pull him back from it.

Ahead of us, Jason and Nose had made it to the bottom of the stairs and were starting up.

Yale wasn't far behind, guiding Emma in front of him and pulling Passion after.

I could see the light at the end of the tunnel. We were almost there.

Marcus reached up with his left hand and hacked at the transparent cord attached to the razor using the sharp medical instrument Dr. Julian had tried to stab him with. The razor came away, its edge imbedded in the glove, and Marcus moved to the next one.

"What are you doing?" I cried. "We have to get out of here."

"Just one more," he said, hacking at another cord.

The second blade came away and he pulled me through the gap he'd cut, running toward the stairs.

We fell up the steps and tumbled out of the freezer into Mike Palmer's garage.

Marcus banged the freezer door shut, and we ran into the living room, slamming the garage door behind us.

"Are we safe?" Yale asked, panting. Everyone was panting. Nose and the girls were slumped on the couch in a pile. Yale and Jason were bent over it.

"I doubt it," Marcus said. "We're standing on top of a minus meter the size of a house. And he rigged the blades to it, like an amplifier or something. It has range."

"But it hasn't done anything yet. Maybe it doesn't work," Jason said.

"Maybe," Marcus didn't sound hopeful. "Or he just didn't factor in how long it would take for something that size to power up." There was fear in his eyes. I could see it. Fear, not for himself, but for the rest of us. This was the way he'd lost his sister. He could always reboot. He would come back. But we wouldn't. I looked down at the silver cube I'd pulled from Dr. Julian. The things I pulled from people found their power in answer to my need, and I was very much in need. I needed us all to get away. To be safe and far away. But that was the bullet's power, and it only sent things to Jason, which wouldn't help at all. What I needed was an all-purpose bullet. One without that rule. A bullet that could function outside the box. *Outside the box.*

I scrambled in my pocket, pulled out the bullet, and placed it on top of the silver box, pressing them against one another with my thumbs.

From the depths of Palmer's house came a sound, a concussion of air and energy just like the sound my burning house had made when it had imploded into my basement behind me.

"What are you d—" I heard Marcus say as I closed my eyes, and wished real hard, and the world went black.

33

A COUCH IN THE WOODS

I woke up with something digging into my side.

My back and butt were cold and damp, and I wondered how my bed had gotten wet.

I opened my eyes and saw stars, real stars, spread out above me like the universe had just been rendered in high definition. It was beautiful, but I had no idea why I was sleeping outside on the wet ground next to a couch.

Someone stirred near me, moaning, and withdrew their foot from my ribs.

I sat up slowly and looked around.

I was in the middle of the woods somewhere. Wet leaves were sticking to the back of my head, and I brushed them away. It must have rained while I slept. Except, my topside was completely dry. Next to me was a tacky couch, covered in dark lumpy shapes. One of the shapes moved and moaned again. People. A whole pile of them. On a couch in the woods.

In front of me, branches rustled and parted, and a dark shape came out of the trees.

"You're awake," Marcus said, the relief on his face clearly visible by the glow of my ghost hand.

"What—" I started to ask, but it all came crashing back then. The plan to rescue Emma. The discovery that Marcus wasn't Marcus. The showdown in the hospital room under Mike Palmer's house. The giant minus meter in the ceiling and the run for our lives. And finally, my crazy idea to combine the power of the bullet with Dr. Julian's box to get us out of there. Well, apparently it had worked. I still had my ghost hand, and we weren't dead. At least Marcus and I weren't. "Are they okay?" I asked, glancing toward the couch.

"They're fine," Marcus said.

I still thought of him as Marcus. I couldn't help it.

"Everyone's still breathing anyway," he clarified. He had a pile of blankets in his arms, and he was wearing a sweatshirt and jacket. He looked warm. I, on the other hand, was beginning to shiver.

"Where are we?" I asked, my teeth chattering a little.

"Just outside of camp. You have pretty good aim."

"Everyone made it?"

"Even the couch," he said, unfurling one of the blankets and wrapping it around my shoulders. He tossed the others over the forms on the couch, then came and sat down next to me. "How'd you do it?" he asked, his warm shoulder brushing mine.

"I used the—" I looked down at my hands. They were empty. I glanced around on the wet ground, searching for it.

"Looking for this?" Marcus asked, holding the smooth silver cube up in front of my face. He shook it and something rattled inside, metal clanking against metal.

I took it from him and shook it myself. "It's inside," I said, turning the cube this way and that, looking for an indent or crack, searching for any indication that the thing had an opening. There was nothing. It looked exactly like it had before—an impenetrable, solid, metal cube. Except the bullet was inside of it now, rattling when I shook it.

"What's in there?" Marcus asked.

"The bullet."

"Jason's bullet?" he asked, sounding alarmed. "Then don't shake it," he snatched the cube from my hands. "That's live ammo in there."

"You shook it first," I pointed out.

"Yeah, because I didn't know what was in it. How'd it get in there?" he asked, looking for an opening like I just had. When he didn't find one either, he handed the cube back to me, the question still in his eyes.

"I used them in combination," I said. "The bullet and this. To wish us all out of there. I guess somehow they fused together."

"How'd you even know to do that?"

"I have no idea," I said. "It just came to me."

"Well, good job. You saved us," he said, admiration in his eyes and his voice, but with undertones of something else too. *You saved us when I couldn't.* Is that what he was thinking?

"It never would have worked, you know?" I said.

"What?"

"Trading yourself in for Emma. He didn't just want you, or an energy source. He wanted all of us."

"I know," he said, staring down at his hands, "but I had to try. I couldn't lose—" his voice broke off. He reached over and took my ghost hand, weighing it in his bigger, darker palm.

"I'm not her," I said, gently pulling my hand away.

"Where the fuck are we?" a voice groaned, and Jason stood up from behind the couch.

I slipped the cube into my front sweatshirt pocket as Marcus turned and said, "We're back at camp."

Jason stumbled around the end of the sofa and sat on the arm, his gun still clutched in his hand.

"Back at camp? How the—Aw, man. She disappeared us," he said, looking at me accusingly. "Why'd you go and do that?"

"Um, so we wouldn't die," I said.

"We weren't gonna die," Jason grumbled. "Not right away, anyway. I would have had time before we kicked it to blow that asshole's head off."

"Yeah, well, I didn't want to die quickly, or slowly," I said. "Sorry if that ruined your killing spree."

"Fuck yeah, it ruined my killing spree," Jason leaned over me, his eyes glinting in the dark. "But I'm sure I can make up for it when that doctor comes for us with an army of CAMFers at his back."

"Jason, his brain was fried," Marcus said, standing up, trying to reason with him. "He's not coming for us."

"If not him, then some other CAMFer. They're just gonna keep coming until we give them a reason not to," Jason said, pushing past Marcus and marching toward the woods.

"Where are you going?" Marcus called after him.

"To kill him," Jason said over his shoulder.

"It's a two hour walk," Marcus pointed out.

Jason stopped in his tracks, turned, and came walking back toward us. "Good point," he said when he got to Marcus. "I'll take my wheeler."

"Yeah, about that," Marcus said. "It seems to be missing."

"Then I'll take yours," Jason snapped, not even stopping in his stride.

"Jason!" Marcus said, steel in his voice.

Jason stopped, turned, and stared a challenge at him. "You promised me this," he said.

They stood, glaring at each other, hackles up like two dogs ready to fight, Jason with a gun in his hand.

I clutched the cube in my pocket, the hard corners digging into my palm.

"All right," Marcus said finally, nodding. "Just be careful."

A moment later, an ATV's engine roared out of the silent night and faded into the distance.

And everyone on the couch started waking up.

"I'm so sorry," Emma said as she helped me put bandages on my fingers. "I messed up everything." We were sitting on Mike Palmer's couch, which Marcus and Yale had carried back to camp. On the other end sat Nose, his shredded mask discarded, with Passion trying to patch up his face. She was even doing a pretty good job of not staring at his PSS. In fact, she and Emma had been amazingly calm and coherent for two girls who had recently been kidnapped and drugged.

"Em, it's not your fault. And we all got out safe." The cuts on my fingers and arms didn't look that bad. In fact, they looked like they'd been healing for days. I glanced to the side, catching a glimpse of Passion's pale wrist in the moonlight. The gashes I'd seen earlier were already healed over and fading to pink.

"Wait," I said, grabbing Emma's arm and turning it over. I couldn't find the needle mark from her IV. How long had we been asleep in the woods?

"What?" asked Emma, looking down at her arm.

"What time is it?" I asked her.

"Nine thirty-seven," Marcus said, glancing down at his watch as he and Yale handed blankets and warm clothing to Emma and Passion.

Nine thirty-seven? We'd gone into Palmer's house around six. Had it really taken less than three and half hours for all that to happen?

I looked up at Marcus. He was still staring at his watch.

"I need to go check something," he said, looking up and catching my eye just before he turned and disappeared into the dark.

"Help them," I ordered Emma, pushing her toward Nose and Passion. "I'll be right back." Something was up, and Marcus was not going to keep me out of it this time.

I followed him into the woods, the ground squishing under my feet. It had been dry and clear in town, but it must have rained pretty heavily out here while we were gone. Marcus was heading toward a tree in a small clearing I knew all too well. He was going to check on Palmer.

"Hey, wait up," I called after him.

He stopped and turned, his face hidden in shadows.

"What's the matter?" I asked, coming alongside him.

"You still have Emma's phone?"

"Yeah."

"Look at it."

I reached in my pocket, pulled the phone out, and turned it on. The screen lit up revealing thirty-two messages from Emma's mom. I'd always known Mrs. Campbell was a worrier but—I stared down at the dates on the messages. I scrolled up, then back down. Then I flicked back to the menu screen. "There's something wrong with this phone," I said, looking up at Marcus. "It says these messages are from the last three days. It says today is Friday, September 30th. But that's not right. It should be Tuesday the 27th."

"My watch says the same thing. And so does my phone," he said, holding it up.

"Maybe getting bulleted messed them up."

"Maybe," Marcus said, turning and resuming his walk toward the tree.

I followed reluctantly. I didn't want to see Palmer. Didn't want to remember what I'd done to him. What if he was dead? Or in a coma, like Dr. Julian.

Marcus rounded the last bend in the path and stopped.

I came up behind him, my ghost hand spilling light on an empty tree, ropes coiled in a tousled pile near its trunk. The hydration pack we'd hung to give Palmer water was gone.

"Well, that explains where Jason's wheeler went," Marcus said, stepping forward.

I stood, my mouth hanging open. I'd seen how thoroughly they'd tied up Palmer. How in the world had he gotten out of that?

"He rubbed the rope against the tree," Marcus said, as if reading my mind. "Rubbed it clean through," he held up a frayed end of the thick rope. "See here," he said, pointing to a place where the bark on the tree had been worn smooth down to the wood.

"How could he do that in only a couple of hours?"

"He couldn't," Marcus said. "It would have taken days."

"But—I don't get it," I said, staring at him.

"I don't think our phones and watches got messed up," Marcus said, staring back. "I think it's been three days since you bulleted us out of Palmer's house."

"What are you talking about? The transfer is instantaneous. We proved that with Palmer, and my dad's painting, and the Frisbees."

"Yeah, but that was without the cube."

"Oh shit!" I said, looking down at Emma's phone

again. The dates and the messages. The healed wounds and Mike Palmer's escape. The rain that was everywhere but on us. None of it made sense. None of it matched the timeline of events we'd experienced. Even if we'd been unconscious in the woods all that time, it had rained. We should have been wet too. Unless we hadn't been there at all. "What the fuck happened?" I asked, looking up at Marcus.

"You saved us," he said.

"But where have we been?"

"Your guess is as good as mine," he said, taking my hand and squeezing it.

Everyone else took the news of the three lost days much better than I had.

Back at camp, Marcus let Yale build a small fire, and we all huddled around it in camp chairs and on the couch. None of us were tired, and I guess Marcus figured the warmth and morale were worth the risk.

"So, we've been somewhere for three days," Marcus said, after briefly explaining to Passion and Emma about the list, and the CAMFers, and Dr. Fineman. Thankfully, he'd managed to be vague about what my ghost hand had done, and to whom, though I could see Passion looking at me, a million unanswered questions in her eyes.

"What do you mean somewhere?" Emma asked.

"We don't know," Marcus answered. "In limbo, I guess."

"You mean outside of this world?" Nose asked, leaning forward.

"Or outside this time," Yale added.

"Oh come on!" Emma protested.

"If you fly from the US to New Zealand," Yale argued, "you cross the International Date Line and lose an entire day. And when you fly back you gain one. Distance and speed and time are all connected. It isn't completely crazy, given our unusual mode of travel, to believe we lost three days."

"Three days," Passion said. "Just like Jesus. That's SRT— Standard Resurrection Time."

"Nah, we weren't dead." Nose said, "So it wasn't resurrection. It had to be time travel. And we discovered it. We're the world's first fucking time travelers."

Emma didn't really believe any of it until we let her listen to all the phone messages. Of course, she immediately wanted to call her mom, but Marcus said no. "We have to come up with a solid cover story for you first," he explained. "But even before that, we have to find out if it's safe for you back in town. The CAMFers may still be there, and they know you can identify them. We'll see what Jason says when he gets back. He should be able to tell us something about what's happened since we left."

Holy shit! I'd completely forgotten about Jason. When he'd stormed out of camp to go kill Dr. Julian, we'd still had no idea we'd lost three days.

"Yeah, but I have to go back home," Emma said, looking around the group for support.

No one said anything.

"I have to go back," Emma said, desperation in her eyes.

"Well, I'm not going back," Passion said. "My parents handed me over to that psycho." She looked down at her wrists, now covered by the long sleeves of one of Yale's sweatshirts. "They could never handle—what I do—or what I am. I'll never be their good little Christian daughter." She looked up, embarrassment shining in her eyes. "I mean, I'd like to come with you guys, if that's okay."

"Of course it is," Nose blurted, the bandages making his face look all bulgy and weird, like a new mask. "I mean, right?" he said, deferring to Marcus, but with a hopeful look. Someone liked Passion.

"Yeah," Marcus agreed, looking at me. "I don't see a problem with that." Did he think I didn't want Passion along? Or was he just trying to prove he was willing to help someone even if they didn't have PSS?

"Hey," Emma said, "You guys are cool and everything. And I admire what you're doing. You saved Liv, and you saved me, and I don't want to seem ungrateful, but I have to go home."

"I understand," Marcus said. "But it's not safe, and I just don't see how you're going to explain being gone this long. I doubt anyone would believe you about the CAMFers, and outing them puts you in more danger than you're already in. Obviously, you can't tell your parents about us, or Olivia, or the time thing. So, where does that leave us?"

"She could tell them about me," I said. "She could say she found me hiding out, and she camped with me a few days, trying to convince me to come home."

"It would never work," Marcus said to me, and then turned his attention back to Emma. "If they think you've been with Olivia, they'll ask questions. There will be some kind of investigation, and you'll be smack in the middle of it. They'll want to know why she didn't come back with you and where she went. You'd have to lie to your parents, Olivia's mom, and the police, and you'd have to maintain that lie indefinitely," he paused, his eyes slipping back to me. Was he thinking about his own carefully constructed tower of lies? "Do you really think you could do that?" he asked, looking back at Emma.

"If I have to," she said. "If it's the only way to keep Olivia safe and get my life back. Yeah, I could do it."

"I don't think so," he said.

"Why not?" I said, unable to keep my mouth shut any longer. "You did it."

No one said anything. They just stared from me to Marcus, waiting.

"You lied about everything," I went on. "You lied to me. You lied to the guys. You even lied about who you are. At least she won't have to do that."

"We all have aliases in this camp," he said, calmly. "How was calling me Marcus any different than calling him Nose, or him Yale? Those aren't their real names."

"Really?" I laughed bitterly. "You don't know how that's different? I'll tell you how it's different. They don't have aliases. They have nicknames."

"Same thing," Marcus said dismissively.

"No, it really isn't," I was so angry at him, I didn't care who knew. It didn't matter that poor Passion and

Emma were there, squirming on the couch. As for Nose and Yale, they were next on my shit list anyway, after what they'd done. After what they'd let Jason do. But ultimately, even that tied back to Marcus and his tendency to mistrust everyone. I'd held it all in while we'd struggled for our lives because I'd had to. But now we were safe, and Marcus had a lot to answer for.

"So, if you found out Yale's real name, or that Nose has two sisters, you wouldn't be this pissed at them?"

"No, I wouldn't!" I said, standing up and getting in his face.

"Why not? What makes me so special?" he asked, raising his voice to match mine.

"What makes you so special?" I asked, poking my finger at him, tempted to poke it right into his chest. "What makes you different from the guy who tied me up and gagged me?" I jabbed my finger in Nose's direction. "Or the guy who let Jason kick me in the ribs?" I pointed at Yale. "Or the guy who keeps sticking loaded guns in my face?"

"Yes," Marcus said, sounding momentarily confused as he looked from Nose to Yale. There hadn't been time to tell him about the events in the garage. "Why aren't you this pissed at them?"

"Well, let's see. Maybe because they didn't kiss me while they did any of that!" I yelled. "They didn't hold my hand, and call me babe, and undress me, and share their fucking tent with me."

Marcus stared at me, his eyes wide with surprise.

The others looked anywhere but at us.

"If you really don't know what makes you different from them," I said weakly, the fight gone out of me. "What makes *us* special, then you're not just a pathological liar, you're a complete idiot."

34

TRUST ME

I left them all there in the dark and marched straight to Marcus's tent. I untied the flaps, ducked in, and found *The Other Olivia* staring back at me.

"What are you looking at?" I snapped. Then I started packing my stuff.

I was kneeling on the floor, cramming the last of my clothes back into the Campbells' bag, when I heard him come in.

"What are you doing?" he asked, sounding alarmed.

"Packing."

"Packing?" He said it as if he'd never heard the word before. "Olivia, don't be—you can't leave. Palmer is out there somewhere. There may still be CAMFers in town. It's not safe."

"Why? Because I'm on the list? Is there really even a list, or was that a lie too?'

"You think I lied about the list?" He sounded pissed off, and that made me very happy.

"You lied about everything else," I said, turning to look at him.

"No," he shook his head. "Not everything."

"Whatever," I said, jamming a pair of jeans into the bag.

"You want to see it?" He went over to the tubs next to the trunk. "Fine. I'll show you," he said, shoving the top one aside, and picking up the keepsake box, the one I'd snooped in that first morning. He yanked off the lid and looked down into it. Then he glanced at me, embarrassment flashing across his face before it closed up, snapped shut as quickly and firmly as the lid he'd just snapped back on the tub. "We should look at it later," he said.

"See, that's what I mean." I cinched the bag of clothes and stood up. "There's no reason for me to stay here."

"You're leaving because I won't show you the list right now?" he asked, anger flaring in his eyes.

"No. I'm leaving because you have serious trust issues." I slung the bag over my back and moved toward the tent flaps.

"Olivia, don't," he said, dropping the tub in a camp chair and stepping in front of me.

"Get out of my way," I said, trying to step around him, but he moved with me, blocking my way again, his chest in my face. It was exactly what Jason and Nose and Yale had done to keep me from leaving the garage. "Get out of my fucking way," I said. "Or are you going to tie me up like they did? Here, you want to see?" I threw the clothes bag down, yanking my shirt up to show him my ribs. "This," I pointed at the fading purple, yellow and green bruise on my side, "is where Jason kicked me while I was tied up and lying on a garage floor completely helpless. He did that because you didn't trust me. What they did—they were following your orders and your lead. I trusted you, and you did this to me." I gestured at the bruise, trying to keep the tears jammed down in my throat. "And now you expect me to just hang around for more of that?"

He reached out his right hand and laid it over the bruise, his palm gentle and warm, his eyes looking haunted. "Shit," he said. "You're right."

"I know I am," I said, wishing he'd remove that hand before I fell into his arms and ruined all the progress I'd just made knocking sense into his head. Thankfully, he dropped his hand, but then grabbed mine with it.

"Come here," he said, pulling me back to the middle of the tent. He picked up the keepsake box and held it out to me.

I stared at it, then at him.

His eyes were the deep, dark pools of intensity I'd first fallen into. He was making me a trust offering. This box was the summation of his life. All the important, private things he'd secreted away and kept safe from everyone. And he was holding it out to me.

I reached out and took it.

He got me a camp chair, and sat down across from me, our knees touching.

I opened the box.

On the very top was something that had not been there last time. It was my hospital bracelet. He must have cut it off while I lay unconscious in his tent that first night.

He touched it, uncurling the plastic so I could clearly see my name in crisp, stark, medical letting. "That night at the hospital," he said softly. "That was the night I knew I was falling for you."

This was why he'd snapped the lid back on the box earlier. It hadn't been the list he was hiding.

"Why that night?" I asked. He was falling for me. It wasn't a ploy or a plan or a strategy.

"I don't know," he said, his eyes finding mine. "I guess because you're a survivor. The CAMFers burned down your house, and you were still roaring to go after them and the blades all by yourself."

So, did he want me as a girlfriend, or as a superhero sidekick? Then again, maybe someone who'd lost everyone they'd ever loved, and pretty much couldn't die, was looking for both. But I wasn't both, was I?

"You don't think it's creepy that I kept it?" he asked, running his fingertips across my name.

"No," I said, touching it too, our fingertips brushing against each other. I didn't think it was creepy; I thought it was sweet.

He slid the bracelet gently to the side, and there was the picture of him and his sister—just two, scared, homeless kids.

I picked it up, understanding the look in their eyes now. It was the will to live. The determination to survive against all odds. "Tell me about her. About the two of you," I said.

"It's not—a nice story." he said, his eyes so vulnerable.

"Tell me anyway."

"Okay," he sighed. "We grew up in Oregon, in the foster care system. You already know that."

"What happened to your parents?"

"There was a train-car collision when I was seven and Danielle was five."

"Oh my God! They got hit by a train?"

"*We* got hit by a train. Danielle and I were in the car too."

"And you survived that?"

"One of us did," he said. "The train hit toward the front of the car where my parents were. Danielle was in a car seat in the back. I was in the back too, but my seatbelt wasn't clipped in properly. I was thrown over the front seat and out the windshield. I sustained severe internal injuries."

"And you died," I said.

"Yeah. That was the first time my PSS rebooted."

I tried to imagine it. A boy of seven, waking up at the scene of such an awful accident, finding his parents dead.

"I also had a broken arm," he continued, his voice monotone. "And a broken leg. There was a lot of glass in my head. My skull was fractured in multiple places. And I had a blood clot behind my left eye."

"What about Danielle?"

"She had a few minor injuries. Nothing like mine. Which was good because she wouldn't have been able to come back."

"She had a PSS hand and arm." The pieces of the puzzle were finally falling into place. "That's where you learned the Vulcan nerve pinch. Could she reach into people?"

"Yes," he said, "but her ability was different than yours. She could fix things inside people—physical things."

"You mean like heal them?"

"Not always. It depended on what was wrong with them. But, yeah. She's the reason I recovered from the accident so quickly, though the doctors took all the credit, of course. That was the first time she used her ability. But even at that age, we knew better than to tell anyone. Then much later, she got sick. She was diagnosed with leukemia, and she used her hand on herself."

"She healed herself of cancer?" I asked, incredulous.

"It wasn't a one-time cure. She had to keep tweaking things to keep herself in remission."

"That's incredible."

"I guess so," he said, shrugging. "Our abilities didn't keep our parents alive. Or keep us out of the system. Or keep us safe. Instead they landed us straight in the hands of the CAMFers."

"How did they find you and take you without anyone knowing?"

"We had run away from foster care again. We'd stolen a car that time, and we got caught. The cops who pulled us over were scumbags, and when they saw Danielle's PSS—" he stopped, giving me an anguished look.

"What?" I prompted gently.

"First, they handcuffed us," he said, his jawline growing tight, his eyes gone cold and distant as if he were seeing something else, someplace else. "Then they took turns—hurting her."

I wanted to stop him. Wanted to wrap him in my arms and tell him it was all right. But that would have been a lie.

"I was handcuffed to the car," he said, his voice breaking. "I couldn't do anything. I screamed at them, but that just made it worse. Then I screamed for help, but we were on some back road somewhere."

My heart felt mangled inside my chest. This was the truth I'd been after. The truth he always kept buried in lies. And now I understood why.

"After that, they put us in the car," he went on, "but they didn't drive us to the police station. They drove us to some kind of compound, with gates and walls around it—a CAMFer research facility, and that's where I first met Dr. Julian."

"He was in charge?"

"No, he was lower down. Just one of the researchers. But that didn't stop him from killing Danielle."

"He told me she died from the leukemia," I said.

"He did?" Marcus laughed bitterly. "I guess I'm not the only liar. No, he extracted her. He sucked the life out of her right in front of me. And then they took her away, tossed her body somewhere."

"I'm so sorry," I said and immediately wished I could take it back. When my dad had died, I'd gotten so tired of people saying that. Sorry was a kid's game, or something you said when you bumped into someone. It didn't hold a fucking candle to death. I reached out and took his hands in mine, stroking his long brown fingers. I could see it in his eyes. He was stuck there in his mind, in that place where Danielle had died. "How did you get out?" I asked, calling him back.

"They extracted me," he said, squeezing my hands. "But they didn't know I could reboot. Some idiot took his lunch break and just left me there on the table. Their security was shitty. It only took me a couple of hours to get out of the facility."

"And that's when you found the list?"

"Yeah. Just by accident. I had to sneak through this room, and the list was there. So, I memorized it, and later I wrote it down."

"And then you went to find Yale?"

"Not at first. I hid out for a while. I tried to come up with a plan for blowing up the compound, but after I escaped, they beefed up security a lot. Eventually, I had to give that up. And then I turned eighteen, and I got the settlement from the accident," he said, his entire body coiling with anger. "One million dollars plus interest that no one had ever told us about. The letter from the lawyer said it had been kept out of our file to protect our assets. All we'd had to do was wait a few more weeks, and we would have had a life."

"There was no way you could have known that." I said. "What happened wasn't your fault."

"It was my job to protect her. And I didn't."

"But you've protected me, and Nose, and Yale, and Jason. I know that doesn't bring her back, but it's something."

"I guess," he said, lacing his fingers in mine. "I've never told anyone any of that before."

"Thank you for telling me."

"Olivia," he said, setting the tub aside and pulling me across the gap between our chairs into his lap, "I never meant to hurt you."

"I know."

"Does that mean you're not leaving?" he asked, burying his face in my hair.

"I don't know," I answered. How could I leave Greenfield and everything and everyone I'd ever known? But if I stayed, the CAMfers would come back for me, and I wouldn't have help this time. If I went with Marcus, I'd be doing something. Maybe that was what the power of my hand was for.

"I'll talk to the guys," Marcus said, his voice growing fierce, "and I swear to you that no one in this camp will ever hurt you again."

"Good," I said, reluctantly extracting myself from his embrace and returning to my own chair. "But I'd still like to see the list."

"Okay," he said, picking up the tub, shuffling past the picture and most of the other things. At the bottom was a crumpled, worn piece of paper, rubbed soft from handling. He pulled it out and handed it to me.

At the very top, Danielle Elizabeth Jordon was scrawled in Marcus's handwriting. Written next to her name was Portland, Oregon, February 14. He and Danielle had been taken on Valentine's Day. Of course, by the time he'd copied this down, she'd been gone. Under her name was his—David Marcus Jordon, Portland, February 14. So, Marcus was his middle name. That made me feel a little better.

The third name on the list was Gilbert Lee Ling.

"Yale's real name is Gilbert?" I asked. "No wonder he goes by Yale."

Gilbert was followed by Trey Emmanuel Faison (aka Nose), Jason Williams and then me, Olivia Anne Black, all with dates and locations. After my name came Samantha Eva James, who apparently lived in Indianapolis, Indiana, and would be accosted by the CAMFers just in time for Halloween. The last name, Kaylee Pasnova, had no location or date next to it.

"What's with this one?" I asked, pointing at it.

"That's how it was on their list, and I haven't been able to find anything about her on the internet. It's like she doesn't exist."

"These locations move in order from west to east. Portland is west of Fresno by a little, and then it keeps moving east to Colorado, Texas, Illinois and Indiana."

"I noticed that too," Marcus said.

"So, if it keeps to that pattern, Kaylee is somewhere east of Indianapolis."

"Probably," he nodded. "But I have no idea how we'll find her."

Samantha and Kaylee. They were girls like me. Girls with PSS and no idea their world was about to come crashing down around them.

"I want to help you do this," I said to Marcus.

"Good," he said, smiling.

I leaned forward, about to kiss those gorgeously curved lips, when I heard the shuffling of feet and muted voices just outside the tent.

"Hey, can we come in?" Emma called through the canvas.

Poor Emma. And Passion. I'd left them out there in the dark with a pack of strange boys.

"Come in," I said, tucking the list back in the box and handing it to Marcus.

"I thought the three of you could sleep in here tonight," he said, putting the lid on the tub as Emma and Passion entered. They glanced between me and Marcus, and I suddenly remembered my outburst in front of everyone where I'd rattled off every intimate moment Marcus and I had ever had.

"No," I said, knowing my face was bright red. "What about you?" I didn't want to displace him, but it was more than that. I'd gotten used to his tent being our place.

"I can crash in Jason's tent until he gets back," he said. "And don't worry. We'll have someone on watch all night." Because Palmer was still out there somewhere. And he struck me as the kind of guy who had acquired a taste for revenge.

"If you're sure," I said, trying not to sound disappointed.

Marcus put away his keepsake box and crossed to the door. "Good night," he said, slipping through the canvas flaps into the dark.

35

JASON RETURNS

"Liv," Emma said, glancing around the tent, "you're not actually going to go with them, are you?" Her eyes landed on *The Other Olivia* and she frowned. "I mean, are you sure they know what they're doing?"

"No," I said, sitting down in a chair and putting my head in my hands. "But I can't stay here, and I think I'm safer with them than on my own."

"What about your mom?" Emma said, sitting down in the chair across from me, just like Marcus had.

"I don't know," I said. "She won't believe any of this. She's been dating the guy who killed Marcus's sister and then kidnapped you. She might still be dating him."

"Yeah, that would be awkward," Emma said.

I looked up and realized that Passion was standing over us, a girl I didn't really know, and she was looking at me with some kind of weird worshipful awe in her eyes.

"What?" I said, staring back at her.

"I'm sorry," she blushed. "I just think what you can do is amazing. I wish I had something like that. Some special power."

I couldn't believe it. Passion Wainwright was some kind of groupie. My groupie. Was it possible she didn't know what my hand had done to her? Dr. Julian had said she knew. He'd said it right in front of her, but then again, she'd been drugged out of her mind. And he could have been lying. I looked up, searching her face. If she didn't know, then I had to tell her.

I looked across at Emma, hoping for some help.

She raised her eyebrows at me.

"I—thanks—it's not that great," I said to Passion, lamely. I couldn't do it. Not like that. The timing just wasn't right. At least, that's what I told myself.

That night we had a very awkward slumber party in Marcus's tent.

Jason came back during breakfast the next morning. One minute we were all eating bacon and eggs, and the next minute there he was roaring up on his ATV.

He got off the wheeler, marched up to the couch where I was sitting, and said, "What'd you do with him?" leveling his gun at my head. There was alcohol on his breath. A lot of it.

Next to me, Emma cringed against Yale, terrified.

Passion stood frozen, like a deer in the headlights.

Nose looked ready to jump Jason, but Marcus caught his eye and gave a little shake of his head.

I just sat, looking down the barrel of Jason's gun. It was becoming a regular thing. I was practically used to it.

"Put the gun down," Marcus ordered. "She didn't do anything."

"Oh, she did," Jason insisted, his finger hovering over the trigger. "She disappeared them. They weren't there. Nothing was there. It looked like they'd been gone for days."

"They have been gone for days," Marcus said.

"What are you talking about?" Jason demanded.

"He's talking about this," I said, reaching into my sweatshirt pocket and pulling out the cube.

"Olivia," Marcus warned.

"What the fuck is that?" Jason asked, lowering his gun a little.

"I don't know exactly," I said, "but I pulled it out of Dr. Julian. That's my ability. It isn't disappearing people. It's reaching into them and pulling things out." From the corner of my eye I could see Passion staring at the cube, hanging on my every word. Yale and Nose and Emma were listening too. Jason just looked confused. "My hand pulled those blades out of—someone." I could at least give Passion that much anonymity. "And when I needed something to protect me from the minus meters, they started blocking minus meters. They took on that power." This was harder to explain than I'd thought it would be. "Then I stuck my hand into you," I said, staring into Jason's eyes.

"You took something out of me," he whispered, his eyes looking past me as if he were remembering it.

"Yes," I said.

"You took something out of me," Jason repeated, his voice growing louder, rougher.

"Yeah, but I didn't mean to."

"It's in there, isn't it?" Jason asked, looking at the cube wide-eyed.

"How did you—"

"I can feel it," he said, taking a step back, his left hand clutching at his chest. "Ever since that day you grabbed me, I could feel it on you. Like you had a hold on me."

"Here, take it," I said, trying to hand the cube to him. I didn't want a hold on Jason, or Dr. Julian, or Passion.

"You keep the fuck away from me," Jason said, raising his gun at me again, warning me back. Marcus had circled around behind him while we'd been talking.

"But it's yours."

"I don't want it," Jason said, looking away from me, swaying a little. "I don't want shit from you. Just tell me where the CAMFers went." He sounded tired. He looked dazed. "I asked someone in town," he said, letting his gun slant toward the ground. "One of the neighbors."

"What did they say?" Marcus asked, and Jason turned, looking at him.

"They said an ambulance came. They said that CAMFer doc was up at the hospital in a coma, that he'd been like that for days. That's when I knew she'd done something. That's when I came back."

"What about the other CAMFers?" Marcus pushed.

"Looked like they'd run. There wasn't no sign of them in the house. Wasn't no sign of anything. Not even the hole or the stairs or the room underneath. The freezer was full of food," Jason said, looking at Marcus. "There was a cement floor under it. Like she made it never happened. Like she disappeared it all."

"They got rid of the evidence," Marcus said. "Covered their tracks so we couldn't prove anything if we reported them. Olivia didn't do that."

Except, really, I had.

I hadn't meant to, but not only had I stolen Jason's bullet, I'd stolen his one chance for revenge.

We all stood at the ATVs, except for Jason. Marcus had taken his gun from him and escorted him to his tent where he'd fallen into a drunken sleep. Even from the other side of the camp, we could hear him snoring.

The others had already said their goodbyes to Emma. Yale was helmeted up and sitting on his four wheeler. Emma was standing next to it.

I reached out and hugged her, trying not to cry.

"It'll be fine" Emma said, patting my back. "I'm an actress, remember? And I'll keep an eye on Dr. Fineman for you."

"Just stay away from him, okay?" I said. "No heroics." The thought of my best friend living in the same town with that guy, even if he was in a coma, was hard to deal with. But it was even harder to imagine my mother sitting at Dr. Fineman's bedside, just like she'd sat at my dad's. What a fucking joke that was, because this time it really was my fault. I'd done that to him.

"I gave her one of the blades," Marcus said from behind us. "It should warn her if any of the CAMFers come back into town."

I wanted to turn around and hug him. We only had two blades, and he'd given one to Emma. But I resisted the urge and handed a folded piece of paper to Emma—a note for my mother. Marcus had helped me write it. Made sure I didn't give any important information away. It said simply:

> Dear Mom,
>
> I am safe and I love you, but I could not come back with Emma. She doesn't know where I'm going, so don't bug her or blame her. I'm not doing this to hurt you. It's just something I have to do. And I know you love me.
>
> Olivia

"I'll give it to her first thing," Emma said, pulling me into another embrace. "And I'll be fine. It's you guys I'm worried about. Be careful," she said, pulling away. "And let me know you're still alive once in a while. You're the only best friend I've got."

"I know. I will." I said. I hadn't told Emma we were going to Indianapolis. The less she knew, the safer she'd be. Also, Grant was there. If she knew, she might contact him and try to get him to watch out for me, and that was the last thing I needed. "When we come back, we'll tell you how we saved the world," I joked.

"Cool," Emma said. "I knew that first day back in third grade that making friends with you was going to pay off big someday."

"You did not," I said.

"Yes, I did," Emma said firmly. "See you later, Liv."

She put on her helmet and climbed on the back of Yale's wheeler, wrapping her arms around him. The motor roared, the ATV surged forward, and Yale and Emma disappeared into the woods toward Greenfield.

I turned back toward camp. We had a lot of packing and planning to do. Indianapolis was two hundred miles away, and the CAMFers already had a head start on us.

But Marcus took my arm and steered me toward his wheeler. "We have one last stop to make," he said, handing me a helmet. "The others can break down camp without us."

I climbed on and wrapped my arms around him, burying my head in his back. I didn't have to ask. I knew where we were going long before we pulled up to the wooded west gate of Sunset Hill Cemetery. We left the wheeler there and went the rest of the way on foot, winding our way, hand in hand, between barren trees and stumpy tombstones. The weight of the recent rain had pulled almost all of the leaves down.

When we got to my dad's grave, I sat on Melva Price, and Marcus stood behind me, his hands warm on my shoulders. He had known I needed to come here. We understood each other in so many ways. Ways my father and I had understood each other. Marcus wasn't replacing him. And I wasn't taking Danielle's place. But both of us were moving on. Together.

"Goodbye, Dad. I love you," I said.

Then Marcus put his arm around me, we walked to the wheeler, and headed back to Piss Camp.

THE END

Coming in 2013:
Book Two of The PSS Chronicles.
Go to www.ripleypatton.com
for more details

ACKNOWLEDGMENTS

This book is my dream and it has finally come true. But this was not a dream dreamt alone. It simply would not have happened without the support and help of the following people:

My husband and the love of my life, for supporting me financially, emotionally, and creatively, and for believing I was a writer long before I did.

My children, Valerie and Soren, for loving my stories, for putting up with mom living in her bedroom and her head for years on end, and for being my inspiration to write YA.

My Dad, for teaching me to think and for encouraging me to devour literature at a very young age.

My extended family, for loving me and for being my first fans.

The speculative fiction community of New Zealand, particularly SpecFicNZ, for backing me in every way possible. Writers need writers. You taught me that.

All those who supported my *Ghost Hand* Kickstarter, both familiar and strangers. Thank you for buying into the dream. I don't think you'll be disappointed.

All those who who gave of their skills and talents to make *Ghost Hand* the best book it could be: Angel Leigh McCoy for very early readings and for convincing me I was a novelist. Kura Carpenter for the most amazing cover ever. Debbie Marshall and Tricia Grissom for their passionate creative and content editing. Edwina Harvey for her proofreading magic. Catherine Langford for the beautiful typesetting, and Simon Petrie for turning *Ghost Hand* into an e-book I could be proud of.

And to the many other writers who have influenced and encouraged me throughout the years, particularly and more recently Helen Lowe and Juliet Marillier.

ABOUT THE AUTHOR

Ripley Patton is an award-winning author who lives in Portland, Oregon with two teenagers, one cat, and a man who wants to live on a boat. During a five-year adventure in New Zealand, Ripley and her family survived the Canterbury Earthquakes (a 7.1 and a 6.3) that rocked their home city of Christchurch. While in New Zealand, Ripley won the Sir Julius Vogel Award for Best Short Story of 2009, and the Sir Julius Vogel Award 2011 for Services to Science Fiction, Fantasy, and Horror. *Ghost Hand* is Ripley's first novel, and the first of a three book series.

To learn more about Ripley and read some of her short fiction be sure to check out her website at www.ripleypatton.com. You can also sign up for The PSS Chronicles series updates by sending an e-mail to ghosthandupdates@gmail.com.

Made in the USA
Charleston, SC
12 December 2012